Vik

**Book 7 in the
Dragon Heart Series
By
Griff Hosker**

Published by Sword Books Ltd 2015
Copyright © Griff Hosker First Edition

A CIP catalogue record for this title is available from the British Library.

Cover by Design for Writers

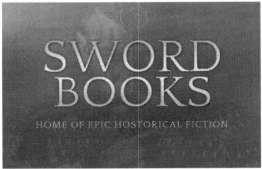

Prologue

Ragnar's Spirit brought them. It was the sword touched by Odin himself which drew them. It was always the sword. They might have said it was for other things: our land, our iron, our sheep, our women but the real reason was always the sword. We knew this for the ones who came were always either Danes or Norse. The legend of the sword touched by the Gods pulled them towards the land in the hills and the waters. It brought them to my land. And when they came, they came to kill. For the sword they sought was wielded by a warrior renowned from Miklagård to Lundenwic.

Haaken blamed himself for it was he who had begun the songs. He had made them up to celebrate my success and to honour me. They were told in every Viking home whether Dane or Norse. He thought his stories drew them. His most famous saga was of the sword touched by the gods and the warrior who could not be killed whilst he wielded it. It was all nonsense; I could be killed as easily as any man... if my enemy was good enough. So far the spirits, the gods and the Weird Sisters had watched over me and I prayed each night that they would continue to do so. I did not fear to die. I would go to Valhalla and see my old comrades and Ragnar the old man who had trained me. My fear was for my people. We had come to this land which was Valhalla on earth and we had yet to make it secure. When it was secure then I would go to meet my wife and the others in the Other Place.

Each day when I strapped on the sword I both cursed it and kissed it. It was a curse and it was a blessing. It attracted enemies who wished to rip it from my dead hands but it protected my people. It was a fine line which separated those emotions. As I watched my son, Arturus, grow I feared for him. Would he have the burden to bear when I was gone or would some other Viking wield the mighty sword? Such things were out of my hands. The Norns, the Weird Sisters who wove our destinies, would decide such things.

One thing was certain the young warriors, Jarls and Princes would keep coming to Cyninges-tūn to try to take my sword from me and I would have to fight every day to stop them. Such was the life I had made for myself; such was the life of Jarl Dragon Heart and his sword, Ragnar's Spirit. It was my destiny and a warrior was a fool if he thought he could hide from his own destiny.

Each time I touched it I remembered those who had died because of the sword. Beorn Three Fingers had suffered the blood eagle and he had been one of the handful who had followed me from Mann. His friend Snorri had smiled, "He will not mind. We have another Bjorn, Bjorn the Scout and he can do what Beorn did. I am certain that, in Valhalla, he will watch Bjorn with great interest."

Chapter 1

It was the end of Gói. We had had the first fine day of the year and I noticed that the birds were beginning to nest. There was a touch of spring in the air. Arturus was now a man and spent more time with the warriors in the warrior hall than in my hall. Since my wife had died it was big and it was empty. I rattled around within it. Apart from Aiden and my slaves I lived like a hermit. It was lonely. I decided to ask Arturus to go hunting with me. I might be the jarl and rule Cyninges-tūn but I still felt foolish having to make an excuse to have some company. The first spring like day seemed a good excuse to me.

I went to the warrior hall where each of my Ulfheonar was busy. Some were repairing or replacing leather straps. Some were carving. One or two were playing dice or nine men's Morris. Arturus was sharpening his seax.

"Arturus, should we go hunting today? I have a desire for wild boar."

He was now almost as tall as I was and he was broader. That was his mother's influence. Her brother had been a broad, stocky warrior. Half of my blood came from the old people, the Britons, and the other half from a Saxon who had forced himself upon my mother. I had not one drop of Norse blood in my veins but I was a Viking. Old Olaf had once told me that being a Viking was a state of mind. He accepted me as one and that was good enough for me.

"Aye father. A good idea."

Haaken and Cnut, my two oldest friends, laid down the scabbards they were decorating. "Should we come, Dragon Heart?"

I shook my head, "No Haaken. You need to spend more time with your family."

He looked disappointed. In truth I was being selfish. I wanted Arturus all to myself. I felt a little guilty, I knew that Haaken's children were at the clinging stage and he desperately wanted an excuse to be out. "Perhaps later in the week. We may not even find any wild boar today. Call today a scouting expedition to prepare for a bigger hunt."

He brightened a little. "Then I will tell my wife that the Dragon Heart needs Haaken to go hunting later in the week."

I shook my head as I left the hall. That was not what I had said. My oldest friend was fierce and courageous when it came to war but he was a mouse when it came to his wife. Since he had married he had shown me a different side to the rock that would not budge in a shield wall but would quake if his wife gave him a hard look. If I did not know better I would have said he was afraid of the shrew.

We went without helmets and armour. You needed to hear and smell when you were hunting and the armour and the helmet would get in the way. I took my sword because I always did. I doubted that I would need it although I had once used it to slay a wild boar which came upon us unobserved. The most important weapons we would take would be our boar spears and our bows. My seax would come in handy when we had to gut the animal we slew. We had arrows which Bagsecgson our smith had made especially for boars. They had heads which were both longer and narrower than our normal hunting arrows. We believed that they penetrated further. Arturus and I were good archers and we would aim for the eye or the heart. The new arrows would, hopefully, kill instantly. A wounded wild boar was very hard to kill. It was like trying to bring down a berserker; they never knew when they were finished.

We took three ponies and Arturus' old dog, Wolf. He had had him since before Arturus had gained the name Wolf Killer. That had been the day my son had become Ulfheonar.

"Where shall we hunt today then, my son?"

"It was your idea." I smiled and shrugged, "Cnut said that there were signs of wild pigs at Tarn Haugh."

"And there are some oaks near there. We will see if my old friend is correct."

The Tarns were less than two miles from our home. We could be there and back in half a day if we were successful. We had a choice of routes. We could drop down to the side of the Water or we could make our way through the forest. The forest route would be easier on the ponies and we took that path.

I had words I needed to say to my son but I knew not how to begin them. I could have used his sister, Kara, for she understood how to put ideas into words. Had my wife, Erika, been alive then it would have been easy. She would have taken him to one side and he would have understood. She had a way about her that I did not have. She had been taken from me so that I had to be father and mother to my son. It was not easy. I had always found that the best way to get something difficult over with was to tackle it head on. I used that approach.

"Time is passing, my son. It is time you took a wife."

He gave me a sudden look of surprise. "Why now? I am still a young man."

"Look at Haaken. He is my age and yet he has children who are barely three summers old. That is because he delayed in finding a wife and having children. You and Kara mean more to me than anything. I would have you experience the same joy."

He looked suddenly sad, "I would, father, and last year, before Yule, there was a girl from the other side of the Water..."

"Excellent!"

"No, you do not understand. She was one of the ones who died of the coughing sickness last winter. She was one that Kara could not save."

"Kara knew?"

He nodded, "She knows my heart father and she said that it was *wyrd*. The spirits have told her that I will find a wife and soon. We both need to be patient. I promise you grandchildren."

My wife, Erika, was amongst the spirits and she spoke to Kara all the time. She had come to me, too, once to save my life. I relaxed. This was good. If the spirits and Kara had foreseen a son then I would soon be a grandfather. I felt a warmth within and a smile returned to my face.

I noticed that the wind was blowing into our faces. A north wind oft times brought bad weather. I hoped this was not a false spring. We needed to go trading and raiding soon and bad weather would prevent that. We were just coming out of the trees and I halted the ponies.

"We had better string the bows. We do not want to be surprised by an animal. If we see one we must strike quickly."

As we dismounted he laughed, "I think you taught me that eight summers ago. I have hunted before, father."

"I forget. Perhaps I am becoming like Olaf the Toothless and as forgetful."

"You have many years to go before you are as lost as he was at the end."

We took our bows from the spare pony. I took the opportunity of untying my boar spear. I still remembered the wild beast launching itself at me. This time I would be ready. It was hard to fit the string to the bow. That was a good sign. It showed that the bow was still powerful. I took an arrow and nocked it just to test the pull.

At that moment Wolf growled. Arturus did not need telling that there was danger. My bow and nocked arrow were levelled in an instant as was that of Arturus. We were saved by the fact that Wolf warned us and we were in the shelter of our ponies. A small warband suddenly emerged from the bushes where they had been hiding. They were less than fifty paces from us. Had the north wind not been blowing then Wolf might not have smelled them. *Wyrd*. Even as I pulled back on the bow I counted them. There were twelve of them. Only one had any armour on but they all had a shield. We had none. I also saw that they were Danes. The leader, who wore a half face helmet, had a double handed war axe. It was important to know your enemies so that you could deal with the most dangerous.

There was little point in wasting arrows on the armoured warrior and I loosed my first arrow at the warrior to his right. He was thrown back by the force of the arrow plunging into his chest. It was a boar arrow and would have gone straight through him. Arturus was loosing as fast as I was. My second arrow was nocked and released when they were twenty paces from us. My third when they were ten paces. There were three men pierced by my arrows and three by Arturus. We had halved our enemies. The slope had slowed them down. I grabbed the boar spear as Wolf leapt at one of them.

The leader was a big man and his lightly armoured men beat him to us. I held a spear two handed and thrust it into the chest of the first warrior while whipping the end around to the right and the other warriors. It struck two of the Danes who tumbled down the hill and took the legs from the leader. I saw that we had felled seven of them. Not all were dead but it left the big Dane and four others. We had a spare boar spear each and I threw the one I held. It was not a perfect throw but it struck a warrior on the thigh and he fell screaming and pouring blood from the wound. He held it tightly to staunch the bleeding.

I hefted my second spear as a cautious warrior holding his shield and short sword circled me. He was trying to make me present my side to his leader who was now rushing towards me. I feinted with the spear at the man's eyes. He pulled the shield up instinctively and I rammed the point at the shield with such force that he fell backwards. I knew that the axe was being swung even as I turned. Arturus had his sword out and was occupied. The Dane was mine. I swung the haft of the spear horizontally and it smacked into the belly of the

Dane. Although he was armoured it was a powerful blow and it winded him. I reversed it and, while he was still recovering, thrust the wicked head at him. He was no boar but it penetrated his armour and began to enter his body. I saw him wince and he swung his axe to shatter the spear in two and then he pulled the broken head from his side and hurled it at me.

I drew Ragnar's Spirit. I saw his face crease in a grin of triumph. "You are the one they call Dragon Heart. You are the one with the sword which was meant to be mine. I will not kill you. I shall make you a blood eagle!"

I knew his type. They liked to frighten you with threats and words. I preferred to remain silent and use my sword to do my talking. My advantage was my speed and my weakness was his armour. Ignoring the sounds of combat behind me I lunged forward to use the tip of the sword. My enemy had to swing; he had an axe. I had a choice of strikes. He did not try to deflect the blow. He ignored it and brought the axe down to split me in two. Even as my sword scored a line through the metal links I was hurling myself forward to follow the blade. The axe was so close that it almost shaved my kyrtle.

My dive rolled me down the hill up which the Dane had just come. An unfriendly rock arrested my fall and I felt a rib crack as I struck it. I jumped to my feet. It was much easier to stand quickly without mail and I raced uphill. My enemy had seen my fall and in it saw victory. He ran down towards me. That was a fatal mistake. He was in armour and he came at me too quickly. I saw the axe swinging and I stepped towards him and under the axe. I ripped Ragnar's Spirit across his middle. My earlier blow had severed some of the links and now the edge ripped open more. The sword went into his padding and his momentum helped it to tear into his stomach. I was knocked to the side but I held my hilt still and the sword continued to open him up as he tumbled beyond me to land in a heap at the bottom of the hill.

I walked down the hill with my sword ready for any threat. He lay on his back and I could see his entrails lying in a trail following his fall. He was alive. His helmet had fallen from his head and I could see that he was a young man; little older than Arturus. He gripped his axe still but that was for his passage to the Other World and not to strike me.

His eyes opened. "They were right. You are a powerful warrior." He laughed and coughed up blood at the same time. "We waited for seven days to catch you alone and without armour and still you defeated us. I will have a good tale to tell when I am in Valhalla."

"What is your name, Dane?"

"I am Elli the Mighty." He closed his eyes in pain and then opened them. "And I was felled by Ragnar's Spirit. It is a good death. I..." And then he died.

I turned to trudge up the hill. My ribs were sending shafts of pain with each step. I had not heard combat while I had been talking to the giant and I saw a bloodied Arturus half way down the hill. He stood over one of the wounded warriors. There was anger on his face. "Wolf is dead! He died protecting me! I will make this one pay."

7

"Wait, my son. Use your head and not your heart. We need to find out where they came from. He will die but first we ask questions."

He sighed and nodded. "You are jarl and you are right." He gave a nod of his head. "I have much to learn."

The warrior was little more than a youth. Elli the Mighty had been young too. I glanced at the youth who stared defiantly at us. He was the one whom I had hit in the thigh. His life blood was slipping slowly away. He had not long for this world and I had to question him quickly.

"Elli the Mighty died well, warrior."

He nodded. "We came for glory and he has it now. End my life and let me follow him in death as I did in life. Give me my sword."

I picked up the seax. It was a poorly made weapon. It looked brittle. Had he used it then it would probably have shattered at the first blow. I held it by the blade. "First I want to know where you came from and are you alone?"

He dropped his hand. "I will not betray my chief."

"You cannot betray him now for he is in the Other World. If you want to join him then answer me. Your wound is slowly killing you. Soon the darkness will enfold you and you will find yourself staring at Hel and not Elli."

His eyes widened in terror. He was too young to have gone a-Viking. I glanced up the hill and noted that they were all young. This had been a band of young warriors on their first adventure. They had been ill led. Elli might have been Mighty but he was not Elli the Clever. You did not take such a young band without an experienced warrior to give advice. I saw that their weapons were all of the poorest quality and their shields badly constructed. Many leaders, such as Elli, wanted to reap rewards without learning their trade. It had cost eleven young men their lives.

"We came across the sea for we heard that there was land and treasure here. In the big town they call Jorvik, a man told Chief Elli of the sword touched by the gods. He said it would be easy to take." He tried a laugh but the pain was too much. "He lied. We could not even take it from two men who had neither armour nor shield."

"And what was the name of this liar?"

"He was the chief of the town and his name was Wiglaf. He was a Saxon."

I gave him his sword. "Send him to the Other World."

My son swung his sword as the youth gripped the seax and hacked his head from his body. It rolled down the hill and rested next to the feet of Elli the Mighty. It seemed appropriate somehow.

Arturus looked at me. "Wiglaf! That Saxon lives still."

"So it would seem." We had first met Wiglaf in Lundenwic where we had helped King Egbert to capture that city. Wiglaf had fled north with my old enemy Rorik. Rorik was dead, I had slain him myself, but the Saxon, who was both cunning and treacherous, had built up his strength by inviting Danes to serve him. I waved a hand. "These were young boys on an adventure. They heard the sagas and thought that they would be in one too. Their leader was trying to gain a sword and thereby a kingdom."

Arturus looked to Wolf. "He should be honoured. He was a brave hound. He died protecting us."

"Aye but he lives still. Look at his pups and their pups. That is how we build our strength my son."

He looked at me and nodded. "You are talking of me again. I have heard you father and I will act."

First we built a pyre. "We shall take the armour and weapons and pile them on their leader. We will lay Wolf on the top so that the Spirits know he died victorious. Then we shall burn them."

We used the Dane's war axe to chop down some trees which looked as though they were either dead or dying. After stripping the Dane of his armour we placed his body and then the bodies of his men on the top. Finally, Arturus reverentially laid the body of his faithful dog to crown the pyre. It was a fitting funeral for a hero.

We always carried kindling and flint in our saddles and we soon had flames licking the wood at the base of the pyre. I nodded to Arturus, it was his dog. He should be the one who spoke the words and sent Wolf on his way.

He held his hands in supplication, "Great Allfather, I am Wolf Killer, I pray you take my dog, Wolf, and let him join the other heroes in Valhalla and tell him to wait for me. I will come one day and take my place at your table."

The flames began to lick around the top of the pyre and smoke started to rise. Although we had chosen the wood which appeared dead it was spring and the wood was still damp from winter rains. Palls of smoke began to rise. That was good. The spirits of the dead would have a safe and rapid journey to the heavens. They had come to kill us but they had died well and I wished them no further harm. When the flames took hold and the bodies began to burn we gathered the armour and weapons. The helmet and the axe were the only items worth saving. The rest, including the damaged mail, would have to be melted down and reused.

We were about to begin packing the ponies when Haaken and the Ulfheonar appeared from the woods. "We saw the smoke and sensed danger. What happened here?"

We told him. He shook his head wryly. "Then the saga I will make will have to be second hand. I knew I should have come with you, Dragon Heart."

Haaken One Eye always took things lightly. It was his way. He was not a shallow creature by any means but it was his way of dealing with such events. He had been the same when, as a boy, fighting alongside me, he had lost an eye.

Cnut, on the other hand, was more serious. He had been with me in the tower when the lightning had struck my sword. He felt protective towards both me and the sword. The Allfather had chosen him to be there with me that day on the mountain with me in Man. He saw the dangers. "This is worrying. If Wiglaf is sending warriors here we should do something about it."

"We should, Cnut, but we will wait until tonight when we are safe within our walls and I can ask Kara to seek guidance from the spirits. And I can ask Aiden; he is becoming wiser each day." I shook my head, "It seems, my son, that we were not meant to hunt this day."

"We did father, we hunted men. It is *wyrd*."

Chapter 2

Kara was waiting for us outside my hall. She and her women had their own hall where they cared for the sick. She also had the two women who had been nuns of the White Christ who made our cheese. Most of the women were the older widows whose husbands had died as warriors. With their sons in the warrior hall Kara gave them a home and purpose in their lives. She saw the laden saddles. "I sensed a disturbance last night, father, but I could not find the danger." She looked at Arturus. "Where is Wolf, my brother?"

"He died saving my life."

"That is a good end for a fine animal but you must take a pup from his seed and raise him. He must be called Wolf too." He nodded. Everyone respected Kara for she was a Volva. "You wish some counsel?"

"Aye. Come to my hall with Aiden and Arturus."

I went to get changed. My clothes were covered in blood. By the time I had changed they had found Aiden. He had been an Irish hostage who had been abandoned by his family. He chose to serve me and he was as close to me as my children. He was no warrior but he had a mind as sharp as any and he knew magic. He and my daughter made a powerful pair. If they could not divine an answer then there was no solution to my problem.

The four of us sat around the large table my wife had had made for us before she died. I think she had anticipated having a huge family and imagined all of us sitting around and eating. *Wyrd*! I told them all again what Elli the Mighty and the youth had told me. They nodded. "I do not know if this is just an accident. It may be that this Elli is the only one who will risk death to take the sword."

Aiden looked thoughtful. "Then one course of action might be to do nothing until someone else tries."

Arturus showed his displeasure at that. "We were lucky this time. It was close to home and they were inexperienced warriors. Suppose it had been a larger band and we had been further from our home?"

Aiden had this great ability to come up with solutions quickly. "That is simple enough. We make sure that Dragon Heart has the Ulfheonar with him when he leaves the stad."

"So I am to be a prisoner in my own home. I am never allowed to be alone."

Aiden inclined his head. "I go back to my original point. This is a temporary measure until we discover if there is a threat."

That pleased no-one. I was not even certain that Aiden liked it but it was a solution. "Kara you have said nothing yet."

"I am still thinking."

"There is one solution; I could sail into the middle of the Water and drop the sword to the bottom. There it would be no threat and would not attract the moths who wish to own the glittering light."

She smiled, "That would not do. The sword is a symbol of our people. If you discard the gift of the gods then you discard the gods themselves and that is a road that only a berserker follows. There may come a time when the sword must be thrown into the Water. It will make that journey but not yet. It will go through fire and blood before that time. Odin has not finished with the sword he touched." She spread her hands, "I have had time to think and my father's words have spurred me to action. I see more here than a band of young warriors trying to make a name for themselves. There may be a higher purpose in all of this. I am sorry that I cannot give you one of Aiden's quick answers. I need to sleep and speak with the spirits."

If Aiden was upset by Kara's comments he said nothing. Arturus just looked troubled. I was sure that the reason was the death of Wolf. He had had him since he had been a pup. The animal had been adored by both Kara and himself. Kara showed no emotion but she never did. Once she found her gift she was always calm and always serene. She was like the heartbeat of the stad.

"Very well then I will stay close to my men." I rose, irritated, and walked out to stand and watch the Water. My wife, Erika, would have said 'stormed' out because I was not happy. She would have known what to say to calm and settle me. My children and Aiden just sat there and let me go. It was probably for the best. I could be like a wounded boar at times and lash out at anyone. It was at times like this I sought Bjorn Bagsecgson the smith. His forges were down by the shore. He had been a rock since his father had been killed on the island of Mann where we had all once lived. His skills brought us great wealth and he was someone I could talk to. It was like speaking with Thor himself for Bjorn was a mighty smith with huge arms and a chest that was like a barrel.

I saw the metal we had just brought in the corner when I walked in. He had four smiths working with him. Two were his sons. He saw my troubled face and said to them, "Go and get some food. Let the jarl and I talk." He gestured to the metal as they took off their leather aprons and left. "I hear you had some trouble this morning,"

"Aye a young band of warriors were keen to have my sword."

"Inevitable. Most young warriors crave a blade such as that. You were the exception, probably because you were only raised Norse, but any young warrior would willingly give a limb to own such a sword and to kill Dragon Heart. To own the sword is a death worthy of a saga. That is probably why the gods gave it to you."

"Depressing. It means I will always be looking over my shoulder."

"You are safe here in this ring of mountains and Waters." He pointed to the discarded metal in the corner of his workshop. "If they all come with metal of such poor quality then we can send our women to fight them." He picked up a seax and bent it in two until it broke. "Why I am not even certain that a smith made this one. If he did then he was piss poor. Perhaps we should ask for more money for our blades."

I was pleased I had come to see him for he made me smile and put events in perspective. I still had the same enemies. The difference was they were coming for me and not my people. I could live with that. I smiled.

Bjorn clapped me across my back, "And I have some good news for you. Aiden was walking to the north and west of Lang's Dale, close to the Gill there and he discovered this." He proffered a lump of rock.

"Good, a rock. We have many of them already. I would not call this a great find or a reason to smile."

He shook his head much as one would do when explaining something to a child and took the rock from me. "It is iron. There is a seam of it. We need no longer trade for it. We have our own."

I grasped it again. Suddenly it felt like holding a piece of gold. "Can we mine it?"

"That is the only problem. It will need labour and lots of it."

"Slaves?"

"Slaves!"

I would need to go to sea again. Mindful of the advice of my family I sought Haaken and Cnut. They were happy to accompany me. Haaken, for it meant he could quiz me about the fight and Cnut because his life was as bound in the sword as mine. We rode our ponies around the water. We could have sailed the small boat we used to travel up and down the Water but it was still a pleasant day and I wanted to talk as we rode. It was me who did most of the talking, at least, until we were just a short way from the boatyard.

"It is good news about the iron and I do not see the problem with having us with you at all times."

"I think, Haaken, that all of you would find it taxing. However, I intend to go raiding soon. We need slaves and I have an idea of my own about the sword."

While Haaken was intrigued Cnut was worried, "Do not be reckless, Dragon Heart. Since Erika was taken I have noticed that you fight and act with more abandon than you used to."

"Cnut! You are not Dragon Heart's mother!"

"He is right, Haaken, but now that Arturus is a man then there will be a jarl when I am taken. I will not be leaving my people leaderless. However, Cnut, do not worry, I am just thinking of ways to discourage others from seeking the sword." I hated lying to my oldest friends and the most senior of the Ulfheonar but I already knew what I would do. The only change would come when Kara had spoken with the spirits. I had learned never to go against them.

Bolli, our shipwright, greeted us with an apologetic shrug. "I am sorry Jarl; I have not yet had time to look over the drekar."

I smiled, "Do not worry. I will not need either of them until Ein-mánuðr but I want *'Josephus'* and *'Heart of the Dragon'* ready for sea by then."

"They will be. They are both new drekar. I will haul them from the water and have the weed taken from them. Will you be carrying cargo?"

"Slaves."

"Then I will leave the ballast."

"We will need a spare mast and spars; we sail to Frankia and needs must we have to be swift." He nodded. "When you are with the ships tell Pasgen we shall be sailing to Frankia in case he wishes to send any of his knarr."

Pasgen was the headman of Úlfarrston. Although not Norse he was a good friend and protected our drekar for us during the winter. We headed back to Cyninges-tūn satisfied that we had planned all. "Frankia?"

"There is a plan to this, Haaken. The lands to the south have been raided already by our brethren. I have heard that they have settled some areas there already. I would not fight Norsemen. I have enough Danes and Norse who covet my sword without drawing others to me. The northern coast of Frankia is close and will provide slaves for us. Since we killed Rorik I suspect that there will no longer be one leader who controls that coast; the Emperor controls only the Rinaz. Others will soon find that this plum is ready to be picked and we shall get there first and then we sail to Lundenwic."

Haaken laughed, "You have a mind like a bear trap. I can see that this will make a good saga."

The next morning Kara came as soon as I was awake. I was always the first up and when I saw my daughter I saw that she had had a troubled night. The spirits had visited her. The spirits were always welcome but their messages could sometime be either unclear or unpleasant. Her face suggested the latter.

I pushed over the cheese and the small beer but she shook her head. "It was not just my mother who came last night. Prince Butar came too and," she paused, "your mother."

I felt the hairs on the back of my neck prickle. I had only recently discovered that my mother had been a Volva. Descended from the last Romans, the last British Warlords, she only came when it was life threatening.

"You have to leave Cyninges-tūn. If you stay then others will come."

She spoke with a passion I had not heard for some time. Her dreams had frightened her and that frightened me. It confirmed my decision to leave. "If they come and I am not here then will it not be worse for my people?"

"I do not make these judgements. I am told what must be. Prince Butar said that the people would be protected." Her eyes pleaded with me to listen. I would have anyway but I heard, in her voice, my dead wife.

I was confused, "How?"

"I know not but the spirits have yet to let us down. Let us believe them. It is important for Arturus that he accompanies you." She frowned. "Your mother said, and I do not understand this, *'the sword must sing and be forged again in blood and fire'*. She looked at me as though I would know the answer. I shook my head. I had never spoken to my mother of swords.

I put my hand on hers for I could see that she was troubled. "Fear not Kara for I have planned a slave raid to Frankia. I will take Aiden with me and between us we can unravel the knot of this riddle. Thorkell can watch over my land and I will have Rolf train up more men to protect our walls. Now that we have our own iron then Bjorn can make good helmets and swords for all."

"There was something else. *'Beware the knives from the north'*."

"The Hibernians?"

"I know not. That was the last message I received. I am sorry, father, this does not help. I have let you down."

"No you have not. The spirits are not always clear. There will be a reason for that and I daresay that the Norns will be at the back of all this. Be at peace. I am settled. Not knowing what to do is a problem which can destroy lives. I know what to do and as the spirits are in accordance then I am happy to leave. It is *wyrd*."

Chapter 3

The inactivity of winter was replaced by the hectic preparations for a raid. I sent Arturus and Aiden to ask Thorkell the Tall to watch my land. I had Bjorn working from dawn until dusk producing the weapons and armour we would need for the voyage and for those who would protect our lands. Siggi and Trygg, our knarr captains, were sent to trade with our friends in Cymru and along the Sabrina. I wanted any enemies to think that we were unprepared for war and having our trading ships travelling unaccompanied would do just that. Haaken and Cnut had their hands full with the warriors who wished to be Ulfheonar. Along with Bjorn the Scout, they were the ones who made the final decision. They would be replacing brave warriors who had fallen. I spent as much time as I could with Rolf. One of my oathsworn, he had been badly wounded and could no longer move as well as he would like. He was the perfect leader to leave in command of my home.

The last of my jarls whom I saw was Windar at Windar's Mere. He was a good leader but he was now so fat that his name had become known as Windar the Fat. He did not need a waist to protect the land to the east and he was happy to do so. He also provided me with half a crew for the Josephus. When we sailed in eight day's time we would have a full crew for both drekar.

Arturus and Aiden were still in the north when the handful of miners we had sent to the new iron workings rode into the stad, their horses lathered and sweating. It was one of Bjorn's youngest sons, Karl, who stood before me. He was not yet fourteen summers and yet he was built like an ox. I had no idea how the pony had managed to carry him. "Jarl Dragon Heart. We saw Vikings heading from the sea."

A chill came over me despite the warm afternoon. "Were they dressed for war?"

He looked confused, "They had their shields over their backs."

That could mean they came in peace but equally it could be just making life easier for themselves. I would heed the words of the spirits. They came from the north and we would prepare to meet them in battle. If they came in peace then I would apologise.

"You have done well, Karl. How many were there?"

He held his hands up five times. There were fifty and that was a large number. "Rolf. Send messengers to Windar and the outlying farms. Tell them there may be danger and to prepare."

He looked troubled, "What is it Jarl?"

I held up Ragnar's Spirit. "I fear it may be this flame drawing them on. But we will see."

The commotion had attracted some of my Ulfheonar. "Is there trouble, Jarl Dragon Heart?"

"I think so, Cnut. Have the Ulfheonar prepare and we will meet this new threat."

"And the ones we have not yet decided upon?"

"Bring them with us. This may be the opportunity to see how they perform. Have the men bring their bows."

As I dressed I knew that Arturus would be angry to be missing this. With him gone and the new warriors we would have just thirty warriors to face what could be a large warband. It would have to be enough. Kara came with Rolf as we assembled. "This may be nothing but we had better be prepared, if they are coming from Lang's Dale then they will come by Skelwith. I will meet them at the beck. Watch my home, Rolf."

"With my life, Jarl."

Kara kissed me on the cheek. "It is the threat from the north, father."

"I know."

We made good time to the beck. There were many places where it could be crossed but the old Roman Road from the coast came this way and I assumed that these warriors would choose the easiest route.

"Sigtrygg, take six warriors and wait on the other side of the beck in the trees." I pointed, "There to the east. Watch for my signal."

"Yes Jarl."

"Bjorn the Scout, take six warriors and do the same to the west."

After they had gone Cnut nodded with a smile upon his lips. "When they come they will see but eighteen of us here and they will outnumber us by more than two to one."

"They will be overconfident and, if they come for war will try to attack us. Erik Dog Bite and Bjorn Carved Teeth take three men each and stay on this side of the beck. You go east, Erik and you go west. Stay behind the bushes."

My warriors nodded and slipped away. Cnut said, "They will see them."

"Of course they will and they will think that is my trap and not know that twelve of my best warriors are behind them."

Haaken frowned. "And you have the six new warriors here with us. That means that half of the warriors who meet them will be without experience."

I smiled, "Surely that is a good test of their skill, Haaken. Can you think of a better?"

I was not even certain if this band of warriors represented any danger. If they were travelling down the road which the Romans had built then they were not hiding. The main reason I had brought armed men was because of the warning of the spirits. I strung my bow as we waited. I did not have hunting arrows I had arrows with a head like the ones on the boar spear. If they had armour it would penetrate the links. Bjorn had discovered the method when one of the warriors had loosed an arrow without a metal tip. It had managed to penetrate the links easier. Bjorn liked them as they were easier to make than barbed ones.

I heard the whistle of a blackbird from across the beck. It was a signal from my men. "They are coming, prepare."

I recognised the design on the shield and I relaxed a little. It was Jarl Harald Blue Eye from Hrossy in Orkneyjar. We had parted as friends when I had helped to rid him of some usurpers who fancied his land. However as they approached the bridge I noticed that, whether by accident or design, they were making a wedge formation. My hair prickled.

"This may be a warband. Watch for treachery and keep your bows to hand."

I heard Cnut growl, "You new warriors listen for commands and do as Haaken and I do!"

I saw, as they approached that the front ten each had a metal byrnie but the other forty appeared to have either leather armour or none at all. Only half had a helmet. I was about to speak when the Jarl swung his shield around and shouted, "Have at them!" So much for the help I had done him. They were here to catch us unawares.

"Loose!" All eighteen of my men loosed their arrows. The wedge formation meant that some of the arrows struck shields but at least three of the mailed warriors were felled and two of those behind. We managed a second flight before we had to discard our bows and swing our shields around. The men of Jarl Harald Blue Eye had to descend into the water and then climb out. While they had been in wedge formation it had helped to protect them from arrows. The loss of the warriors and the descent into the beck meant that they no longer had a cohesive front. They were easier to hit.

"To the bank." My new warriors had their spears with them as did many of my other warriors. The warriors from Orkneyjar struggled to cross the water, still icy from snow melt in the hills. They were jabbed and struck with spears. I wanted them in the beck before I committed Sigtrygg and Bjorn the Scout to the attack. Bjorn Carved Teeth and Erik Dog Bite were still able to use their bows and the warriors towards the rear were being struck as they loosed arrow after arrow at men without armour. It bunched them in the middle as they tried to avoid the missiles. It was futile; my men were too good and many warriors fell. I saw two of the band turn and prepare to run back up the road. That was time enough for my reserves.

"Sigtrygg, Bjorn! Now!" I waved my sword above my head as a signal. Perhaps it was an accident but a sudden shaft of sunlight shone and lit the blade making it seem alive and afire. The first warrior who climbed the bank came directly for me. I swung Ragnar's Spirit diagonally across his neck. He held up the shield to protect himself. As he placed one foot on the bank I punched him with my shield and he fell backwards. He made a spectacular splash as he landed in the water, knocking over two other warriors too. I saw that my men were now approaching. I heard Jarl Harald Blue Eyes yell, "Back to the ship!" His trick had failed and he saw that he was surrounded. He had always been too cautious as a jarl. Sven Knife Tongue had nearly out manoeuvred him.

At least a handful of his warriors shook their heads and stood their ground. They had lost barely ten warriors and they still outnumbered us. The rest formed on their jarl and made a wedge which was able to negotiate the other, lower bank. Sigtrygg and Bjorn the Scout ran at them and there was a mighty clash of metal on wood as they met. My men were outnumbered and the men from Orkneyjar had the incentive of the safety of their ship to motivate them. Sigtrygg and Bjorn the Scout could not contain them without help from the rest of us.

"After them!"

Three warriors stood in the middle of the beck. Their jarl might have had no honour but these three would go to Valhalla when they had killed some of us. Three of my new warriors ran, bravely but recklessly at them. I jumped into the water to go to their aid. The three they fought had the death wish upon them. They were not the opponent for a novice. The first of the new warriors, Oleg, still held his spear. He jabbed it at the middle warrior who imperiously swept the head aside and then brought his sword around backhand to slice deep into Oleg's neck. The beck flowed red with his blood. I pushed through the icy water. I wanted no more of my young men to die needlessly. These three were going nowhere. We could finish them with arrows if we had to. As the second, Sven the Wild, died, I swung Ragnar's Spirit over my head. The warrior who had killed Oleg held his shield above his head. My blade made it shiver and he had to step back. I punched with my shield as he was off balance and he had to take another step west, towards the bank. I used my sword backhand and, this time, when he brought his shield up it was not quite quick enough and the tip of my sword sliced through some of the mail links. He was still going backwards and his blow with his sword was weak. I pushed it aside with my shield and, seeing a gap, plunged Ragnar's Spirit into the tear made in his byrnie. I twisted as I withdrew it. He fell into the beck and my blade was covered in his entrails. I turned and saw that Haaken and Cnut had despatched the other two.

"Erik Dog Bite, take your men and pursue them." I looked and saw that Oleg and Sven the Wild had been joined in Valhalla by Harold Sigisson. Their deaths had been unnecessary and I felt Haaken's accusing eyes on my back. He had known they might die. Had this been the fault of my arrogance? Did I think we would always win and always survive unscathed? Perhaps so.

On the other bank were two wounded warriors. I waded through the water to question them. I chose the one who was about to die anyway. "Why did Jarl Harald Blue Eye forget our friendship and come for war?"

The elder of the two, a warrior with white flecks in his beard gave a wry smile. He had a stomach wound and was not long for this world. "He came not for war, Jarl Dragon Heart. He came for the sword touched by the gods. He was convinced," he winced in pain, "he was convinced that, with it, he could conquer Orkneyjar. He would become as invincible as you."

Haaken shook his head, "Then if Dragon Heart is invincible how did he expect to take it?"

The man shook his head, "We were oathsworn and we followed." He winced again and gripped his seax. "I am in pain. End it Jarl with Odin's sword. I will join my sons in Valhalla."

I nodded, "You were faithful to the end. Go to the Allfather." I slid the blade across his throat and he died with a sigh.

We placed our dead on cloaks which were supported by the spears and I had my warriors take the five of them home. Taking off my helmet I joined Haaken and Cnut to burn the fourteen raiders who had been slain. I wanted to wait for the return of my warriors. We watched the smoke rise from the pyre and said a prayer for the dead. I wanted no blood feuds in Valhalla. We occupied the time sorting through the items we had taken from the dead.

Haaken shook his head as he held up a mail shirt torn by my strokes, "Dragon Heart, if you would just take their heads then Bjorn could use the armour. This is another byrnie you have ruined."

I laughed, "I will remember that next time."

"These were not impoverished warriors, Jarl. Look at the warrior bands and the fine amulets. Perhaps we should raid Orkneyjar."

"No, for I would not wish Norse slaves who could try to run home or whose families could try to rescue. The people of Frankia will forget their lost ones and the slaves will forget their home."

"But think of the treasure."

I sat on a rock and took off my wolf cloak. "I fear that we will have treasure enough for it seems my sword draws men on. They seem to forget everything in their desire for Ragnar's Spirit."

Cnut watched the water of the beck begin to clear as the blood was swept away to the sea. "And you think that if we go to Frankia then it will draw the sword seekers there."

I nodded, "And if we go to Lundenwic and spend some time there it will draw them south too. By the time they have come to seek us in the south we shall have sailed for home again."

Cnut nodded his approval but Haaken said, "I can see a flaw in the plan. It delays them, that is all. They will still come."

"But by then it will be winter and nature herself will protect us." I held up my hand. "We are alone and I will tell you two for there are no secrets between us; I intend, next winter to travel to Jorvik and to slay Wiglaf. If we stop his tongue then we limit the threat."

Cnut pointed to the north. "Blue Eye did not learn it from Wiglaf."

"It will not stop all but it will limit their numbers. I am not going to give up this home as we did Mann because of threats from enemies. This is our land now and we will keep it. More men are flocking to farm here and there is plenty of land. We will only grow stronger."

Cnut threw a stick into the beck and watched it flow downstream. "Until, Dragon Heart, you are slain and then what?"

"By then Arturus will have learned how to be jarl."

Haaken laughed, "And that shows that you are not Norse. Most Vikings give their son a sword when he becomes a man and then says go and make your fortune. You will hand your sword and wealth to your son; is that it?"

Cnut smiled and lay back on the bank, enjoying the shafts of sunlight which peered through the thinning clouds. "Of course he will and that is why he is Dragon Heart and you sing songs about him."

I smiled at their jibes, "Why else does a man choose to have a family if not to make their life better than his. I was born a slave and look at what I have achieved. My son is born the son of a jarl...."

It was late afternoon when my warriors returned. I saw that there were two missing. I would find out who they were in due course.

Sigtrygg bowed his head, "I have failed you, Jarl Dragon Heart. We could not capture them and we lost Erik and Siggi."

They were both seasoned Ulfheonar and would be hard to replace.

"Did they die well?"

"They died well."

"Then do not mourn them."

"We killed four of his oathsworn and five others but they fled on their drekar."

"Do not worry, Sigtrygg. They will not return. We questioned one of his warriors. He came for the sword to make him invincible. He will find it hard to hang on to what he has. This will be the last we hear of Harald Blue Eye. He has gambled and he has lost. We will return home and celebrate our friends who are now telling the Allfather of our deeds."

We feasted long into the night. We had lost Ulfheonar. Some were new to us but we celebrated their lives and their glorious deaths nonetheless. I saw Cnut and Haaken with the three new Ulfheonar who had survived. I wandered over to listen. Haaken punctuated his words with his finger.

"Ulfheonar are not reckless. We are brave and we are fierce fighters but we do not rush into combat. We have lost three young warriors who might have become great Ulfheonar and that is a tragedy."

"Haaken is right, live for your brothers. We are the best and we have high standards. Meet them." Cnut had such a serious look on his face I thought the new warriors might recoil in fear.

I put my arms around the shoulders of my two old friends. "They are right but remember that we do what we do for our people. That is why we need to live. For in living we keep them safe. You did well today and I am proud that you are my oathsworn. Enjoy tonight for once we sail south there will be no such nights. We feast and we drink when we are safe here in Cyninges-tūn. Everywhere else is a place of danger. You will learn as we all learned and when you have your wolf skin then you will know what it is to be Ulfheonar."

Arturus was most disappointed to have missed the skirmish. He had done what I had asked of him. Thorkell and Windar would watch our lands whilst we were away. Both had new warriors. Every day disgruntled Vikings came from Jarls who did not offer what we did: good land and a code by which we lived. We had no kings and princes. That had appeal to those who sat beneath the yoke of tyrants. Rorik had not been the only one. We heard of the privations Wiglaf was inflicting upon his people. He was far crueller than any Viking. He surrounded himself by vicious killers who cared not for the old ways and values. They were there to extract all the gold that they could from their people. It explained the reason why he had begun to spread the legend of the sword so that all the malcontents would try to get the sword for themselves. They would leave Jorvik and his power would only increase. My decision to leave was a good one. My decision to slay him an even better one.

It took much organisation to prepare our ships for sea whilst ensuring that our homes were safe. Our voyage would take many weeks. The three new Ulfheonar went hunting their wolves while the rest of the warriors went hunting. Our farmers and fishermen were too busy to be able to forage for wild food for us. Our smiths and miners were equally busy. I left Arturus and the Ulfheonar while I went with Aiden to my ship and to see the headman of Úlfarrston, Pasgen. Kara insisted that I take the small ship down to the end of the Water. She was mindful of the allure of the sword. As Aiden and I strode through the forest the sword felt like a heavy weight in my baldric.

I walked in silence as I was trying to plan for the future. Haaken and Cnut were both correct; my plan would only delay the arrival of other seekers of the sword. I could not sail the seas of the world until the end of time.

Aiden frightened me sometimes. He suddenly said, very quietly, "This will pass, Jarl Dragon Heart. There will always be those who seek the sword. There have been before. Think how many warriors have challenged you to single combat. Wiglaf is the problem for he is feeding the fire of warrior's envy and desire."

"You have entered my mind again."

He laughed, "Let us say that I know your moods and I have spoken with Kara. She knows your heart and your mind as well as any for she speaks with the spirits. This is good, Jarl, this is *wyrd*."

Erik Short Toe had been the ship's boy on the "*Heart of the Dragon*." He had been trained to be captain by old Josephus, the Greek slave we had rescued. The old Byzantine had done a good job for, despite his youth, Erik was the best captain I had. He was consulting with Bolli as Bolli's men scraped away the weed from the hull of my drekar. Thanks to the concoction Aiden had made and we had smeared over the hull there was less than one might expect. When the weed had been cleared the hull would be treated again. It was what made my drekar the fastest afloat. She and her consort, *"Josephus"* could out sail any ship that we met.

Erik looked eager to sail. He hated the inactivity of winter. He was born to the sea. He seemed to understand what the wind would do before it changed or swirled. He rubbed his hands as he came to greet me. "Jarl Dragon Heart! We sail soon?"

"We sail soon, Erik. Have you your ship's boys?"

He nodded and then looked at me apprehensively. "They are not from our people, jarl. They come from Úlfarrston."

I laughed, "Erik, you forget I am not from our people as you say. I am not Norse. Half of my blood comes from the same people as Pasgen. So long as they are good workers I care not where they come from." I pointed to Aiden. "Aiden here is from Hibernia; does that make him not of our people?"

He smiled, "I am sorry! And Josephus was Greek! You are right. When do we sail?"

I cocked my head on one side. "You are the captain and Bolli is the shipwright. You tell me!"

"Then three days from now."

"Good! The hunters will be back then and we can salt the meat. I will see Pasgen. Come Aiden."

I told Pasgen of the attacks on our land and explained that I was raiding for slaves. "If you have ships you wish me to escort to Lundenwic then I can do so."

He shook his head. "Trygg and Siggi went with our boats as soon as the weather became clement." He frowned, "Are we in danger when you are gone?"

"I hope not but we have put plans in place to have Thorkell and Windar have promised to protect my land."

We did not have three days. Had we not been preparing for war we might have been caught unawares. If we had been out hunting or working on the Water then disaster might have struck us but we were preparing for war and we had two boat crews inside our walls. The twenty raiders slew the two guards at the open gates with arrows and slipped silently into the heart of my home. I was trying on my armour. Bjorn the smith had made some improvements to make it lighter and he was in my hall with me as we adjusted it.

Padraigh my slave rushed in clutching a bleeding arm. "Jarl, there are raiders!"

I drew my sword and picked up my shield. Bjorn picked up the hammer he always carried. "Stay here Padraigh." We stepped into the main hall and there were six warriors there. None wore armour and all were ready to kill. They were Norse and had the tattooed bodies favoured by the men of Northumbria. All of them carried a sword, held a shield and sported a helmet.

Bjorn looked at me and smiled, "Only six of them, Jarl."

Their leader had carved teeth and an enormous scar running down his body. He wore battle rings on his arms. "We have warriors enough outside. When I have the sword touched by the gods then we will enjoy your women!"

Just then there was the clash of arms beyond my hall. I smiled. It was my men and they were already falling upon the Vikings who had made the mistake of trying to beard me in my own den. "Did you think I was alone? Did you hope to creep in like an assassin, murder me and take my weapon?" I shook my head. "The gods would not allow that. The man who prises this sword from my dead fingers will be a great warrior and not a posing, preening warrior who carves his teeth, cannot afford armour and was almost killed by some Saxon." Part of my insult was guesswork but I must have hit a nerve for he launched himself at me.

His reckless charge played into my hands. I parried the blow from his sword as I spun and swung my sword horizontally. He was past me when my blade bit into the bare flesh of his back. I caught sight of Snorri and Sigtrygg as they charged through my door and fell upon the others. The leader turned and saw the blood dripping from my blade. His eyes narrowed as he realised that he had been wounded. It sometimes happens in the heat of the battle that you are struck and do not know it.

He roared and charged at me. I noticed that the strike he had made on my shield had bent his sword slightly. I parried hard with Ragnar's Spirit as I punched with my shield. The sword bent even more and he stumbled backwards. I brought my sword around in an arc and rammed it into his middle. He sank to his knees and he looked at me in surprise. I swung a third time and took his head in one mighty blow. It was over and the raiders were dead.

We had no one left to question for my men had outnumbered them. The fact they came from the east told us that Wiglaf's poison had done its work. We took their bodies and burned them on the beach. The Water would scatter their ashes into the depths. Bjorn took the poorly made weapons and melted them down. Their treasure was poor. Kara had nodded when she had seen their bodies, "They were poor warriors who saw the sword as a means of becoming rich and powerful."

I worried that more might come now whilst we were away. Scanlan and Rolf reassured me. "We can keep the gates shut from now on. It is a small inconvenience to open and close them each time someone wishes to enter. I have more men and boys I can use as sentries. The young see it as a way to become one of your warriors."

Kara had agreed, "I sensed danger but I said nothing. This is my fault, father. I thought that the danger was for you on your voyage. Fear not I will heed all the messages that the spirits send to me. I will not let you down again."

We left a day before Ein-mánuðr. The weather was good with a wind from the north east. It was a cold wind but it came from Ragnar's home in Norway and we all took that to be a good sign. It had also passed over our home and carried with it the good thoughts of our people. Best of all, according to Haaken, was that the Ulfheonar did not need to row. I was torn because Arturus was with his own crew on the *"Josephus."* It was hard to get used to the fact that my son had his own oathsworn. They were not Ulfheonar for they did wear the skin of the wolf, but they had proved themselves when they had manned the eastern fort and fought off Ragnar Hairy Breeches and Rorik. This would be their first raid. I knew that my son needed to stand on his own feet and lead his own men but the father in me wanted me close by to watch him.

I stood on the opposite side of the drekar to the steering board; from there I could see the *"Josephus"* and my son and his crew. Aiden came to me. "You had no father to watch over you when you led your first warband, jarl"

I shook my head as my mind reader did it again. "No, but I had Prince Butar and Olaf who were there to offer advice."

"And he has you. He is as a brother to me and he has strength within him. Never fear."

"Ah, but I am a father and there is something within me which will not let go."

"That is from your mother and the Warlord of Rheged. The spirits favour us on this raid. It will bring great success."

Inevitably the first part of the journey was always the most dangerous for we passed Mann. Once our home, it was now the haunt of the Dyflin Norse and the men of Orkneyjar. They were led by warriors like Sihtric Silkbeard who were treacherous and cruel. If they were what the world thought of as Viking then I did not wish to be called a Viking. We passed the two islands of Mann and Calf of Mann without incident and then round the island now called Angle Sey. They were not seafarers but they had closed their harbours to us. We were the wild men of the north who were to be feared and not to be trusted.

Ironically some of the men of Cymru were our allies. We had traded for iron with them although we did not need to do so any longer. After three days of favourable winds we had to navigate the Scillonia Insula. I always felt a shiver when we passed these low-lying islands. It had been here where the spirit of my mother had come to me. A sorceress inhabited them and I was tempted to land and seek advice. I knew that the Norns did not wish it for they had directed me with storms and foes before. It did not do to try to cross the Weird Sisters. If they wished it then it would happen. When we saw them receding in the west then I knew that we would not be landing there.

Once we had passed the ragged rocks and boiling seas Haaken's face fell as he was forced to row. Although the wind still sent us south it was now coming across our bows and the crew had to row. Cnut set up the chant and the men rowed with vigour. It was a simple chant but it was unique to my boat. It spoke of the pride they felt in their status.

'Ulfheonar, warriors strong
Ulfheonar, warriors brave
Ulfheonar, fierce as the wolf
Ulfheonar, hides in plain sight
Ulfheonar, Dragon Heart's wolves
Ulfheonar, serving the sword
Ulfheonar, Dragon Heart's wolves
Ulfheonar, serving the sword'

The chant would be repeated until Cnut or Erik needed to change the beat. We would not need to do so for the seas were empty. The chant was almost hypnotic. When I rowed the chant seemed to give extra strength and my warriors told me that they could row for longer when they chanted.

Danger came when we neared Wessex. King Egbert was an ally. We had helped him defeat Mercian raiders. However, he was engaged in a bitter war with the men of Corn Walum. We were sailing to the south of the island called Wight when the five small ships appeared from the east. They were pirates from Corn Walum. I guessed, much later, that they had been raiding Wessex. It was unusual to meet another ship unless you were approaching or leaving a port.

As soon as I saw them I yelled, "Archers!" I donned my helmet and strung my bow. Half of the rowers left their benches and took up their bows. I hailed Arturus and pointed to the east. He waved and acknowledged the threat. "Danger!"

With only half the rowers we were going slower and, as the wind was coming across the bow's quarter it meant we were crawling along. The five pirates, all of them half the length of ours, were able to sail without using rowers and were travelling much faster. Aiden smiled, "The Allfather watches over us, Jarl Dragon Heart."

"Aye Aiden. We have a stable drekar from which to release our arrows and if they misjudge their attack then they will sail beyond us and have to turn into the wind." I was relieved that we had prepared for war and our shields were hung along the side. The rowers would be protected.

Haaken stood next to me. "Do the men of Corm Walum use bows?"

"They may do but I wager that they are not as good as my Ulfheonar."

"We will see."

I had the barbed arrows to hand. Only a fool wore armour in a sea battle. It was too easy to fall overboard and then you would be dead. We had twenty archers ready and we gathered at the bow. There the figurehead, hand carved by Bolli's father, would give us extra protection. I nocked an arrow and prepared to draw. They were just a hundred paces from us and their intention was clear. Each of our drekar would be attacked by two of theirs leaving the third to support whichever was having the hardest time. These pirates had done this before for they shortened their sails.

"Release when you have a target!"

I did not need to tell them who to target for they were all experienced warriors. The three new ones rowed still. I allowed for the wind and I released. I aimed at the steersman and he ducked. Sadly for him he was struck by a second arrow, probably from Haaken. As he fell his dying hands tugged on the steer board and the small ship lurched to the steer board side. The wind caught the sail and, beam on to both the wind and the waves it heeled over. In their desperation they ran to the steersman and the extra weight capsized the boat, hurling the occupants into the sea.

The fifth boat now tried to close with us and we concentrated our arrows on the second of our attackers. We discovered that they did have archers but their speed and their small size meant that many of their arrows were wasted. We had four times the number of archers and the deadly missiles rained down upon their packed decks.

Aiden suddenly shouted, "Jarl! The last one is closing." I glanced to the side and saw that the last of the ships of Corn Walum was almost alongside us. The leader must have been aboard and he had risked more sail to close with us. It had worked and our attention had been on the other ship.

"Snorri! Take half of the archers and keep the other ship at bay. Haaken and the rest come with me. This is sword work. Let us show these pirates how real warriors fight!"

The rowers suddenly began chanting "Ulfheonar," over and over. I felt the blood surge through my veins. I loosed a last arrow and dropped my bow. Aiden would pick the dropped up and take them to the stern where he would guard, along with the boys, Erik Short Toe. Our captain was the most important man on my drekar and that included me.

I drew my sword and felt its power rush into my arm. As the first hook snaked over the side I roared a primeval cry and leapt to the side. I saw a hand grasp the side and I was swinging before I even reached the pirate. My blade ripped across the man's head and into his hand. It severed his arm, the rope and opened his skull. He fell back in a heap. More ropes were now joining us but the pirates were struggling to climb our higher sides. I brought Ragnar's Spirit down on to the skull of the next pirate and this time his whole skull was split asunder. Those around him were showered with the grey, slimy contents of his head.

Suddenly I heard a warning shout from Aiden. Their chief had boarded us with three of his men. He was a huge half naked barrel of a man with an old Roman helmet and a long sword, the kind the Romans had called a spatha. He made straight for me and swung the long sword. It had a longer reach than mine but the deck of a pitching, rolling drekar is no place for such a weapon. I ducked beneath its swing and, holding his arm with my left hand I plunged my sword into the vast chasm of his stomach. When my hand touched his flesh and the blade ground on bone then I knew I had severed his spine. His body shook and then he fell backwards into his boat.

That was enough for the men of Corn Walum. The ones who had boarded with their chief now lay dead and the half empty boat drifted south. I ran to the other side and saw that Snorri and his archers had driven off the second attacker. I fearfully looked north and felt relief when I saw that *'Josephus'* was alone. My son and his crew had driven off their attackers.

"Well done Ulfheonar! The pirates are no more."

Haaken clapped me on the back. "And he was a big one, Jarl. I wondered how you would get through the layers of fat."

Tostig Wolf Hand wiped the blood from his sword and said, "How did we sink a pirate, drive off four others and only have four wounded men."

"It was the sisters, Tostig. It was *wyrd*."

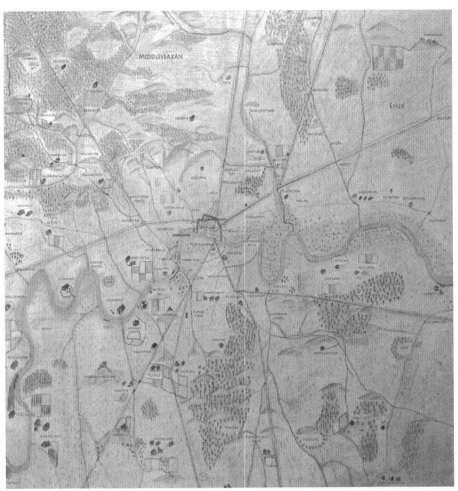

Anglo Saxon London

Chapter 4

We hove to in a little bay half a day's sailing east of the island of Wight. We had maps which Aiden had been making. They had begun life as old maps we had found in a chest. They had been made in the time of the Warlord and in the times of the Romans. Aiden could read Latin and the old language; he had transcribed them for the originals were too fragile to risk at sea. The old Roman port of Gesoriacum had long since vanished and in its place was a small fishing village called Bononia. It was clearly marked on the old maps. I had chosen it as I assumed and hoped that its small size would mean it would be overlooked by raiders seeking treasure. We sought not treasure but people. Fisher folk were strong and hard working. They could be trained to be miners.

We decided that we would sail across under cover of darkness and strike in the middle of the night before the fishermen went to sea. We would be well to the south of any ships which might contain armed warriors such as the ones we had met in Frisia. It was the mouth of the Rinaz which was filled with such ships. As the two drekar bobbed up and down on the waves which lapped the shingle beach I tried to sleep. I knew that it was impossible. My mind was racing with the dangers and rewards of what we were going to do.

We left as the sun set and we rowed, for the wind had veered during the day to become a headwind. The mast was removed and laid on the mast fish. It made us harder to see and we were faster without it. Erik and the men we left on board could replace it while we raided. We had prepared for war before we sailed. Our eyes were lined with red and black and our weapons were sharpened. We shunned our armour for we did not expect armed opposition. We wore our leather byrnies and our wolf cloaks. They would be enough. It took some time to row across the short channel to Bononia. The headwind did not help but it was relatively calm and that was a good thing. Aiden navigated us to a beach which was close to the village. We passed the village on our way north. The smell of wood smoke drifted on the breeze as we approached but the place was in darkness. They kept no watch. They would pay for that mistake; it was a harsh world in which we lived.

The gods watched over us for it was low tide when we approached. Six men from each boat were chosen by lots to wait with the boys and captains. Four of them were the warriors wounded in the sea fight so this time it was only two disappointed warriors we left behind. While we were away they would step the mast and then sail the drekar around to the port. It was the reason we had landed to the north so that the breeze would do all the work for the two drekar.

I jumped ashore and smiled as I did so. I remembered when I had been a ship's boy and it had been my job to take the rope and secure it. Old Olaf the Toothless had been an unforgiving captain. Once my feet were on the sand I began to trot, knowing that my men would soon be behind me. I raised a hand and Snorri and Bjorn the Scout sprinted ahead. They were our eyes and ears. Once they disappeared from view I slowed a little to allow the rest of my men to catch up with me. Arturus appeared at my shoulder. We said nothing for sound travels long distances at night but he nodded and grinned. It was still a game to him. We moved forwards towards the village we knew was over the headland.

Snorri rose like a wraith from behind the rock. He pointed ahead and I could see the huts. There were ten of them. They should contain at least twenty who could be taken as miners. I had already told them that we would only kill if they resisted. I hoped that our wild and fierce appearance would drive all such thoughts from their terrified minds. I waved Arturus and his younger warriors to the far side of the huts where I knew Bjorn the Scout would be waiting. I led my Ulfheonar to the heart of the village. Each dwelling was surrounded by five warriors. They were all watching for my signal. The Gods were smiling as the moon appeared and bathed the beach and the village in a beautiful blue light. I raised Ragnar's Spirit and we stepped into the huts.

After the brightness from the moon it seemed incredibly dark in the hut. There was just a glow from the embers of the fire. There were six people in the hut. An old couple, two children and a man and woman. I had my sword at the man's throat even as he was waking. Tostig picked him up and bound his arms. The movement awoke the others and they screamed.

Einar asked, "Do we take the children and the old man?"

I looked at the old man. He might not even survive the voyage and the children were less than six summers old. It was not worth the effort. "No. Just the man." They stared at us not understanding a single word but obviously terrified.

The old man struggled to his feet and tried to grab Tostig's arm. Einar drew his sword but I restrained him. I looked at the old man and I shook my head. He said something I could not understand. I pushed him to the floor. He reached into his tunic and pulled a knife. I stamped on his hand and took the knife. I knew he would not understand my words but I said them anyway, "Stay here or you die!" To emphasise the threat I drew my hand across my throat. The old woman seemed to understand and she threw her arms around him to prevent any more foolishness. The woman and the children were sobbing.

"Take him out. *'Heart'* should be here soon."

The beach and the village were still bathed in light but it was no longer peaceful. There were screaming women and struggling men. It was a futile struggle. We outnumbered them. They were like helpless sheep and we were the wolves. Such sheep needed a dog to protect them and these had paid the price for having none. I saw that the two drekar were off shore. Their masts were now stepped. "Arturus!"

He ran over to me. "No injuries, Jarl."

"I would have been disappointed if there had been. Take the slaves back to Cyninges-tūn. Then return and meet us at Lundenwic."

"Are we not finished here yet? Why do we not both return home?"

"I wish to advertise our presence and draw the hunters to us. Lundenwic has many traders and is close to the Danes who live amongst the East Angles. If they know where I am they may come south for me. I would rather we fought far from our home and keep our people safe."

30

"You will wait for me?"

I laughed, "Make a speedy voyage and you will miss nothing. I am hoping to meet with King Egbert and see how his war with Mercia is faring. We can trade a little while we wait for you."

"We will fly, I promise you that!" He turned to shout to his men. "Sven, get the slaves aboard our ship! Use the fishing ships to ferry them. Why should we get wet?"

The unfortunate captives were dragged somewhat unceremoniously over the sand to their own boats. "Haaken, get the men into the other fishing boats and we will return to our drekar."

The old men and some of the older boys whom we had not taken were shouting at us and waving their fists. The women restrained them. We were being kind. Had I chosen I could have slaughtered everyone in the village and fired it. As it was they would have a hard time for a while but we had left them their boats and they could still fish. They still had a roof over their head. Perhaps they would learn their lesson for if other Vikings came then this village would cease to exist. I was the last to board my ship. We pushed off the fishing boats; the incoming tide would take them inshore but, already the young boys were hurling themselves into the surf to recapture their boats.

"Erik, head for Lundenwic!"

I watched my son's drekar as it headed west. With the wind at its back it moved with the speed of an arrow. He would make good time. As we slowly headed through the night and dawn towards the coast of the land of Kent I thought about the slaves we had just taken. I had been a slave and I had been freed. Scanlan and his family had been enslaved and now, not only were they free, Scanlan was my reeve and ran my estate. We lived in hard times and the families we left behind would learn to build walls and protect themselves from wolves such as us. If they did not then this would happen again. As for their men, they would not be mistreated and, if they worked hard they would win their freedom. The world was filled with many who could be enslaved as easily as we had taken these fishermen.

The Temese was a wide river and, as dawn broke, we were able to avoid the smaller boats heading out to sea as we sailed west towards the fort. In truth it was they who did the avoiding for we were a Viking Drekar. As we passed many of the ships I saw the followers of the White Christ making the sign of the cross. It made me smile as though waving a hand in the air could ward off evil. For that you needed Thor's Hammer or a treasure touched by the gods; I wore such a treasure at my side.

We passed the old Roman fort and headed for the jetty. We had arrived propitiously for many ships and boats had recently left and we had space to berth. Although Siggi and Trygg traded extensively here they were knarr and the drekar still inspired fear. The people who did not live within the Roman wall hid behind their wooden doors. I knew that they would be wondering if we came for trade or for war.

I took off my leather byrnie and, after hauling up a bucket of river water, I washed my face of the red so that I would not terrify those that I met. "Haaken, keep the warriors on board until I have met with Egbert's man. I will just take Aiden with me."

"Aye Dragon Heart. It will give us time to make ourselves irresistible for these Saxon wenches."

"Haaken! You are married!"

He laughed, "Aye but the children I make down here will not be so demanding of my time as my own and the world needs more of my blood. It will put poetry into the hearts of these dull Saxons."

He was a dear friend but Haaken had a high opinion of himself and his skill as a singer."Have you coin, Aiden?"

"Aye, Jarl."

We had learned that using silver coins made us more welcome. Erik's boys had put the gangplank down and we headed for the gates of the town. I noticed a few faces peering from cracks in the door as the two of us strode through the wooden buildings which proliferated around the river. Passing the sign of the barley I knew where Haaken and the others would be found later. They had an ale wife here in Lundenwic who brewed passable ale. It was not as good as that which we brewed but it was better than most we found on our travels.

There were armed guards at the gate. They wore no mail but held spears and shields with their seax in their scabbards. Without my cloak and helmet I was not recognisable.

"You are bold, Viking, to come into our town and stride up to the fort. Do you have the death wish?"

"I am Jarl Dragon Heart of Cyninges-tūn. I am a friend to King Egbert."

Those words changed the warrior and his attitude in an instant. He bobbed his head. "I am sorry, Jarl. I did not recognise you." He stood aside, "Please pass." He looked and sounded terrified. I knew that there were stories about me which were not true. They told of how I had leapt aboard a drekar and slain every warrior within. That was not true. It had been Rorik's ship and I had leapt aboard to enable my own knarr to be saved. I killed but a couple. However, as it had happened on this very river and had been witnessed they had built the tale into something it was not. It was further enlarged by Haaken's song which made it sound as though it had been a tale of the Gods and not a battle between Vikings.

I strode through the narrow streets of the old Roman fort. The wide-open spaces of the old Roman fort had been filled with tiny stalls and shops. The barracks were either filled with the warriors and their families or had been converted. Either way the neat lines which had been planned by the Roman engineers were no more. It was no wonder that folk were building outside the walls when inside was more cramped than a double crewed drekar. I headed for the hall. It stood on the site of one of the barracks. It was not made of stone but timber, lath and tiles taken from demolished barracks. I knew that Egbert had his own eorl here. He changed them frequently for he was a clever king. This was a powerful place and he did not want one of his own men to use it to usurp him.

Once he conquered Mercia then he would be King of Britannia. Of course there would be one part which would not be under his control and that was my land. I bowed the knee to no king.

There were more guards at the hall and I pre-empted any confusion by speaking first. "I am Jarl Dragon Heart of Cyninges-tūn and I am here to speak with King Egbert's man."

"Eorl Edward is within." He glanced at my sword. "Is that the sword touched by the gods?"

"It is."

I saw that as well as the cross of the White Christ he wore about his neck there was another thong which showed beneath his kyrtle. This Saxon was not a committed Christian. He still adhered to the old ways. I believed that he wore Thor's hammer. It was confirmed when he asked, quietly, "May I touch the blade my lord?"

I nodded and drew the blade. It was the most beautiful sword in the world and both guards gasped when they saw it. I held the blade so that the guard could touch the hilt. I saw him feel the power and he nodded as he withdrew his hand. He viewed it as though it had been burned by some magical fire. "Thank you, my lord."

He led us into the hall. I saw Aiden smile at me as we went. He knew why I had acceded to the guard's request. This would announce the location of the sword quicker than anything. He would tell all that he knew that he had touched Ragnar's Spirit. By nightfall the story would have been spread throughout the city and beyond for the sailors who heard it would repeat it. It was the fastest means of telling Wiglaf where the sword was. The second part would come when I spoke with Egbert's eorl.

I recognised him as soon as we entered the hall. It was Edward. He was one of Egbert's illegitimate sons. He was a little younger than me but he had been with us at Grenewic when we had routed Rorik's raiders. He knew me and that was important.

He left his counsellors and strode over to me. Like most Saxons he wore his hair long and bound. His clothes were of finely made linen. I felt like a dirty barbarian by comparison. Most Saxons would have agreed with me; to them I was a dirty barbarian. The eorl clasped my hand. Behind him I saw that not all of the counsellors were smiling. One or two were scowling at me. Aiden would find out their names. Not all of Egbert's people were happy with Wessex rule. Some still hankered after the Mercians who had been ousted. It was part of the reason that this city was now part of Wessex. Lundenwic and Lundenburgh were in the middle of what had been a number of Saxon kingdoms. Some thrones were bigger and more powerful than others. These counsellors and advisers would still play the game of politics. There would still be plotting and hidden alliances. It made me yearn for my home even more.

"Jarl Dragon Heart we did not know you were coming."

"We have been in Frankia. We had a little trade to do."

I got no further. Edward put his arm around my shoulders and led me away from prying ears. "You know that King Louis the Pious is encouraging the Danes and the Mercians to attack Wessex? He hopes to weaken my father. It is said that he is also trying to make an alliance with King Coenwulf of Mercia."

I did not but it was no surprise. Egbert and Wessex were a threat to the Carolingian Empire. "I did not know the news. My home is far from such events and we hear little of the outside world. What is the king doing about the threat?"

"He is first subjugating the men of Corn Walum in the west to make that border safe and then he will defeat the Mercians once and for all."

I smiled, "We had a run in with some of the pirates of Corn Walum on the way here. They have now learned to be wary of my dragon ships." He nodded and I could see that there was a question on his lips. "The Mercians your father can deal with but what of the Danes. That is the thought in your mind."

He laughed so loudly that the counsellors looked over in surprise. "My father says that you have a mind like a bear trap. Yes we fear the Danes. Your people are of the same ilk and we know how fierce you are. One Viking can be worth five Saxons in a battle and you are all so unpredictable." He hesitated, "We would like your advice on dealing with them."

"Advice or our swords?"

He laughed, "My father's assessment of you is accurate. Yes Jarl Dragon Heart. We would like your swords and your advice."

"I had intended to return to my home; this was a courtesy visit only. I will wait for my son and his ship; he is raiding Frankia." That was lie but it would hurt no one to tell it. Then we will see if we can do something about the Danes and their voracious appetite for Mercia." I smiled. Perhaps if your people spread the word that Jarl Dragon Heart is in Lundenwic it might deter any attacks."

"That is a master stroke, Jarl. I will do so. You will receive recompense for your trouble. Will you stay with me in my hall?"

"My men and I will make our own arrangements." I hesitated. "Would we be permitted to build a hall of our own along the river?"

"I cannot see why not. There is land aplenty."

"Good then I will see to that and try to discover who is leading these Danes."

"I will have a chest of coins prepared for you. My man will bring it to your drekar."

As we left I questioned Aiden about what he had seen and heard.

"There are two of them, Jarl, who are most unhappy to see you. One is called Aethelheard but I did not find out the name of the other. They are both older men and were here before the time of Egbert. They are Mercian at heart."

"Good you have done well. We will watch them. We have been given permission to build a hall on the river and the Eorl wishes us to find out which Danes are the greatest threat." I smiled, "He is telling the whole of Lundenwic that Jarl Dragon Heart will be here for a while."

Aiden's face split into a smile. "*Wyrd*!"

"And even better, Aiden, he is paying us for our services. There will be a chest coming to the drekar. Look to it for me."

We discovered that there were not enough trees close by to the city to build our hall and so we headed up river to Windlesore where there were trees in abundance. It did not take long to cut the quantity we needed and we towed them back to the site we had chosen. I did not want to be close to the church of the White Christ and so we chose a piece of higher ground at Celchyth. The site suited me for it was isolated from the town. We would see any who approached. The higher ground afforded us a degree of protection.

We landed the wood and rowed back to Lundenwic. We would sleep on the ship. The men had earned a night in the ale house. Cwoenthryth the ale wife was delighted despite their boisterous behaviour. Inevitably there were fights, mainly with the younger Ulfheonar but Haaken slipped her an extra coin and she was happy enough. I knew that, once the word got out that we were in Lundenwic then such nights would be a rarity. It was yet another reason why I wanted a hall which was away from innocent people. I wanted somewhere to defend when those who wished to take Ragnar's Spirit came.

There were sore heads the next morning as we rowed upstream. My men had celebrated well. We would now have to learn to be self sufficient. Aiden had procured some flour so that we could bake our own bread. We still had salted meat and that would do us until we went to raid the East Angles and the Danes.

Aiden laid out the outline of the hall and while half of the warriors prepared the tree trunks which would form the frame the rest of us dug the holes for the posts. This would not have to last long and we were not fussy about the shape of the trees used for the roof. Once the holes were dug then the younger warriors were sent to cut turf. We gathered as many stones and rocks as we could to make the timbers secure in the ground. One advantage of the proximity of the river was the clay and the mud. It made the manufacture of the daub much easier. By the end of the second day the eight trees had been planted in the holes and stones rammed around them. By the third we had the wood on the roof and by the fourth the turf had been laid. We now had shelter from above. I left Aiden in charge of the building. He would have the men make willow and hazel hurdles for the walls and daub them with mud and grass. I took Snorri and Bjorn the Scout to explore the land and go hunting.

We took our boar spears and our bows. Salted meat paled after ten days. We needed fresh meat to augment our diet. I was also keen to explore the land to the north. The border between Wessex and Mercia was only vaguely defined. Many of the villages owed allegiance to both Coenwulf and to Egbert. It ensured their survival. We had no mounts and our exploration would be limited. We headed north towards Wemba Lea. It was a small village, or so Cwoenthryth had told us, and was surrounded by forests. She had heard that they teamed with game.

It was a Roman Road we followed although once we neared the forest we took a track to head into its heart. Bjorn the Scout and Snorri were in their element. They soon found the spoor of some small deer. These were not the huge red deer we had at home. These were much smaller. They were almost like big dogs. He looked at the tracks in the muddy ground and worked out where they were heading. Snorri took us so that we approached them downwind. At times I thought that Snorri was the most wolf like of us for he could smell game long before the rest of us. He nocked an arrow and I knew at that moment that the animals were near. We spread out, quite naturally. Bjorn the Scout went to Snorri's right and I to the left. We watched our footing as we approached them. A snapping twig would send them scurrying away. I was a good archer but my two companions were the best and so I would wait for them to release first.

We saw the small herd. There was a large male with four females and four young. We all crouched. They were just sixty paces from us. We all made a silent plea to the god, Ullr, to guide our arrows and make a swift kill. I knew that my companions would not aim at the stag. That would be like killing the whole herd. They would choose an older female and one of the young. It ensured that the herd would continue just as we had left the young of the fishing village. It was a poor farmer who harvested all and had nothing left for the next year. The gods did not approve of such a waste and the goddess Eostre would punish us for such disregard.

The two arrows sped towards their targets and the deer began to flee. One of the young came in my direction and I released. It struck it in the head and it crumpled in a heap just twenty paces from me. Ullr had indeed listened. We quickly gutted the three of them and then slung them around our necks. Our wolf cloaks would absorb any blood and smell. It would help us disguise ourselves when we hunted again.

We had seen few people as we had travelled north and I asked Snorri to lead us east on the way back to our new home. We had only travelled a mile or so when we all smelled smoke. This was not the smoke of a cooking fire or a fire of charcoal burners. This was a fire of destruction. We dropped our burdens and, hefting our spears we ran in the direction of the smoke. It was an easy trail to follow for the smoke came in our faces. When we heard the screams and the shouts then we knew that it was human predators.

The small settlement was in a clearing next to the Roman Road which headed north to the land of Cymru. Two of the huts were on fire and it was their smoke which had drawn us. I saw the helmets and the axes. It was a band of Danes. There were fifteen of them. We could have turned and returned to our catch but that was not my way. We strung our bows and jammed our spears into the ground. The Danes were so busy with their privations that they had failed to set a guard. This was not a slave raid. They were intent on destruction, pillage and rape. We released our arrows together and, even as they were in the air released three more. When the first two warriors fell with arrows piercing them they turned to look for the danger. The second flight took out two more while a third was lucky to be able to raise his shield in time. We sent three more in their direction before dropping our bows and grabbing our spears.

"Ulfheonar!"

There were but three of us and now there were eight of them but we feared no man be he Saxon or Dane. My mind took in that only one had armour and the rest were dressed as we were in leather byrnies. I ran at the armoured Dane who had his shield across his back and his war axe above his head. My boar spear was longer than a man. If used in two hands, as I held it now, it was a powerful weapon. I saw Snorri's spear as it sailed by me and plunged into the chest of a half naked warrior. The armoured Dane's eyes flickered to the side and I took advantage of the momentary lapse of concentration to feint with my spear. He saw it at the last moment and he committed his axe to a block. The swing opened up his chest and I jabbed forward with the spear. It punctured his mail and his leather byrnie. He was a young warrior and he stepped back so that only the tip of the spear drew blood. I reversed the spear and swung the wooden haft at his head. It smacked the side of his helmet and he staggered. Suddenly I sensed a movement to my left and I swung the head to tear into the throat of the warrior attacking me on my blind side. I dropped the spear and drew my sword.

My opponent had regained his composure and was advancing towards me more confident now that I had lost my spear. I held my left hand before me as a shield. It drew his eye. I kept Ragnar's Spirit horizontally behind me. I could see blood seeping from the slight wound I had given him. I knew where I would strike. I feinted with my sword but he was wise to that manoeuvre and he did not commit his axe. Instead he whirled it above his head and advanced. If he thought to intimidate me he was wrong. I spun around as though I was going to flee in the face of his attack. With an exultant cry he moved rapidly towards me. I had spun out of the space he was attacking and I brought my sword across his back, just below the shield he carried there. This was not the tip, it was the edge but the force made him cry in pain and more of the links were shattered.

I dived and rolled forward to take me away from his flailing axe. As I stood I saw four dead Danes and Snorri and Bjorn the Scout chasing the other three into the forest. There was just me and the Dane left. He was in pain. I must have broken a rib when I had hit his back. Certainly his mail byrnie looked the worse for wear. Its integrity gone it would not take many more blows to render it useless. Links hung down making him unbalanced.

He advanced on me more slowly now. His gritted teeth told me that he would either kill me or die in the attempt. He had the look of death upon his face. He held the axe in his right hand now and swung his shield around. I had taught him caution. He knew that I had skill.

"Before I kill you Norseman, tell me your name so that I can tell others of this fight."

"It is a name you would fear to hear Dane."

He laughed, "I am Cnut son of Guthrum and I fear no Norseman!"

"Then fear me for I am Jarl Dragon Heart and I bear the sword which was touched by the gods. I will see you in Valhalla!"

He had a mixture of shock at my name and joy at the opportunity of killing such a renowned Viking. He came at me and tried to punch with his shield which he had pulled around while he talked. It was predictable and I stepped backwards so that he punched into empty air. He would soon find that using a war axe in one hand was tiring. I reached behind me and took out my seax. His eyes flickered between the two blades. I was happy for him to wait. A Danish war axe is meant to be used in two hands and I could see the sweat on his brow as he held it in one. I feinted with my sword and he swung his axe at me. My left hand darted in and the seax I had taken from a dead Saxon ripped and tore into the hole made by my sword. The curved blade enlarged the wound and he screamed in pain. I twisted it as I pulled it out. He punched with his shield and sent me tumbling but it also pulled some of his guts with it. He was mortally wounded and I had to finish it.

I regained my balance and swung Ragnar's Spirit at his head. He brought up his shield to block the blow and I charged my shoulder into his chest. He tried to step back but he tripped over one of his dead warriors. His arms fell open so that he looked like the cross the Christians wear about their necks. "I will see you in the Otherworld." I plunged my sword into his bare throat and he died instantly.

I cleaned the blood from my weapons and sheathed them. I saw Snorri and Bjorn the Scout returning alone from the forest. Snorri looked angry. "They had ponies waiting. They escaped."

"We did well enough. The villagers were all within their walls too terrified to emerge. There were five villagers lying dead outside the huts and I did not blame them. I spoke in Saxon. "You are safe now. I am a friend of King Egbert. I am Jarl Dragon Heart."

Gradually the braver ones came from hiding. One man was nursing a cut arm and he approached me. "Thank you Jarl. I thought that the Danes had us then."

"These are dangerous times my friend. I would build a ditch and erect a wall. What is the name of this place?"

"Willesdune."

"I will tell Eorl Edward what has happened here. You can keep the weapons and the mail although it will need repair." I knew that Snorri and Bjorn the Scout would have searched the bodies for treasure and we could not carry both the deer and the weapons back. This way they would be better protected and they would remember my generosity.

We retrieved our deer and headed back to Celchyth. "Did you find aught of value?"

Snorri grinned, "The young Dane you killed had a golden torc around his neck and the others all had either copper or silver rings. His axe was well made too. This was a profitable encounter."

I nodded, "We were meant to find them. The Danes now know we are here. They will have recognised our cloaks and their spies will discover our names. This is *wyrd*."

Chapter 5

There were walls on the hall when we returned. Aiden and my men had worked hard. I sent Snorri and Bjorn the Scout to tell Eorl Edward what had transpired. When Snorri handed me the torc Haaken shook his head. "Next time Snorri can make daub and I will hunt."

"If you were half as good a hunter as Snorri then I might consider it." We prepared the deer as I told them of the fight.

Aiden looked thoughtful. "The Eorl is right. They are intimidating those who might favour Wessex over Mercia. Do you think this Guthrum is their leader?"

"He may be. When Arturus joins us we will raid the Danish villages of the South Folk. It will please our allies and it might reward us with treasure."

It took another four days to complete the hall and to have it dry out. Eorl Edward came to visit us but this time just with his oathsworn and without the counsellors. He stood back to admire the hall. "You build differently from us. Why do you use turf for a roof?"

"It is the only material we have in Norway. At home we use stone for we have it in abundance."

"It is interesting." His face became serious. "But now you must tell me of the dangers from the Danes. Your warriors said it was Willesdune which they attacked."

"Aye. And that seems perilously close to Lundenwic. My men thought that it was an attempt to make the villagers change their allegiance."

"It would not take much. What the people want is to be protected from raiders." He gave an apologetic shrug, "From people like you."

"I am not offended and it is our way. It is for that reason that I tell you to make your villages less appetising for the Danes. Use ditch and wall."

"Do they stop you?"

I laughed, "No but we are Ulfheonar and nothing stops us. If we choose to take somewhere then we take it but they would have stopped the Danes we bested today."

"In another warrior I would take that as boasting but I know that you are merely speaking the truth. My father is happy that you are an ally for he would fear you as a foe."

"And I am happy to be Wessex's ally for you are far from my land. If Wessex ever cast covetous looks in my direction...."

Eorl Edward smiled, "I do not think my father would risk such a reckless act."

I led the Eorl to one side. "Some of your council are Mercians; you know that?"

He looked astounded, "I did but how did you know?"

"Aiden is a clever man. He keeps his eyes and ears open. Aethelheard is one but Aiden did not know the name of the other."

"Osbert. We know of them and we watch them."

I shook my head. "If they were my enemies then they would be dead already."

"My father hopes that they will lead us to other traitors."

"No, Eorl Edward, if you have poison then cut it out for it can spread." I shrugged, "This is your land and I only offer advice."

"I believe you are correct Jarl Dragon Heart but my father is king and it is his decision."

We were left to our devices for the next few days until a messenger came from Lundenwic to tell us that Arturus had arrived. We had managed to construct a simple jetty from the wood we did not need for the hall. It meant that he could tie up and our boats would be protected. "Snorri. Go to Arturus and tell him to moor here. It is safer."

"Aye Dragon Heart."

The men were ready for action. The work on the hall had occupied them but the raid on the port in Frankia had not been exciting enough for them. They all envied Bjorn the Scout and Snorri. We had fought Danes and we had won. "Haaken, have the weapons sharpened. We sail on the morning tide."

Arturus had had an uneventful voyage. The slaves had soon been cowed and Bjorn Bagsecgson was not a man to be crossed. They would be treated fairly but they would work. Scanlan would be their taskmaster as they toiled in the hills above Lang's Dale. Our miners would begin to extract the metal almost as precious to us as gold. We quickly gave an account of our time and, like Haaken and the others, he was envious.

"We have been able to bring another eight warriors for it was peaceful when we left Úlfarrston. There were no more raids at home, Jarl. Perhaps the news of our voyage has spread."

"No, Arturus, it is too soon. Word will take time to reach the odious Wiglaf. But I now believe that it was *wyrd* that brought us here. The Norns are weaving their webs. This is our destiny; for good or ill we need to be here until winter."

Aiden had not been idle and had won the ear of the ale wife. With so many sailors passing through her house she had a great deal of news and gossip at her fingertips. Aiden was adept at eliciting such information. He had discovered that there were a number of settlements along the east coast. The easy one to attack would be Lothuwistoft; the most heavily defended was Here Wic. Naturally we chose Here Wic. It had a wall and a garrison. If Guthrum did not live here then he valued its importance for he had a warband within its walls. It was not as risky as it sounded for we would probably have more men than in the garrison. It would be enough to protect the walls from most; not the Ulfheonar.

Aiden found an old widow who, for a few copper coins, watched our hall for us. She was there to keep the vermin outside and to keep a fire going. The daub walls were still drying as was the timber. Arturus had also brought more arrows from home for we had used many during the sea battle.

We slipped out in the darkness and we sped seawards on the receding tide. We would sail north and identify the port and then wait offshore until the hours of darkness returned. We stood far enough away from the coast for us not to be a threat but close enough to identify where we could land. This was a low lying and marshy coast. The fishing ports were perched precariously on little banks which looked as though an unusually high tide might wash them away.

It was mid afternoon when we first saw Here Wic. It was a fort which guarded a fine harbour and estuary. I could see why it had been chosen for it was the highest piece of earth we had seen so far. Within it we saw the masts of at least three drekar. We continued north as though we were raiders heading back to Norway. Aiden's sharp eyes and the old maps we had helped us to deduce that we had to land to the south of the port for the estuary was a death trap. We would be seen and could be attacked by the crews of the drekar. Instead of a direct attack we would march over the dunes to reach the fort. I felt confident. It was a strong defensive site but that very strength gave it its weakness. They would not expect to be attacked, especially not from the landward side. We could only do this once for they would be ever watchful after but we had a chance and it would draw the glory hunters south to find this impudent Jarl Dragon Heart who attacked a Danish stronghold.

As darkness fell we lowered our sails and rowed in to the shore. The lots drawn, the twelve warriors who would be aboard the ships took off their armour. They would not need it. They would be there to help Erik to move the drekar and to fend off any attacks. The sea, sky and the dunes were black when we reached the surf. Two of the boys jumped in to ascertain the depth. We were able to edge in just a little further when they found that they had to swim.

"Erik. Stay off shore and watch for our signal to close with the beach. The closer you can get to Here Wic the better."

"Yes, Jarl. What will be the signal?"

"Watch for fire. It will be a big fire and not just a signal fire. We will escape when there is confusion and mayhem."

Snorri and Bjorn the Scout jumped into the sea first. They would scout ahead. We followed and landed in waist deep sea. The water was still cold. It would be some time before the summer sun warmed it. Half of Arturus' men had bows. They would rid us of anyone who interfered with our plans. My Ulfheonar had other tasks to perform.

We headed north. We had seen our scouts disappear and we followed their line. Once we had crossed the dunes then we moved through thin and spindly pines and sand. The land was flat hereabouts and the fort could only be dimly made out but Snorri waited for us. "It is less than a thousand paces from here. Bjorn the Scout is waiting beneath the walls to the west."

"Arturus, take your men and go to Bjorn the Scout. You know what to do?"

"Aye, Jarl Dragon Heart."

"Make sure that you light the fire as soon as the sentries are dead. That is the crucial part of the plan."

He cocked his head on one side. "I am a man now father and I lead my own oathsworn. Trust me to do this well."

I clasped his arm, "To me you will always be a son and I cannot help worrying about you." He nodded and led his men off at an easy lope. Snorri led us east towards the tower at the end of the fort.

As we neared it I could see that it was not Roman. It had not been built of stone. Therein lay its weakness. It was wooden and the ditch was too shallow. It would not deter a child. The towers did not jut out which created many blind spots. I intended to exploit those.

The flaw in my plan was that there was no way of coordinating our two attacks. I just hoped that we would confuse them. It was likely that one of our two attacks would have to bear the brunt of the Dane's ire. I hoped that it would be us.

There was a ditch which ran beneath the ramparts. However, the driving sand had filled in most of the ditch. It might have originally been built deeper but it had not been maintained. The complacency of the garrison would come to haunt them. Half of the Ulfheonar approached the walls. Snorri and Bjorn the Scout had bows strung and arrows nocked in case the sentries showed an interest in the landward side. They seemed more concerned with the seaward side and that suited us. Cnut waited with half of the men while Haaken and I led the other half. We sank a little in the damp, sand filled ditch but it was a minor inconvenience. Tostig and Erik Dog Bite held their shield for me and others did the same for Sigtrygg, Haaken and Bjorn Carved Teeth. I stepped on to the shield and they raised it to their waist. My shield was upon my back and I held Ragnar's Spirit in my hand. The sentries were still at the tower which overlooked the sea.

I nodded and I was thrust upwards. I grabbed the top of the ramparts with my left hand and sprang on to the walkway. I must have landed silently for no one sounded the alarm. I did not wait for the others but moved towards the tower. I was almost at the tower and the guards when I heard a piercing scream from the western end of the fort; Arturus and his men had struck and been seen. One of the Danes came rushing from the tower and ran into my sword before he even saw me. I thrust him to the courtyard before me and stepped into the tower. There was a brazier burning. The four Danes must have had a shock when they looked up and saw a monster wearing a wolf cloak with burning red eyes. I swung my sword horizontally and was sprayed with the warm blood of two of them. I punched them with my shield and they fell in a heap. One was mortally wounded but the other three tried to get to their feet. Haaken and Bjorn were behind me and all three fell dead.

We could hear the noise of battle at the main gate. All was eerily quiet where we were. After helping the others over the ramparts we clambered down the ladders into the heart of the fort. The Danes were leaving their warrior hall and running to the gate where they perceived their danger. Sigtrygg stabbed a surprised Dane in the back as he stepped from the hall. He pulled the body away and stepped inside. "Haaken, Cnut, keep at their backs." I stepped into the warrior hall. Half of the Danes had already left and the ones who remained were struggling to rise. The evening's drink had weakened them. "I am Jarl Dragon Heart and I wield the sword touched by the gods! Fear me and my oathsworn!"

Normally I would have just attacked but I needed my name spreading. The bait would have to be laid thickly if I was to draw the danger towards me. Sigtrygg and I slew four warriors who lurched sleepily towards us with just their swords. Their blows bounced harmlessly off our weapons and armour. They died. Sigtrygg ran to the fire and used his sword to stab a burning brand. He hurled the brand high and it fell against a wall. The dry interior soon began to burn. Erik Short Toe would have his message. He would be able to head in and pick us up.

We hacked our way to the door as the ones who remained inside tried to beat back the ever growing flames. Outside the hall we saw that Arturus and his men had set fire to the gate and were driving Danes towards us. We had them surrounded. Had they had a leader they would have formed a shield wall but there appeared to be no one left to organise them. Snorri and Bjorn the Scout ran to my side. "Our ships are coming."

"Good. I want a prisoner. Get one."

"Aye Jarl Dragon Heart."

"Sigtrygg, take a dozen men and burn their ships."

I saw him run towards the water. Haaken and Cnut took their places next to me. We began to hack, slash and stab our way to Arturus. It was not that the men we fought were not brave. They were, but we had better weapons and armour and my men had a leader, they had me. The warriors broke before our ferocious attack. Those that could, disengaged and ran towards the walls. Others tried and were slain as they ran.

My men began to bang their shields and chant, "Jarl Dragon Heart" over and over. The ones who survived would take the stories of the wolves that appeared in the night and brought death to them. Wiglaf would soon discover where I was and my enemies would come for me.

I greeted Arturus, surreptitiously checking that he was unwounded. "You did well, my son."

He frowned, "I lost six warriors."

"They died as your oathsworn with swords in their hands. They are in the Other World now and they are happy. Come let us get to our boats."

We made our way down to the sea. Already the Danish drekar there were burning. There were dead and dying Danes showing that they had tried to defend their ships. Our two drekar came around the headland slowly for they were only crewed by a handful of warriors. I turned and looked at the Danish stronghold. It was burning. I had no doubt that there were survivors who would come and put out the fires but the damage had been done. As a fort it was now redundant and Guthrum would have to rebuild. He had two reasons to hate me now: I had killed his son and destroyed his stronghold and drekar. I saw that our warriors had stripped the bodies of those they had killed and were carrying weapons and treasure. That had not been our aim but it was welcome reward for our brave men.

We boarded at dawn. No one tried to stop us. The few survivors had fled the fort and were hiding. Our sudden attack had had the desired effect. The winds were from the north and whilst not strong they meant that we did not need to row. We would save that for the river. We stripped ourselves of our armour and drank from the small barrel of beer we had bought from the ale wife. Men slept where they could, even Aiden. As we headed south I had Snorri bring the prisoner we had captured. There were just five of us to question this prisoner. The rest lay beneath their cloaks.

He was not a young warrior. I saw the lump forming on his head from the blow Bjorn the Scout had given him. "What is your name?" he remained silent. "I am Jarl Dragon Heart. You have heard of me?"

His widening eyes told me he had. "I have heard of you. That is the magic sword." He nodded, "Now I know how you captured our fort. It was witchcraft. You have a powerful witch who protects your home and you have a Galdramenn."

I smiled, my Galdramenn was asleep less than six paces from him. "Then it will do no harm to tell me your name."

"I am Siggi Ulffarson. Now kill me, Jarl Dragon Heart."

"Who says I am going to kill you? You have no sword in your hand. If you know my reputation then you know that I am a fair man."

"Then what do you wish of me?"

"Two things: I wish information and then I wish you to take a message for me."

"Why should I do either?"

"If you do then it will save your life. You will live."

I saw him weighing up the alternatives. "Ask your question and I will then decide if I should answer."

"Is your leader, Jarl Guthrum?"

He frowned as he tried to see the trick in my words. Of course there was none. He nodded. I smiled, "And why was he not at your stad? Or did we kill him?"

"Guthrum is a mighty warrior. You would have lost many warriors had you tried to kill him. You were lucky that he and most of the band were to the south west."

Already he had told me more than he intended for the land of the Middle Saxons was close to the land of Wessex. Their leader was on the borders of Wessex. Coenwulf was using him to threaten Wessex while he supported the men of Corn Walum. He was a wily king. I smiled, "Then you have answered my questions. Now I need you to take a message for me."

"Where? And why should I?"

I shrugged. "It is a message for this Guthrum. You cannot object to returning to your jarl can you?" Again he was looking for the trick and, of course, there was none.

"Very well but what is the message?"

"Tell him that Lundenwic is under my protection now and if he tries to attack it or the lands of my friend, King Egbert, then he will answer to Jarl Dragon Heart and his sword, Ragnar's Spirit."

The man's mouth opened in amazement. I was challenging this leader of the Danes. He obviously had more men than I did for we had had to fight many men in the fort and more were with this Jarl Guthrum. He nodded, "I will do as you ask. You are a strange man. I do not understand you."

"Good then that is how I like it. Erik, stand in to the shore. We will drop off our passenger." We dropped him in the shallows and watched while he waded ashore. I waited until he had disappeared into the swampy area behind the beach.

I waved Snorri and Bjorn the Scout forward. "Follow our friend there and find out where this Guthrum hides. Stay hidden and do not take risks."

Bjorn the Scout cocked his head to one side. "Jarl Dragon Heart, no one takes more risks than you. We will stay hidden."

They slipped silently into the water and trotted after the Dane. They would not be seen unless they chose to be and his trail was easy to see. "Now we head back to the hall. It has been a good night."

The men had to row up the river and they did so without a chant. They were weary and this was a job which needed doing. Each warrior was thinking of his fight and how he could have fought better. That was the Ulfheonar way. They also thought of the warriors we had left behind. There were just two Ulfheonar who had died and they were two of the newer warriors. It was always the way. We had high standards; once we met them then we had more chance of survival. We had their bodies with us and we would bury them with honour at our new hall. Their spirits would watch over it for us.

Erik watched the mast head and touched the steering board a little to correct our course. "Why did you tell him what you did, Jarl? You told him where we would be. He will come for us."

"He will and he will tell the tale of how Jarl Dragon Heart and his Ulfheonar raided his fort and fled to Lundenwic. Wiglaf and the other seekers of the sword will come to Lundenwic."

"That will put the town in danger."

"It would if we were not there but that fort was built by the Romans. We can help King Egbert to defend it. Who would you back to win: the Danes or the Ulfheonar?"

He laughed, "That is an easy one. The Ulfheonar. Your mind is becoming sharper, Jarl."

"Thank your old mentor, Josephus. He introduced us to the ways of the Greeks and I am a quick learner. We do what we do for our people. The fact that I am helping the King of Wessex is incidental. So long as we draw danger here and away from Cyninges-tūn, then I am happy."

We finally tied up to our crude jetty in the early afternoon. Although exhausted I knew that I needed to speak with Edward. Aiden came with me. I think he was curious about the events of the day and he had noticed the absence of Snorri and Bjorn the Scout. He nodded his approval when I told him what I had done while he had slept. "The maps came in useful then?"

"When I saw the area of swamp marked then I knew that Bjorn the Scout and Snorri would be able to follow him easier than through a forest."

The sentries now granted us admission as soon as we reached the gate. I was delighted to see that the counsellors were not present. I never minded generals, eorls or leaders but counsellors were like politicians. They were always self serving. Edward poured me a beaker of ale and leaned forward eagerly. "Well?"

"We destroyed some of the Danes' ships and we made their fort indefensible but Guthrum was not there."

He looked disappointed, "Oh."

"And there is worse. We believe he is coming here or at least he is coming to this area with his warband."

"I will send a messenger to my father."

"He is in Corn Walum?"

"Aye."

"Then unless your messenger sprouts wings then this will be over before he can get here. I have my men seeking Guthrum. We will have a better idea of our position when they return."

"I will still send a messenger."

"Of course."

He left us alone and I poured some more ale. I was hungry enough to eat raw horsemeat but I knew I had to wait until we had confirmed a strategy to deal with the unknown number of Danes who would be coming.

He returned with Leofric, the leader of his oathsworn. "What would you suggest we do, Jarl Dragon Heart? I know my father values your opinion on matters of war."

"If you have kept the ditch clear of rubbish and if it is laid with traps then Guthrum will find it hard to assault the walls. The bushes should be cut back as far as the tree line. Lay in food, water and arrows." I finished off the ale. "The last time we came those who lived in Lundenwic were kept from the fort. It was a mistake. They should be invited in and protected. It will give you additional warriors."

Leofric snorted, "Tanners and merchants, warriors?"

"If they stand on the wall and hold a weapon then Guthrum will think they are warriors and they can still wield a spear and kill an enemy. At least in the fort they have a chance of survival. The Danes are not like the Mercians. They will show no mercy. The men will be slain, the women raped and then they and the children will be enslaved."

"How do you know this?"

I shrugged. "It is what I would do. It is the way Danes fight. He wants to strike fear in the hearts of your people so that they will side with the Mercians. It is the Danes they will fear."

Edward nodded, "He is right Leofric. And you, Jarl Dragon Heart, will you and your men fight?"

"We have never run away from a fight yet. We will stay." I saw the relief on both of their faces. "We will wait until my men return before making any decisions about how we fight."

"How you fight?"

"Half of my men are Ulfheonar. The Danes fear us for we are shape shifters and they believe we can turn into wolves."

Leofric laughed, "What nonsense. Men cannot become wolves."

"Ah there you are wrong. We can act and move as wolves do. We can hide in the night and strike when least expected. I did not say we physically turn into wolves but our enemies believe we do and that is all that counts."

I saw Leofric gripping his cross and knew that he was a follower of the White Christ.

"Anything else?"

"Your traitorous counsellors what will you do with them?"

Edward looked a little shamefaced, "They and their families fled last night."

"If you wanted evidence of their perfidy then you have it now. Well it is too late to do anything about them. I hope that no mischief comes of this." I yawned. "I need my rest. I will return when I have news. If you hear of anything then you know where we will be."

When we reached the hall there was a pot of food on the fire. My stomach was aching with the appetising smell. I washed the blood from me and changed into a clean kyrtle. I had an idea that I would be in armour for the foreseeable future.

After we had eaten I sent Aiden to buy another barrel of ale. The men had deserved it. While they feasted I sat with Arturus, Aiden, Cnut and Haaken and I told them of our plans.

"I do not mind fighting, Jarl Dragon Heart, you know that, but why are we fighting for Saxons?"

"A good question and I will try to answer it. Firstly it draws our enemies here and makes our home safer. Secondly, treasure."

"Treasure?"

"The Danes we slew had much gold and silver about them. Were they the best warriors the Danes have?"

"No, they were piss poor. Only a couple had mail."

"So when Guthrum comes he will be bringing his best warriors and imagine what treasure he and his warriors will have." I held up the golden torc with the blue jewels. "I hope it will be more of this. Coenwulf is paying Guthrum and his Danes. They are rich. But we are better and we will reap the rewards of our efforts."

Cnut smacked Haaken on the back of the head, "Why you question the Jarl I do not know. Everything that Dragon Heart does is planned and well thought out!"

I noticed Arturus, who had said nothing, taking it all in. He was learning how to be leader. It was why I made sure he attended all of my councils of war. I sent Arturus and a dozen of his warriors north the next morning. I wanted to be sure that Guthrum was not close by. His warrior had not said when he had left his fort for his raid. I took my men and we went to inspect the fort. As I had suggested the killing ground had been extended and the nearest cover was beyond bow range. Edward joined us outside. "We have cleared the ditches and buried stakes at the bottom."

I nodded my approval, "How far can your archers send an arrow?"

He had a blank look on his face. "Sigtrygg take your bow and go to the walls. Loose an arrow and ask any of the archers of Wessex on the walls to do the same."

"Do you wish to show that your archers are better than ours?"

"No, but it is important that we know the range. If not then we waste arrows and we do not have endless supply of those."

We waited and watched as Sigtrygg climbed to the walls. They were not especially high but they would give our archers an advantage over any archers that the Danes might bring with them. Standing below him we were able to watch the arrow's flight. It plunged into the trees and we did not see it land. The Saxon's arrow landed twenty paces from the eaves of the woods. Three of four others tried it and they had the same effect. "Aiden go and mark the spot with some stones."

Edward asked, "How does that help us?"

"My men can release as soon as they come out of the woods and yours when they reach the line of stones."

Edward nodded, "That way we strike more quickly than they do."

"I do not think that they will do much damage until they are much closer. We can thin their numbers before they even reach the walls. Have your men pour as much river water into the ditch as they can."

"We cannot fill it. We have tried."

"I do not want you to fill it; I want it so muddy and slippery that they fall and the ladders they bring will sink."

Aiden returned. "I have seen the forest; we could lay trips and traps there too."

"Good. Haaken, take the rest of my warriors and make the forest hazardous for them."

I led Edward back inside. "You have done this before, Jarl Dragon Heart."

"We have. Both in attack and in defence. Have you pig fat and seal oil?"

"I think so, why?"

"Build a fire in the yard and have a pot of pig fat ready to heat. Once we know they are coming we can heat the fat. It kills quickly and penetrates even the best armour. You pour it from the walls and when it cools it makes the ground and anything it touches slippery."

He clapped me on the back. "You are teaching me much."

"I hope so for you are paying us well."

He went inside and I carried on with my inspection of the walls. The King had improved the ditches but the walls had not been looked after. The mortar was crumbling. If Guthrum brought a ram he could break the walls. I had to hope that he would be overconfident. I returned to my hall. It was time to prepare for war.

Chapter 6

It was dark when both Arturus and my two scouts returned. I had been more worried by Arturus' absence. I had expected my scouts to take some time to find our enemy.

"Where have you been, Arturus?"

"We found some Danish scouts. There were eight of them. We followed them back to their camp and we met Bjorn the Scout and Snorri. We came back with them."

I was relieved. He had done the right thing. Of course I still worried about him. I was his father but everything he did was correct. My people would have a good leader when I went to the Other World.

"Snorri, how far away are they and how big is their camp?"

"They are fifteen miles away; that is a rough guess for they are not using the Roman Road with the stone markers. They are camped in the forests and using trails. There are almost two hundred of them. We counted at least forty who wear mail and have the double Danish war axe. They have archers and even some slingers and the majority of the men have a helmet, shield and some have two weapons. They look to be battle hardened."

He was telling me that these warriors might well be the equal of us and they would certainly be superior to the warriors Eorl Edward had in the fort. "You have all done well. They could be here before morning. Eat and I will speak with Eorl Edward. Haaken, choose six men for each boat and have them taken over to Suthriganaworc. I would that they were safe." He left. "Tostig Wolf Hand, go and tell our neighbours that there may be trouble tomorrow. They can either cross the river on our ships or go into the fort. It is their choice."

The gates were closed but soon opened when I was recognised. "The Danes, Eorl Edward, are fifteen miles away. I think they will be here before morning. I have told those from Lundenwic to either come into the fort or cross the river. When my men have eaten we shall come into your fort."

"How many do we face?"

"Two hundred and they are well prepared warriors." I looked at Leofric. "How many warriors can you muster?"

"Forty."

"I have fifty. I think that we might need those tanners and merchants, Leofric. What do you think?"

He had the grace to bow as he said, "I think that I have much to learn and I am just glad that we do not have to face your men too."

The gates were opened but guarded as the people of Lundenwic came within the protection of the Roman walls. Annoyingly no one had made any arrangements for them to have a place to sleep. Aiden discovered that the old stables had a good roof and I took the decision to house them there. There were just a couple of horses within. If anyone argued they would have to do so with me.

Cwoenthryth, the ale wife, had Tostig Wolf Hand in tow and he carried a barrel of beer. She kissed me on the cheek as she entered. "Thank you Jarl, you have a kind heart even though it breathes fire. This is for your men. I know it is you who has thought of us. We will remember."

The Eorl had his armour on and he carried his helmet. The mail links did not look as well made as Bjorn's. Bjorn hand riveted every link so that it could withstand much damage. "All is prepared then."

"Not quite, you need to light the fire beneath the pig fat and have some containers ready to hurl upon the attackers."

"Just when I think I have everything in hand you find my shortcomings."

"You will become better."

I sat on the ramparts and closed my eyes. My helmet and my shield were next to me. I would rest. I would not sleep, at least not soundly but I would be ready if they came. If they did not come this night then Guthrum had another target in mind. As I rested my head on the old stone walls, once protected by Roman legionaries, I knew that he would come. I had destroyed his ships, I had slain his son and I had thrown down a challenge. He had to come else his men would begin to doubt him and one might challenge him for the warband. I knew that I was lucky to have around me men such as mine. They were loyal.

We had spread my men and those of Arturus out amongst the Saxons. I knew the worth of my warriors. The men of Wessex were an unknown quantity. I had the impression that for many of them this would be their first real fight.

It was the traps in the forest my men had laid which alerted us. The sudden noise in the dark of night shattered the silence. The first one made me turn. Then there were others and a shout as one of the Danes found the spikes my men had cunningly hidden. I had stressed that we should not make a noise and show that we knew they were coming. I donned my helmet but I left my shield where it lay. I would not need that just yet. I reached down and took my bow. I strung it. I would soon need a new string but this one would suffice for the work we had to do.

I nocked an arrow and then watched the woods. I was pleased with Edward's men. They had held their silence. I suspect my own men had impressed upon them the need to obey all of my orders. I was not certain that they would have had the same effect had King Egbert been within the fort. Eorl Edward seemed a little out of his depth. I liked him and he was an honest man but he was a very inexperienced leader.

Aiden ghosted next to me and whispered close to my ear. "All the men are in place and the pig fat is bubbling well."

"Good then go to the hall and wait. They will need your healing skills. I fear they and we will need one soon." We had discovered that they had no healer within the fort. Aiden would have to fulfil that function. He had many herbs and potions. Kara was better but there were few others who could heal as well as he.

It was Snorri who released the first arrow. It plunged into the shoulder of the mailed warrior who silently emerged from the woods. Suddenly the eaves were filled with the Danes. I released three arrows and then put down my bow. It was hard to see the effect as they were shadowy figures who were our targets. There were others who could loose arrows. I needed to gauge the strength and the direction of the attack. I was looking for Guthrum. I had never seen him but I knew that he would have the best armour and he would be well protected. He would also be surrounded by his oathsworn; large mailed Danes with war axes. When he was not one of the first to move, under the shelter of a shield wall, towards our ditch then I knew that he was not reckless. That made me suspicious. Had the two hundred men we had seen been his only warriors? The ones who moved forward were not the oathsworn. Guthrum was doing as I did, he was waiting and watching.

"Eorl Edward, I will take a walk around the ramparts."

We were lucky having the river so close to the southern wall for it meant we only needed men on three sides. The river protected one side. I wondered why the Dane had not used his ships. That way he could have attacked all four sides at once. He was cautious but he lacked imagination. I was learning much about this Dane and I had never even seen him yet. The west wall was ominously quiet. Lundenwic lay in that direction and the buildings could be used for cover. Sigtrygg was in command on that wall.

"Sigtrygg I have the hairs on the back of my neck prickling. Look for a trick on this side."

Sigtrygg was a clever warrior. He could have led his own war band had he chosen but he was immensely loyal to me for I had saved his people from the King of Northumbria. "I too am suspicious. I have men watching the river."

I had forgotten that there were other ships tied up to the wharfs and jetties. Ours had been moved but they had not. Their crews had merely taken shelter with us. They had left their boats there and that could spell danger for us. "I should have thought of that. Well done."

The east wall had some sign of a Danish presence but the land to the south of Stybbanhype was marshy. They would only use that if they were desperate. By the time I returned to the north wall the shield wall had moved closer. The protection afforded by the shields had saved many lives but it had slowed them up. My men were now only loosing when they caught a sight of flesh.

Edward looked less nervous now. "There are many of them but we have hit at least ten."

"There will be few dead amongst those but we are weakening them. Once they reach the ditch then tell your men to be ready to rain death upon them. They cannot maintain their shields when dropping into the ditch and the traps and the mud will surprise them. Have the pig fat brought up ready to use."

I could see that Guthrum had committed half of his men to this first attack. It would probe for weaknesses. Now that they had closed a little I was able to see that these were not his oathsworn. He had better warriors available when we were softened up. These were the ones he could afford to waste. I slung my shield and drew my sword. "Watch for their archers!"

As soon as they were within fifty paces of the wall his archers rose from behind the shield wall. Our archers had the advantage that they were ready and the first four archers fell to our arrows. Eventually they managed to loose a few arrows. I heard a shout as we took our first casualty. One of the Wessex men clutched his arm. A greater danger were the slingers. They could shelter beneath the shields while releasing their stones and we suddenly found their missiles falling on us. For a man with a helmet it was an annoyance but some of the men of Wessex had no such helmets and some were stunned by the stones. I fear that if my men had not stood with them then it might have gone ill.

The first Danish warriors reached the ditch and this was the crucial time for both sets of warriors. The Danes were cautious. They almost lowered themselves into the ditch. They could not see what was in the bottom and the stakes had been disguised by mud. Even though they took care some of the first to descend were slain. Their bodies, some of them still writhing, protected the warriors behind. Some were half way across when the first warrior stepped on to a stake. He screamed and involuntarily threw his arms open. An arrow plunged into his chest and at such a close range it penetrated the mail.

The Danes were now struggling up the bank towards the wall. "Have the pig fat ready!"

We had assigned Leofric's disparaged tanners and the like to bring the vessels of hot, smoking fat. I saw that Cwoenthryth was one of the first. I should have known it. She was used to hefting barrels around, dealing with hot liquids and, more importantly handling drunken warriors. There was little about a battle which would discomfort Cwoenthryth. She smiled. "Jarl may I be the one to throw it? It is hard to listen to others fighting for you."

"Of course." I held my shield above her. She edged to the stone and then threw the jar of boiling fat to the bottom of the wall. There was a scream of pain which rippled down the wall as the hot fat splashed and spread.

She giggled, "I shall get more, Jarl!"

The warrior the vessel had struck began to scream as the liquid found his flesh. I watched in fascinated horror as he squirmed and writhed in the ditch until he managed, somehow, to impale himself on a spike in the bottom. There was almost a look of peace upon his face.

I began to think we might win as more vessels were hurled at the Danes who sheltered beneath their shields. Suddenly a warrior ran to me. "Jarl, Sigtrygg says they are attacking from the river. He needs help."

I knew that he would not ask for help unless matters were desperate. "Haaken continue fighting. I will take some of these men." I saw his hand raised in acknowledgement. "Have fire arrows prepared!" His waved hand told me that he had understood.

I tapped warriors as I moved along the ramparts. I chose equally from the men of Wessex and my men. "You come with me!"

By the time I reached Sigtrygg I saw that the Danes were trying to climb the wall. There would be a time for explanations later although I did see boats tied up close to the walls.

A warrior of Wessex was thrown from the wall as a Dane leapt over the top. I was the closest to him and I had the warriors I had brought behind me. My sword was on the wall side. I held the shield tightly to me and I ran at the Dane. He had the freedom to swing his sword at me. It smacked into my shield as I hit him hard. He was not expecting that move. The blow had made him a little unstable so that when I swung my sword around he tumbled backwards and landed on the floor below. There was a gaggle of women and boys there. They fell upon him and beat him to death with their hands and their knives.

I saw that Sigtrygg was hard pressed. As I ran to him I shouted, "Fill in the gaps and stop them getting into the fort. If they gain the gates then we are dead!"

I rammed my sword through the back of the warrior who triumphantly raised his axe above his head to finish off Sigtrygg. Bjorn Carved Teeth contemptuously barged another warrior out of the way as he led the reinforcements towards the eastern end of the south wall. A Dane turned, his shield before him and his sword poised to hack into me. I swung Ragnar's Spirit sideways and the edge slid up the shield to knock off his helmet. The press of men was so close that there was barely room to move and I head butted him. I must have knocked him unconscious for he tumbled over the wall to land on his fellow below. He too was hacked to death by the angry women.

I felt a blow on my back. I rammed the pommel of my sword backward and heard an intake of breath. I swung to my right and found myself face to face with a huge Dane wielding an axe. He had a slung shield. As I came around I brought my sword across his body. It sliced through the mail links but his stout leather byrnie prevented any more damage. There was barely enough room for him to swing his axe and the blow which struck my shield was weak. He was however a big man. Even worse was the fact that more Danes had made the walls and Sigtrygg and I were fighting back to back. Guthrum's men knew that we were Ulfheonar and the leaders on this wall. Our deaths would mean they had the wall and thereby the fort. They were almost fighting each other to get at us.

I pushed again with my shield so that the Dane could not use his axe and, as he stepped backwards, I hooked my right leg behind his left. The movement of his arm over his head with the axe was fatal. He fell backwards to the ground. This time there was no need for the women to finish him off. We all heard the crack as his back broke.

The respite was momentary. The space occupied by the huge Dane was now taken by two smaller warriors with swords. Suddenly there was a whoosh from my left and an arrow transfixed one of the Danes. As his companion looked to see the danger I stabbed him with my sword. I now had two bodies before me and I looked to the left. Erik had brought the ships over to the northern bank of the river and he, his ships boys and the guards I had left were sending arrows towards the Danes who were ascending the walls. At the same time there was a roar of flame from the north wall as Haaken ignited the pig fat which had been thrown. There was a collective scream as shields soaked in pig fat ignited.

A young half naked Dane ran towards me and, using his dead companions as steps, he launched himself at me. I swung my sword which deflected his seax and then hacked into his neck. His bleeding body fell to join his companions below. The Danes began to flee. We had held them. I turned to Sigtrygg. He had a bad cut along his lower arm and I saw him wincing as he moved.

"I will get you to Aiden."

He nodded as I took his weight. "I knew they were up to something. They used the boats from the jetty and sailed to the unguarded river. There were not as many stakes there. Had Erik not brought the drekar things would have gone ill." He smiled, "I owe you my life again, Jarl."

"As you have done before for me. It is why we are Ulfheonar." Just then we passed the body of Bjorn Carved Teeth. He too had helped save Sigtrygg and now he lay with a half severed head. The sword in his hand told me that he was in Valhalla. It had been a good death.

After I had taken Sigtrygg to Aiden I went back to the north wall. We had paid a price for their clever attack and we would have empty benches when we returned home. I peered into the ditch. Some of the bodies were still smoking whilst others were blackened, charred, corpses. Haaken had not escaped unscathed. He sported a dented helmet and a hand which had been sliced by a seax. He shrugged, "I was lucky."

I looked into the forest where the Danes were dragging their wounded. They had left behind many fine warriors.

Haaken laughed, "And you were lucky too, Jarl Dragon Heart." He tapped my shoulder. I looked and saw the effect of the Danish axe. "A blow has almost cut through your fine Greek armour. The spirits watched over you again."

"And I am grateful."

A slow, rhythmic banging of shields began as the men of Cyninges-tūn began chanting, "Dragon Heart" over and over. It was taken up by the men of Wessex and only ended when I raised my sword and yelled, "Odin!"

Wyrd!

Chapter 7

My men went over the battlefield despatching those who were dying and binding those whom we could enslave. There were few of the latter. My warriors took the arms, armour and treasure of the vanquished. We had paid a high price. Arturus, in particular, was upset by the loss of five of his young warriors. I left my men to continue their grisly task and sought Eorl Edward. He had survived but his helmet and armour showed that he had done his part. Leofric had a bad wound to his leg for he had worn a short byrnie. Aiden later told me that he would limp for the rest of his life.

"Well, Eorl Edward, we drove them off and the people of Lundenwic did not suffer."

We were walking through their village on the way to my hall. "Aye but they will need to rebuild and repair some of them."

"Daub and wattle are easier to replace than lives. They will be stronger."

My drekar were tied up when we arrived. "Well done Erik, that was smartly done."

"It was young Karl who spotted the boats and he alerted us."

"You will all be rewarded and share in our success." I had wanted Edward alone to talk about our next move. I was not certain of the loyalty of all of the inhabitants. Those who had fled might just be the ones we knew about and there could have been others. "He may be back. We did not kill enough of his men to discourage them. He has more and he can send to Denmark too. There are many landless warriors who will fight for gold."

"I am not certain we could withstand another such attack. They came perilously close to succeeding."

"We learn from their actions and prevent them using our own boats against us. I sent mine to Suthriganaworc."

It was a criticism and Edward acknowledged it. "Perhaps this task is too great for me."

"No, you are a good leader and your father will be proud."

"Hopefully he will return soon."

"In the meantime if you have horses I will take some of my men and follow them."

"I am sorry we have but four."

"Then four will have to do."

I took Snorri, Bjorn the Scout and Cnut with me. Arturus was disappointed when I told him he would be staying.

"I need you here for your warriors. They had a hard fight and will need to recover."

"What you really mean is that I will need time to recover."

I shrugged, "I think that your mind will be on the dead for a day or two and besides I am taking scouts with me. That is the reason for their selection."

The four horses were larger than the ponies we used at home but not by much. We deigned armour. We had no intention of fighting. That also made it much easier on the horses. We found the first dead Dane not far from the fort. He had fallen behind and just died of his wounds. He had been speared in the stomach. That sort of wound was always fatal but rarely immediate. We took his treasures and weapons from him; he had no armour. There was a ditch nearby and we laid him in it and covered him with dead wood. It would not keep the scavengers away but it afforded the dead Dane a little dignity. We found another five before we left the forest. All had laid down with their swords in their hands.

Snorri had shaken his head as we had laid the last one in a ditch by the road along which we travelled. "His brothers in arms could not have thought much of him if they left him."

"None of them were the oathsworn of Guthrum. Many of these would have been hired warriors. Some would have come alone and many of the others might have lost their companions in the fight. We are lucky, Snorri, we fight for each other and we leave no man unburied and no warrior behind."

Once we had found our last body I sent Snorri and Bjorn the Scout ahead. Cnut and I followed more slowly. Our two scouts did not need to be encumbered by our presence. They would move faster and more silently without us. We were now able to speak. "What do you intend next, Jarl Dragon Heart?"

"You do not think we should stay here for a while?"

"I do not like fighting for Saxons. We could go home now for Wiglaf and the other glory hunters know where we are."

"I know your reasons are good but it does not feel right."

"The spirits?"

"Aye and the Norns. When it is right then we will return home but let us wait at least one more moon. We can still make it home for midsummer."

"Or we could raid. We have only found a few slaves."

I laughed, "Cnut, the treasure seeker. Perhaps we will." I rubbed my chin. "I have thought of raiding the east coast, north of the Dunum. We shall see."

Snorri and Bjorn the Scout returned an hour after they had left us. They pointed to the north. "They have made a camp. I think they are awaiting reinforcements."

"I thought that they had given up too easily. You have done well. How many remain?"

"There are at least forty with mail and sixty or seventy others. We saw that some had gone hunting. We had best return to Lundenwic. They might see us and I fear they have no love for Ulfheonar!"

Eorl Edward could not hide his disappointment when I told him that it was not over. "I had thought we had bloodied their noses."

"We did but not enough. We will have to hope that your father returns. What of the fyrd? Could they be called to arms?"

"Perhaps. I will send my men out to find more warriors but it is the season for sowing and working their fields." I said nothing. That was their problem and not mine. "Could you not raid Here Wic again?"

"There would be little point. They will not have started rebuilding and the men who were there will be on their way to join Guthrum. And the traps in the woods will not work a second time. At least they will not come at night next time. It will be dawn so that they can see the ditches and they will bring faggots and bundles to help them across. The Danes are quick learners."

"Have you no good news, Jarl Dragon Heart?"

"Your people did well even those that Leofric thought would not. Use those too." I smiled. "You might think of buying better weapons too."

"Where is the best place to buy them?"

I gave him an innocent look, "Cyninges-tūn."

It took him a moment to take in what I had said and then he laughed, "You make weapons?"

I nodded, "This armour, this sword and those of my men are all made by the Water. If you have the coin then we will sell them to you."

"I will ask my father when he arrives. It seems that hanging on to this town will be expensive one way or another."

We spent a quiet couple of days. My men made arrows and repaired armour. There was little to spend their newly acquired treasure upon and they were in danger of becoming bored. To alleviate that I sent ten out each day, in pairs to watch for the return of the Danes or the Mercians. While we were waiting Siggi and Trygg arrived with two of Pasgen's ships to trade. Although there was little which my warriors wanted the pots which were available were greatly sought after at home. The seal oil and the iron ploughs were highly sought after and I knew that our people would make a good trade. The seal oil, in particular, could now be used as a weapon.

"How are things at home?" I was worried for I was not certain if the ploy was working.

"It is peaceful. We have more settlers and the land to the west of Windar's Mere is filling up. He has reoccupied the fort of Arturus to guard from incursions. We had many lambs and calves this year. Next time we come we will have fine animals to trade."

"Good, then tell Bjorn that Wessex needs to buy armour and weapons. It will please him."

Einar Badger Hair, one of my men, had been badly wounded by a Danish axe. Aiden could not help him further but he felt that Kara could. We sent him back with the knarr. The four ships all rode much higher in the water than when they had arrived. Bjorn's iron and the seal oil were much heavier than the pots with which they returned.

One effect of the visit of the knarr was the sudden upsurge in trade. We saw merchants travelling from every direction to buy the fine ploughs and the ever useful seal oil. Not all were what they seemed. Aiden had finished his medical ministrations and he took to watching the arrivals. Some came by ship but others by road and we were well placed to see those who came from the north west and the west along Waeclinga Straet and the Roman Road to the heart of Wessex.

He saw a couple of merchants who looked less like merchants and more like warriors disguised as merchants. He sought me out immediately. "I think they are Mercian spies, Jarl. They came down Waeclinga Straet and they both have long swords. I think they are warriors."

Arturus was nearby and overheard. "Let us follow them. We may discover news."

I was about to say no and then I realised that this would be like a slap in the face for my son if I allowed Aiden to do this mission and not him. I nodded and unstrapped Ragnar's Spirit. The scabbard was unmistakeable and whilst I might be anonymous without my armour my sword would tell the world who I was. I handed my sword to Cnut. He would guard it with his life. I picked up a Danish blade we had captured the other day. We followed them. I kept back from Aiden and spoke in Saxon to Arturus. His Saxon was good but I had been brought up speaking it. We allowed them to head for the trading hall before we closed with them.

Their identity was confirmed when they only gave a cursory glance at the goods on offer. We saw them head to the sign of the barley. They tied up their horses and pack horse outside. We could not enter for Cwoenthryth would recognise us. Aiden said, "I will risk it. Cwoenthryth is a clever woman. I will speak with her quietly and try to overhear their conversation."

Rather than looking obvious we left Aiden to his own devices and we returned to the trading hall. We were able to see how much the traders were charging for the ploughs and the oil. We would be able to tell Siggi and Trygg when we returned. It was better for us to make the profit rather than the merchants of Lundenwic. They were popular items and the ploughs would not last the rest of the day. As we left I said to Arturus. "We can make even more profit next time."

We did not have long to wait. The two spies left and headed towards Lundenburgh. They did not take their horses. We followed them so that Aiden would appear less obvious. They walked very slowly towards the gates. They looked more like two old men out for a stroll rather than merchants. When they neared the gate they turned right and headed towards the river.

"Arturus go inside and find the Eorl. Tell him of our suspicions and then go around the far side of the fort. You can cut off their exit." He nodded and hurried ahead.

Aiden caught me up. He spoke to me in Norse so that the Mercian spies would not overhear. "They asked about the battle the other day. They seemed very interested in us. They asked Cwoenthryth where you were. I caught her eye and she feigned ignorance. I will speak with her later. She did well. They then asked which the drekar were." I was glad now that I had put the mast on the mast fish. They would have to go down to the river to see them.

We had enough information now and I decided to catch them up. "Have your seax ready. They may run. I hope that Arturus and Eorl Edward are in place."

The two men had reached the river now and they looked upstream. I knew that they would see the two drekar. They did and they turned. When they saw us they drew their swords and then ran east along the river bank. We did not hurry. I hoped that there would be some warriors waiting for them. If they saw them then they would risk the two of us.

I heard a loud shout from the river gate and the two Mercians looked up. Suddenly Eorl Edward, Arturus and four of Edward's oathsworn appeared. The spies did what I expected them to. They ran at us. I only had a borrowed Danish sword and Aiden had a seax. We would be lucky to escape unscathed.

I heard the shout from the gate again, "Stop or we release our arrows!"

The two men hesitated then ran on. The six arrows plunged into the ground at their feet and, effectively, stopped them. Arturus and the oathsworn reached them and then disarmed them. As we approached I heard their complaints. "Why do you detain us? We have done no wrong. We are law abiding merchants."

I smiled, "I heard that you were looking for me and I wanted to save you a wasted journey around the fort. I am Jarl Dragon Heart."

They paled. One reached into his kyrtle and pulled out a seax. I stabbed upwards, instinctively, with the borrowed blade and transfixed his hand. He gripped it with his other hand but the blood still flowed freely between his fingers. He gave me a look of pure hatred. "Now we know you for who you are." Aiden picked up the seax while Arturus searched the other and pulled out his hidden seax. "So, you may now speak the truth. Why are you here?"

"My friend told you before you stabbed him. We are merchants. Men must defend themselves from Vikings."

I smiled, "And you would swear to that?" He nodded eagerly, "You would testify?" The thought of losing his manhood made him shake his head rapidly. "I thought not." I jabbed my Danish sword in the ground. "Now I will ask you two questions more. Why are you here? I know I asked that already but I was not certain if you understood it. You do understand the question do you not?" He nodded. "Then I would answer before your friend here bleeds to death. Now the second question may be easier to answer. Have you heard of the blood eagle?"

This time he dropped to his knees and began sobbing. He had heard of it. "I pray you, jarl, not the blood eagle. Give me my sword and end my life."

I turned to Edward. "This Mercian is no Christian." I shook my head at the man. Answer the first question and I may give you the warrior's death."

The wounded man shouted, "Do not tell him, Aelfraed!"

I picked the sword out of the river mud and rammed it into the wounded man's chest. He fell backwards writhing. I left the sword where it was. "If you do not answer my question then like your friend there you will not go to the Other World but you will see Hel without your lungs and in great pain." I stepped close to him. "Answer me."

His head dropped. "King Coenwulf sent us. He wanted to know how many men were here and if you were still here."

"Because?"

"I answered your question! Give me the warrior's death."

"And now I ask you another. You know that you cannot trust a Viking; especially not one who can change into a wolf. What does the king plan?"

"He is coming with an army to join Jarl Guthrum."

I smiled. "There, wasn't that easy? Give him a sword, Arturus."

Aiden handed him a sword. I saw the hate on the man's face as he contemplated using it on me. I took out my seax and held it at his throat. You would be dead before the hand had moved an uncia!"

"I will wait for you in the Other World."

I nodded to Arturus as I said, "There will be many others ahead of you." His dead body joined his fellow. When we had searched the bodies we threw them into the river. They bobbed downstream to the sea.

"What do we do now, Jarl Dragon Heart?"

"Nothing has changed. We knew that Guthrum was returning. Now we know that he has Coenwulf too. The two men came on horses which means that the army is not within walking distance. We know where Guthrum is. They will need to join up and then attack us. Coenwulf and Guthrum will not risk losing because they rush here. He must know that your father is still in Corn Walum."

"You give me confidence Jarl. I will have my men repair the traps in the ditches and try to get more of the fyrd."

As I returned to my hall with Arturus and Aiden my son asked me, "Are you confident, father?"

"No. We are in a dangerous position for I believe that we have our enemies within a day's march of us. We have delayed them by killing their spies. I think I have gained us a day but that is all. It is fortunate that we have two ships. So long as we hold the river gate we can evacuate most of the people across the river."

"But you sounded so calm."

"There is little point in making a nervous warrior more nervous. This way his people will think that he has control and they will not panic. We need to step our masts and prepare for war. I think that the Weird Sisters are spinning once more."

There was urgency about our warriors as we prepared for an imminent attack. The two hundred Danes had been a serious enough threat. Now it seemed we would have many more enemies. It was difficult to ascertain numbers for we had no idea where Coenwulf was. I had fought him before. The last time his army had numbered five hundred. We would be outnumbered when they came.

I had my scouts out all the next day but they returned without having sighted anyone. Eorl Edward had managed to bring in another twenty of the fyrd. They each had a spear but little else. We had the Danish swords which we would have to let them use. The shields we gave them, for what they were worth. I took all of my men inside Lundenburgh and had our two drekar tie up at the river gate. Half of the men were on watch while the other half were resting. Every weapon had been sharpened and every piece of mail cleaned and repaired. We rubbed seal oil in the mail and cleaned our wolf cloaks as much as possible. We would look like warriors when the end came.

When the message came from Erik Sort Toe I felt my spirits sink. It was Karl the bright ship's boy. "Jarl Dragon Heart, the captain says that there are men crossing the river upstream. He cannot make out numbers but from the sound of metal he thinks they are warriors."

"You have done well Karl. Tell him to prepare to push off for the south bank when I give him the word."

Eorl Edward was eating when Arturus, Aiden and I found him. "We have been duped. Warriors are crossing the river upstream. You have best get your people inside quickly, if you can. I will have my men man the walls. My drekar are standing by in case you need to have any sent south, to safety."

He nodded, shocked. "Perhaps we can make a stand that men will speak of."

"Perhaps."

We heard the cacophony of noise as Edward urged his people into the walls of Lundenburgh. All the euphoria of our victory had evaporated. The Eorl and his men had a panicked look about them. It could not be helped and they could be deceived no longer. I breathed a sigh of relief as the west gate was slammed shut.

Eorl Edward was, however, learning. He had the pig fat heated as soon as he returned. He and his oathsworn were dressed and ready for war. Even a limping Leofric climbed to the ramparts. When Eorl Edward tried to send him back down he said, "If I am to die it will be with a sword in my hand defending my lord and not laying in a bed like an old man!"

Suddenly an urgent voice from the west gate shouted, "My lord! I hear warriors approaching. There seems to be a mighty host."

"Prepare arrows. We will show these Mercians that the men of Wessex can wield a bow."

Then we heard a voice boom out. "Why are the gates of my own burgh barred to me? Open up I am Egbert the King of Wessex and I am both tired and hungry!"

The Norns had played another trick upon us. I think we had all aged five years at least but now we had hope. The king was with us. I hoped he had brought enough warriors.

King Egbert burst out laughing when he saw our preparations for war but when Edward took him to one side and told him the reason his face became dark. He came over to me. "Thank you Jarl Dragon Heart. My men will take over the watch. Your men can rest. We have been marching for days but this is Wessex now and we will defend it."

I nodded. He was right. "Eorl Edward, we will return to our hall. We do not wish to overcrowd you."

Our marching west was a sign for the people of Lundenwic that there would be no attack that night. Many returned to their homes too. The King had returned. We spent a restful night; my men drank and I studied Aiden's maps. When we rose there was a sense of an anti-climax. We had expected to fight and to die. Now the threat had gone. As we ate our stale bread and drank our small beer I made a decision. "Now that the King is here we are no longer needed. We will leave this morning and head north."

"We will raid the north of the Dunum?"

"No Arturus. We will sail up the Ouse and we will raid the lands of Wiglaf." That surprised everyone, including Aiden. I smiled. It was rare that I could astound him. "I have studied the maps and we can sail close to the city. We could sail to the very walls of the fort if we chose. We will sail along the river towards Jorvik and then raid as we head south east again. We will have the river with us and we can outrun any of their ship. It will send a message to Wiglaf and yield us a healthy profit too."

They all smiled, except Aiden. He looked troubled. While my warriors all spoke excitedly my Galdramenn looked askance. "I am not certain that our work here is done, Jarl Dragon Heart."

"The spirits?"

"Aye Jarl. We have thrown a stone into this Mercian pond and the ripples have yet to reach the shore."

"Nevertheless, as the king is here we will sail and we will raid. I have no desire to squat on this river waiting for something to happen. We leave." I stood; happy now that the decision was made and we made preparations to leave.

We were like ants as we toiled to provision our ship. The tradesmen of Lundenwic did well out of us and were sad to see us leave. It took most of the morning to prepare but eventually we were ready. I was just saying farewell to Cwoenthryth when King Egbert arrived.

Wyrd!

Chapter 8

He was followed by Edward and his oathsworn. I recognised many of them. "Jarl Dragon Heart! You are leaving?"

"I stayed for Lundenburgh and Lundenwic needed my protection. Now they have King Egbert and they are safe. I have overstayed my welcome and we needs must sail."

He put his arm around my shoulder and led me down towards the river. "My son has told me all that you have done. I owe you much. Wessex owes you much. This is not finished. Coenwulf and Guthrum come."

"And you have enough men and warriors to defend your town and defeat them."

He spoke quietly, "I did not bring all of my army. I brought my oathsworn and those who could keep up with us. I have just over two score of warriors. They are the best but... The rest are on the road and will not be here these seven nights." I hesitated and I think he sensed that I was wavering. "I will pay you and your warriors to fight for me. At least until my army gets here although I believe that our enemies approach even as we speak."

I looked over his shoulder and saw that his men were shepherding the villagers towards the fort. "Until my men arrive." He waved a hand and two of his warriors walked towards us with two small chests. He opened one. It was filled with coins all bearing his face. "Take this my friend as a reward for what you have done and what you will do."

There was more treasure in the two boxes than we could possibly hope to take from the lands along the Ouse. I nodded and clasped his arm. "I will get my men into the fort."

He smiled and spoke conspiratorially. "I have a better solution." He explained his plan to me.

I watched the king and his entourage hurry towards the fort. I waved Arturus and Aiden over. Pointing to the chests I said, "We fight for King Egbert. Here is our pay put it on our ships. We will divide it up when this is over."

As we headed to our drekar Arturus asked, "Should we get the men into the fort? It seems the king thinks that a battle is imminent."

"Not yet. I have to explain King Egbert's plan to our men."

Had King Coenwulf been a little cleverer he might have wondered why my men and I all wore our armour as we drank horns of ale on the river bank. His scouts must have reported back to him. Snorri and Bjorn the Scout had watched them as they spied upon us and then hurried back towards the north and west. What they had not seen was the ship's boys and their captains aboard the ships already and waiting to cast off. They did not count our men and see that at least twenty were not carousing on the river bank. They also appeared to have failed to see the shields arrayed along the sides of the drekar. Whatever the reason when King Coenwulf and his horsemen burst from the woods to the north he must have thought that he had the vaunted Jarl Dragon Heart. He had not!

Snorri had spied them and warned us. As soon as they emerged, less than a hundred paces from us we ran to the drekar and were aboard before the horsemen were halfway towards us. As we clambered aboard our captains lowered the sails and the twenty archers who had been hidden on the drekar sent flights of arrows towards the horsemen. It was too late for them to halt and they had to suffer sixty arrows before they could retire out of range. There were dead horses and warriors littering the river bank. As we headed downstream, towards the sea, we watched the rest of the army appear and, from the woods to the north of Lundenburgh, the Danish army of Guthrum. He had thought to trap us. He had failed. He would think that we were deserting the Saxons.

As Haaken rowed he could not help laughing. "This will make a fine saga. How the Mercian king was duped by empty beakers."

"Let us hope that we continue to dupe him then or this plan will go seriously awry."

Although the plan was a good one it depended upon many things, not least the moon and the tide. Aiden and I had modified the plan suggested by King Egbert. As we sailed beyond the fort I saw him and his men standing along the walls. There were slightly more men in the fort now than had been there when we had fended off Guthrum's attack but now those besieging Lundenburgh had three times as many warriors. The odds were even more in the attacker's favour than they had been before. We sailed around the bend of the river to Grenewic and tied up there to wait until dark.

I looked at the sky; it was clear. "Are you certain that the clouds will come?"

Aiden was confident. "I am, Jarl Dragon Heart, and they will come when the tide turns. Fear not this is the work of the Norns."

We had listened to the sound of the assault on Lundenburgh and seen the flames rising in the sky. Lundenwic was burning. I daresay that our hall was destroyed too. The sting in our tail had left many of King Coenwulf's best warriors, his horsemen, dead and dying. He would want vengeance. King Egbert's plan had hinged on Guthrum and the Mercians believing that the Norse had fled in their dragon ships. He would ignore the river and yet the river would become a dagger aimed at his heart. We would be that dagger.

I watched the river begin to rise and saw the smug self satisfied smile upon Aiden's face. My Galdramenn had done it again. He knew nature and the spirits had guided him. We pushed off and, without raising the sail, we sculled upstream with the incoming tide. The clouds and the river hid us from prying eyes. The fighting had died down and we saw the watch fires which ringed Lundenburgh. King Coenwulf and Guthrum had them sewn up tighter than a pig skin. Their main camp appeared to be north of the river and north of Lundenwic. We went beyond them to our jetty at Celchyth. Our hall was a burned-out shell; only the shrivelled turf roof remained.

We disembarked close to some willow trees. I waved to Erik as we led our men north. The two captains would have no warriors to protect them this time. They would be reliant upon themselves. They had Sigtrygg with them. His injury meant he could not move quickly enough. He was the only warrior we left behind. I had no doubt they would acquit themselves well. They had no enemies upon the river.

The Ulfheonar led. Terror would be a weapon we would wield. We spread through the woods almost invisible in our black armour with wolf cloaks. Snorri and Bjorn the Scout led. Their task was to find any sentries who might be watching. They returned, as the moon briefly emerged from behind the clouds. "They have no sentries and their camp is sixty paces to the east of us. They are sleeping."

I turned to Arturus. "You know what to do?"

"My men may not be Ulfheonar but we can move silently when we need to. May the Allfather be with you."

"And with you."

With shields slung around our backs we headed towards the camp. We all held a sword and a seax. With our wolf cloaks and red eyes I hoped that we would look like creatures from Hel. We moved silently in a large semi circle into the camp. We would have but a short time to do what we needed before the camp was awake. I saw that the ones through which we passed were Mercians. The Danes were further north. When we were forty paces in I turned to raise my sword. My men did the same and I brought it down on the neck of the sleeping giant at my feet. The first few died silently but inevitably some woke. At the first gurgled scream the camp was in uproar and warriors jumped to their feet. As they grabbed their weapons they stared in horror at the red eyed wolves who wielded swords and were in the middle of their camp. The fear cost many their lives as they hesitated. As I stabbed one half awake Mercian I sensed a warrior from my left and I instinctively brought my seax around in a sweep. My hand was covered in his gushing blood as he fell trying to push his entrails back inside.

I heard the alarm in the Danish camp and knew that we had not long left before we would have to flee. The oathsworn of the Mercian king were donning their armour. They knew better than to take on the Ulfheonar without mail. I felt a blow from a sword across my back. The wolf cloak, armour, and padding cushioned the strike and when I swung with Ragnar's Spirit I saw the fear in the man's eyes. He thought he had slain me and I turned and slew him.

"Back! Ulfheonar, back."

We turned and moved swiftly through the camp. To the warriors who were pursuing us it must have looked as though we had disappeared for all that they saw was the black of our cloaks. It was why I had chosen the Ulfheonar for this task. There were a few warriors before us and we slew them. The men formed on me. I knew that Haaken and Cnut would bring up the rear. They would turn a few times so that the Mercians and the Danes could see our direction. We wanted pursuit.

It was the time of year when the sun shone for far longer than there was night. It had been part of the plan. Behind us I knew that dawn's light would be breaking and that we would be running into the dark. When I heard the low whistle then I knew that we were almost at the ambush site. We emerged into a clearing and when I reached the far side I turned. We had run hard and I was out of breath.

My warriors formed on either side of me. I saw that Harald Thin Neck was not with us. We would see him in Valhalla. When Haaken and Cnut appeared and went to the extreme ends of our line I breathed a sigh of relief. We were drawing the enemy on to us.

We heard them coming down the track, keen for revenge. I saw a faint light to the east. It had worked perfectly for by the time they reached us the first rays of the sun would light our faces and fear would return to the vengeful pursuers.

Guthrum and his Danes led and they were cautious. They had taken the time to arm and don mail. They halted at the far end of the clearing and began to form a wedge. Guthrum, I assumed it was him from his magnificent armour and helmet, shouted, "You may frighten these Mercians with your red eyes and wolf skins but I know you for what you are! You are a half breed trickster. You are not Odin's child but Loki's! I swore vengeance when you slew my son and I will give you the blood eagle. I swear this."

He thought to anger me but I remained silent. I wanted the delay. When the Mercians came they would be terrified despite Guthrum's words. When they attacked Lundenburgh we wanted them afraid of the Wolf Men before they even moved towards the walls.

He saw that he was getting nowhere with his insults and he ordered his men forward. I noticed that he and his oathsworn kept back and the only mailed warriors were the eight at the front of the wedge. They were thirty paces from us when the arrows rained down on them from behind. I saw some turn and look only to be pierced by the black arrows which came from all around them save where their enemies were. The rear ranks of the wedge dissolved as men fled or died. Although the eight at the front were mailed their rear was exposed.

Arturus and I had planned this well. His men had hidden in the woods when the enemy had followed. After releasing their arrows they had run to line the enemy's flanks. Once they had released those they ran behind us.

"Now!" My warriors swarmed around them. I smashed my sword against the haft of the spear from the lead warrior and jabbed forward with my seax. It went into his eye and penetrated the skull at the rear. He died instantly. All eight fell and we stood back in line.

King Coenwulf appeared with his warriors. Guthrum's men were sheltering from their invisible foe. Another shower of arrows fell. Had they not been in a state of shock they would have realised that the arrows no longer came from behind them; Arturus and his men had moved down the sides towards us and were now raining death from the north and the south of the Mercians.

I saw warriors protecting the two leaders with their shields while they argued. Now was the time for a final gesture to inspire fear. We had decided to intimidate and terrify the enemy. They were in the clearing and we knew the effect of a wolf's howl. The Ulfheonar stepped forward. Each warrior began to howl like a wolf and our enemies just kept moving into the centre of the clearing. Behind us Arturus' men were forming up in the woods with their bows ready with nocked arrows.

I raised both my hands. My warriors fell silent as I yelled in Saxon, "The Ulfheonar strike in the night. When you camp tonight, Mercians, keep your weapons close and your armour on for we will come and you will die! No matter how many sentries and guards you have we will come!" A strong ray of sunlight chose that moment to shine on my black armour and revealing my red face. I saw them recoil. We turned as one and ran towards the woods.

"After them! It is a trick!"

King Coenwulf's voice broke the spell and Mercians and Danes ran after us. Two flights of arrows slowed them down. We ran until we reached the ships. We quickly boarded ours and half of the warriors took the waiting bows and nocked arrows. Arturus and his men were right behind us. My archers sent discouraging flights towards the pursuers while Arturus and his crew jumped aboard their own drekar and cast off. The Danes and the Saxons had not brought bows and they had to watch impotently as we sailed downstream towards the safety of Lundenburgh. There would be no attack this day. King Egbert's army was another day closer.

We tied up next to the southern gate. The gates were opened and King Egbert and Eorl Edward awaited us eagerly. I clasped their arms. King Egbert looked over my shoulder as my warriors disembarked. "Did you succeed?"

I nodded, "We surprised them and I do not think they will attack today."

King Egbert looked disappointed. "You did not kill many then?"

I felt my hands clenching into fists. Aiden caught my eye and shook his head. "If you mean we did not lose many of our warriors then you would be correct but we slew many. However each of my dead warriors is worth more to me than fifty dead Mercians."

There was an edge to my voice. Although I had taken off my helmet I had not yet washed off the red dye from my face. That and the blood which had spattered on to me must have made me appear aggressive for the king took a step back. His face creased into a frown. He was not accustomed to being spoken to like this. I would not back down.

Arturus' cheerful voice broke the tension. He had been a little slow getting off his drekar and had not witnessed the disagreement. "We managed to take some of the weapons and helmets from the dead warriors who were in the wedge. We did not have time to take their mail. Look, father, a silver torc!"

King Egbert managed a smile at my son's enthusiasm. "You have succeeded then. Good."

I pointed to the south west corner of the fort. "We need to defend there. I will leave our drekar here but I will not risk losing them." Without our ships we were helpless.

Eorl Edward stepped forward and put his arm around my shoulders. He led me into the fort. "I will have my men build a barrier between the ditch and the river..."

I shook my head. "Have them dig a channel from the ditch to the river and it will fill with river water. That will suffice."

67

I saw the look exchanged between father and son. They had obviously not thought of that. I was tired and I headed directly for the warrior hall. Arturus caught me up. "I am sorry, father, what was all that about?"

"It was not your fault, son. King Egbert did not think that we had lost enough men. Now that he pays us he thinks he owns us. I will put him straight on that but I shall wait until I am less tired. I do not want to say something that I will regret." I looked at the objects he had in his hands. "What do you have there? Treasure?"

He nodded, "These were on the warrior you slew. There is a small golden torc. See how it has the blue stones at the ends. They are the same stones as are on the sword you found and the scabbard from the fort."

"*Wyrd*." It was the second such torc we had found.

"The sword he had was also decorated with gold wire. These Danes are rich if they can decorate their weapons so."

We had reached the warrior hall and he offered them to me. I took the torc. "You keep the sword. It looks well made."

"But you killed the warrior." He was desperate for me to have it. I needed no such treasure. Arturus and Kara, they were my treasure.

"I have Ragnar's Spirit and I have the sword we found. That is enough treasure for me. I am content"

After I had taken off my armour I returned to the river. Taking off my clothes I plunged in. The current was not particularly fast and my drekar were close by. I let my head sink beneath the river water. I felt much cleaner when I emerged, free from blood. The water had wakened me somewhat.

Feeling refreshed I sought Aiden. He had spent the night on the drekar as an extra bowman. He now took me to one side and said, "You should watch your words with King Egbert, Jarl. I have spoken at length with his son. The King has a new wife and she is young. He is keen to show her what a fine warrior he is and what a hero. You are too great a hero for him. The folk of Lundenwic are speaking of you as the hero who saved them. The king does not like it."

I was bemused, "And how does that affect me?"

"She is travelling with his army and your threat to his authority today would not be brooked in front of his young wife. She is young, jarl. She is younger than Arturus. Apparently, he likes young girls. His old wife is now in a nunnery." He shrugged, "I cannot understand it either but poor Eorl Edward has suffered because of it. It is hard enough being the bastard son but when someone young enough to be your daughter is put above you then it is even worse."

"Thank you, Aiden. You have done well. Your eyes and ears are as sharp as any. When King Coenwulf is defeated then there is not enough gold in the world to keep me here. We will return home." I would have left already had I not given my word. A man did not forswear himself. The gods did not like it and a man had to face himself each morning.

That evening, after I had rested we were summoned to a counsel of war. It was punctuated with food and ale but I kept my intake of the latter down to a minimum. Arturus was invited as were King Egbert's eorls. I could not help but compare them to my Ulfheonar. Where my men were powerful warriors without an ounce of fat, Edward excepted, they were all overweight and too fond of their food and drink.

The way King Egbert spoke one would have thought that he had been the one responsible for the attack on the Mercian camp.

"We have weakened them now. Perhaps we could take the army beyond these walls and defeat them in the field." He was asking for praise and for encouragement. He deserved neither. He had done nothing.

I saw Edward look to me. He appeared far less confident when his father was close by. The overweight eorls all sounded their agreement. I introduced a pail of ice cold water. "You do not have an army. You have three warbands. If you met them in the field then you would be slaughtered."

"You and your band survived."

"We did not fight them we tricked them. We led them into an ambush and we took them by surprise. If we leave Lundenburgh then they will know and they will be ready. From what we have seen they have twice the number of mailed warriors as you do. The Danes are a tough enemy. We sent them packing only because we surprised them. We have no more surprises. We have to hold them here until your army reaches us. The question is, when will that be?"

The king looked at me as though I had spoken Greek to him. "How do I know? They could be here tomorrow."

I knew the answer to this question but I had to voice it. "Is it just the army or do you have baggage and," I hesitated, "women?"

"Yes of course we have baggage and we have women. The army protects them both."

"If the army do not reach here in time, your majesty then the baggage and the women will belong to Coenwulf and Guthrum."

When the eorls looked at each other I knew that the queen was not the only female passenger. "So your only solution is to wait behind these walls?" I think the king thought that such a mighty warrior would have a solution he had not thought of. He was wrong.

"We have food, water and shelter. We control the river. If anyone tried to get up or downstream then my drekar can stop them. We have plenty of oil and pig fat, we can burn them as we did before. This is a good, well made burgh. Use it."

As soon as the words were out of my mouth I knew that I had not used the right tone and the king frowned. I was not meant for politics. After this was over I would not fight with allies. I preferred making my own decisions. Within seven days I would be a free man again. We would never serve another again. The treasure was not worth it.

The enemy came in the middle of the next morning. This time they had prepared well and had faggots to lay in the ditches and a ram to break down the gate. They did, at least, come by the north gate which we had prepared better than the others. It was the one entrance which allowed them to use the ram. Although we could only see two hundred warriors I knew that there would be others hiding in the woods.

King Egbert, on the other hand, seemed confident that this was all that Coenwulf and Guthrum had available to them. "We will slaughter them before they reach us!"

Argument with him was futile. I waved to Haaken to bring all of our archers to the north wall. Our enemies were lined up in a long shield wall which bristled with spears. Once again it was not his best warriors whom we could see but, from the helmets in the second rank, I knew that they were close. The ram was visible but it was behind the front two ranks. It would be well protected on its journey towards us. My men waited to release their arrows. We had saved enough for this. King Egbert shouted to his men, "Release!"

Eorl Edward said, somewhat diffidently, "They are too far away. The arrows will be wasted."

"I command here, boy. Do as I say! Release."

Every archer but ours released but they all fell well short of the advancing warriors. Eorl Edward ventured, "There are markers to let the archers know when to release." His comment was greeted by a scowl.

I said nothing but I pulled back on my bow. My warriors would choose when to release. With shields before them and helmets on their heads they were difficult targets. The closer they came the more chance we had of making a worthwhile hit. Snorri sent an arrow soaring. It did not strike any of the warriors in the first ranks but hit one of those pulling the ram in the shoulder. Other Ulfheonar sent arrows at the ram and more of those hauling fell. I saw King Coenwulf wave and shout. Twenty more warriors rushed with shields to protect those pulling the ram on.

The front ranks came within range of the archers. They loosed but all that they did was strike shields or ping off helmets. One warrior clutched at his arm and then threw the broken missile to the ground. The Danish slingers began hurling their stones and I saw two Wessex archers, in the process of pulling on their bows, fall from the ramparts.

"Target the slingers!"

Our Norse archers went to work with ruthless efficiency. Slingers had neither helmet nor mail and they stood no chance. They all died but it allowed the shield wall to advance even closer. The archers of Wessex were now, at least, hitting their targets but barely one arrow in five did any sort of damage. I noticed my archers changing to the boar arrows. The shield wall was less than fifty paces from the ditch and my men were good. It was Bjorn the Scout who scored the first hit through mail. The shield was not held high enough and the arrow plunged through the mail and into his shoulder. He dropped the shield involuntarily and Tostig Wolf Hand sent one into his chest. As soon as he fell there was a gap in the line and two more warriors were hit before the gap was plugged. They were moving much slower now as they concentrated on holding their shields up. The ditch was closer. They were barely five paces from the edge. They halted.

Suddenly every shield was raised and each warrior in the front rank hurled his faggot. Even the archers of Wessex had a target and many of the warriors in the front rank were hit but only a few were fatally injured. Half of the faggots hit the ditch. They all covered the stakes.

The ones with the ram were Danes and I heard them counting. "They are going to run with the ram. Aim for the men on the ram!"

The front rows parted and the Danes pulled the ram whilst running as fast as they could. The Mercians protecting the men, who were pulling, ran alongside. They were hit first. I loosed an arrow and watched it strike a warrior in the middle of his body. They were so close that it penetrated flesh. He fell and I heard a scream as his head was crushed by the wheel at the back of the ram. The ram was losing momentum but the brave Danes were still pulling it. The last two were killed when it was just two paces short of the ditch. It flew over the ditch and struck the gate. I felt the gate shake from my position above it.

King Egbert shouted, "Shore up the gate! Have the pig fat readied." He sounded unsteady as though he was panicking already.

What we could not do, with the ram in the position it was, would be to use fire. We would end up burning down our own gate. I had had a quantity of stones brought up and as the warriors ran across the ram and the ditch my men hurled the large rocks. When they struck there were more devastating than an arrow. Even so some of the warriors made the walls and they made a cover of shields as they started to hack at the gate with their axes. The boiling pig fat sent some Danes to their deaths as it burned beneath their armour. They were damaging the door but they were doing so at a cost. They were paying with their warrior's lives.

They would break through. "Ulfheonar! To me! Arturus keep up our attack." I ignored the men of Wessex. Their king could issue the orders. My men fought for me, no matter who was paying.

I led my men down to the courtyard. There were spears stacked there ready to be thrown. We each picked one up. They would keep an enemy at bay. We would need that edge when the gate fell. Already gaps were appearing in the wood of the gate. "Form a wedge on me."

Haaken and Cnut stood behind me. Sigtrygg would normally have been there but his leg meant that he was in the rear rank. It would annoy him I knew. I slipped my seax into my left hand behind my shield. It was irritating to be kept in the dark. We had no idea how we were doing. We were just concentrating on the gate. I hoped that the new gulley would protect us yet. When that burst open then we would have to race forward and meet the attackers before they had any order.

I watched as two of the villagers carried an amphora of boiling pig fat up to the gate tower. They handed it to two warriors and then I heard a chorus of screams as the men at the gate were scalded by the boiling fat. The hammering of the axes slowed. I wondered what incentive they had used to make the Danes keep coming on. The defenders were now hurling spears but the Danes were winning. One of the planks in the gate was shattered and that gave impetus to their blows. A second one disappeared and I could see them now. One warrior had arrows sticking from his shoulder but he still swung his mighty axe. From behind me one of Arturus' archers sent an arrow into his throat and he fell from the ram. He was quickly replaced.

"Ready. As soon as I give the command we move as one."

I lifted my spear and rested the end of the weapon on my shield. I felt the two spears of Haaken and Cnut slide over my shoulders. The first warrior to face us would need to be a very brave man. When the gate went it went suddenly. It was as though it had held on for as long as possible and simply died.

"Now!" I moved my right foot first. We had trained for this many times. It meant we could run and keep our formation. Few other warriors were as skilled. The others all stepped onto their right foot too. The first two through leapt from the front of the ram and, in their enthusiasm to get to us were impaled on my spear and Cnut's. I released the now useless weapon and drew my sword. I held it up. "Ragnar's Spirit!"

"That sword is mine!" I saw a half naked warrior swinging an axe leaping towards me. He ran into Haaken's spear and ripped the head of the spear from his shoulder where it had stuck. He seemed impervious to the pain and he swung the axe over his head. I lifted my shield to block the blow and rammed my sword into his unprotected middle. The blow from the axe almost drove me to the ground and I had to drop to one knee. I knew he was a tough man and I brought Ragnar's Spirit into his groin and up into his body. I felt flesh and kept pushing and then, as I twisted, I withdrew the bloody blade. It seemed that most of his wriggling insides came out with the sword.

He was such a big man that there was a gap at the end of the ram. I heard Cnut shout, "Another spear." One was passed from behind and we had two spears jutting out before me. We moved to the end of the ram. The spears protected my head and I slashed at the legs and feet of the men who climbed along the ram to get at us. Suddenly the top of the ram was empty as the archers of Arturus and the stones from the walls took their toll.

"Quick. Shoulders to the ram." I shouted up to the walls. "Pour oil and fat on the ram."

"We have little ready."

"Just use it all and then have a fire arrow ready!" I put my shield against the ram. "Heave!"

My men all pushed. I felt the pressure of the men behind and I thought that my chest would burst but inexorably the ram began to move. I saw liquid being dropped onto the ram as it began to move quicker. Mercians were running towards the ram, desperate to finish this; I could see above it now that we were through the gate. The Wessex archers were having more success and the few who made the ram died quickly. Then the rear wheels struck the ditch and the ram fell away.

"Flame arrow!" I turned to my men. "Get some timbers and shore up this gate!" We ran back inside the fort.

Outside there was a whoosh as the pig fat was ignited. Had I not had my helmet on then my beard would have been singed. As it was I was knocked back by the force of the flames. Then the flames leapt along the faggots so conveniently laid by the Danes and the Mercians. By the time the gate was finally shored up the whole of the ditch was aflame and we could hear the screams of dying, burning warriors.

By the time I reached the gate tower the battle was over. Guthrum and Coenwulf were retreating to lick their wounds. The fire meant that they would not be fighting until the flames had gone and, thanks to their own endeavours, that would not be until the next day. We had bought another day.

Chapter 9

They came again the next morning just after dawn. This time, however, they came for a truce. They wished to talk. I saw that there was King Coenwulf, Guthrum and another Dane. I wondered if he was the new leader of the oathsworn. He certainly looked like a tough warrior. He had a short byrnie and his helmet was a well made one with a mask for the eyes. He too had a gold torc around his neck. Working for King Coenwulf appeared to be profitable. They approached with no shields, no helmets and their hands at their sides to show that they came to talk. They halted twenty paces from the still smoking ditch. I knew that we would have to clear it as soon as possible for it would allow the enemy to swarm over the ditch and the gate's repair was but temporary. King Egbert was summoned and he joined us at the gate tower. Eorl Edward was a quick learner and he had ten of his archers with their bows levelled at the three of them in case of tricks.

"What is it that you want, Coenwulf?" King Egbert shouted.

"I want my town and my fort back." He spread his arms towards the ditch. "Soon we will walk over the ditch and destroy the gate again. This time we will triumph. You have less than a hundred warriors you cannot last long."

"And how many more of your warriors do you wish to smell burning? You have lost many too. We will wait. These walls were Roman built and they are built to last."

King Coenwulf turned to the new Dane. "We have new allies. This is Magnus Skull Splitter and he is come from the north. He is here with fifty of his men. What say you now?"

"I say bring as many of these Danes as you wish. They die as easily as women anyway."

I saw Guthrum begin to become agitated. His eyes burned hatred towards me. Each day I heaped more pain and misery upon him. I had killed his son, sunk his drekar, destroyed his fort and now I had drubbed him twice. I could see that he was barely able to contain himself. He wanted to leap at me and kill me. The new warrior, Skull Splitter, turned and said something in his ear. He quietened.

King Coenwulf shouted, "You use the Vikings too. Magnus here would like to fight a single combat against your Dragon Heart. What do you say, Viking?"

Every eye turned to me. King Egbert nodded that I should speak. I smiled as I considered my words. "I have fought many men in single combat and I have always won. I will let this Magnus Skull Splitter live. If he wishes to fight me then let him lead your armies. I will be at the fore of the defenders."

I had spoken in Saxon so that both armies could understand me. I had given an answer which satisfied the Saxons on both sides. There was something about this Dane that made me suspicious. My suspicions were confirmed when he spoke directly to me. "Half breed, I will have this sword of yours. When I hold the sword touched by the gods then I will be invincible. I will come for you when this battle begins."

"Then you will end your life beneath these ancient walls. And the only time you will possess it is when it ends your life."

King Egbert looked at me and asked, "What was that all about?"

"He wants my sword."

King Egbert nodded and turned back, "It seems King Coenwulf that we will have no entertainment. You will have to try again and more of your warriors will die."

"And when we enter we will slaughter all! It will not just be your warriors who will die. Those who are not slain will be given to the Danes here. They yearn for prisoners!"

They turned and departed. King Egbert turned to Eorl Edward. "How many men did we lose yesterday?"

"Fifteen dead and ten wounded."

"Jarl?"

"One dead and three wounded."

"He has not hurt us yet."

"No, but today he can. By noon the ditch will have cooled enough for them to cross. They will not need a ram today. The gate needs replacing. They will send fresh Danes with sharp axes."

"Then we use arrows to thin them out."

Eorl Edward said, "We do not have many arrows left. We used too many yesterday." I knew that the king would rue the profligate use of his arrows.

We were walking back towards the walls and the still smoking ditch. Beyond the walls and the ditch I saw the river. I had a sudden idea. "Then we cool the ditch down quicker."

"What?"

"If we break through to the river on both sides of the fort then we make a defence of water. He will need to build bridges to cross it."

"Have we time?"

"We waste time by talking. Leave half the men on the walls and have the other half connect the ditch to the river at both ends."

In the end it proved relatively simple. We had men using anything they could, including Bjorn's ploughs, to dig through the earth. The god Ran helped us for he sent a high tide to surge down the river. It raised the levels of the water. Even though we had not dug much out the rising river flooded over the banks and filled the ditch. The waters steamed as the smoking wood was doused. The tide would continue to rise for an hour or so by which time the ditch would be completely filled. In fact it had worked to our advantage for when the river receded the water would still remain as it had two small dams to hold in the water. They would have to build bridges. Before we ate we sharpened all our weapons and gathered our arrows. We would be prepared when they struck.

I ate in the warrior hall. King Egbert came to me. "This sword of yours, it draws men does it not. Why?"

I nodded to Haaken who told him the tale. He concluded, "The sword can never be defeated."

Eorl Edward asked, "Then who ever fights you is doomed to die?"

I washed the food away with a horn of ale. "Each one who tries believes that there is a moment when my strength will fail and they are also arrogant enough to believe that they are great warriors already. With Ragnar's Spirit they hope they will become greater. Oh they are good warriors, Eorl Edward, but they are big fish in a small pond. Guthrum is a leader who has not fought great warriors. That is why he is rarely at the forefront of his men. He allows others to do the fighting for him. He hates me more than anyone for I killed his son and yet he did not challenge me to single combat. Now Magnus Skull Splitter is a warrior; I can see that. This Magnus has fought in a few raids. He may be a skull splitter but that does not tell me that he can handle a sword. An axe or a hammer is a weapon to terrify a nervous warrior. If he leads the attack and comes at me with an axe then he will die."

"You seem confident, Jarl."

"King Egbert, I know my own weaknesses and my strengths. I do not enjoy fighting but I know how to do it well. I do not boast which is another reason I did not accept his challenge. I have done it too many times already."

One of the guards from the walls came running in. "King Egbert, we can hear chopping. They are cutting down trees."

I smiled, "As we knew they would." I emptied my beaker. "Let us go to the wall and watch them. It will tire them out if nothing else and we are well rested."

The Weird Sisters weave complicated webs. We stood on the walls and, by noon, the chopping had ceased. I say noon for we assumed it was so but large black clouds had rolled in from the south west. Haaken mused, "It will not be long now."

Whoever had directed the building of the bridges had been clever. They had split logs and made them as long as the ditch was wide and as wide as the body of a man. Those way ten warriors could carry the wooden structures like a giant shield. With their own shields slung across their backs and only their helmets showing they would be a difficult target for our archers.

"We will need to use our best archers to hit them when they try to lay the bridges. Once they get them across then they will use the Danes to race across them."

King Egbert looked at me, "You think King Coenwulf would waste his allies so?"

I stared at the king. "He has paid for them; I daresay he will use them as he sees fit. He will certainly not risk himself or his own bodyguards. He has men he can use as he will." The king almost recoiled and I wondered if I had gone too far but he nodded. In that moment he understood.

The wall of bridges advanced. They had built just eight of them. Behind the eighty warriors who carried them we saw the Danes advancing in a shield wall. There were two lines. The first was led by Magnus Skull Splitter and the second, surprisingly, by Guthrum. That alone told me that they were confident. They thought that they could span the ditches and scale our walls. I strung my bow and selected an arrow. Eorl Edward had had a supply of stones brought to the ramparts and they were ready to be thrown down as men tried to cross the bridge.

I looked at the water in the ditch. It had mixed with the ash to make a grey sludge which lay across the surface. If anyone fell in then it was hard to see them getting out easily. The sky continued to darken as they approached. The Christians did not appear to notice but my men sensed the gods at work.

When the eighty men reached the edge of the watery ditch they halted. I saw archers run from behind the first line of Danes. "Archers!" I wondered where he had got the archers from. There were few but they were a surprise.

Arrows began to fall upon the Saxons but some reached the bridges and began to send arrows back. As the bridges began to be laid we loosed arrow after arrow. The men of Wessex had no more to send and they could do no damage to the bridge with the stones we had; it was too far to reach with the large stones which had been gathered. There were too many targets for our few bows and, inevitably, the bridges were laid. I saw that they were spreading their attack out this time. The bridges were spaced along the length of the wall. Their reinforcements had made the difference. They all waited along the ditch. They would attack us all at once. I saw that Magnus Skull Splitter had chosen the North Gate. He knew where I was. The wolf on my shield marked me out clearly. He was desperate to get his hands on my sword.

"Save your arrows. Arturus, I will take the Ulfheonar to the gate. If we get the chance I will lead a sortie and destroy this bridge. If I do have half of your men support me with their bows while you and the others guard the gate."

"Aye Jarl."

I saw him glance at King Egbert who seemed resigned to waiting for an assault. Arturus shook his head. This was not the way for a leader to lead.

I took Haaken and Cnut to the western tower of the gate; the better to see where they were going to place the bridge. "There is no way we can stop them rushing across there in a wedge. I want Arturus to conserve the arrows we have. They will break through again and this time they will be quicker for they will not have to stand on top of a large tree trunk. We will use the same tactic we did yesterday. Arm every warrior with a spear and we form a wedge but we will stand closer to the gate." I paused, "I want to weaken the gate."

"Weaken it?"

"Aye Cnut. If we weaken it then they can break through all the quicker and we can then rush them. It will not be their best warriors who break in. They will conserve those. They will wait behind the shield wall until they break through the gate. Our best chance to hit those warriors will be when they try to cross the bridge. We will hit them there and drive them from the far side so that we can pull the bridge back and use that as a gate."

"But we will be on the wrong side of the fort."

"I intend to get rid of the other bridges too. That is why Arturus is saving his arrows so that they can support us."

"And how do we get back inside?"

"We do not. We make our way around the wall to the south gate and we board our ship."

Haaken laughed, "I hope we survive for this will be a glorious saga!"

We quickly made a wedge. Arturus' men formed up behind us. "When we charge the enemy, your task will be to stop any from breaking through. We will bring the bridge back and you will use it to make a new gate."

"How?"

I shrugged, "You are young and clever you will find a way. It does not need to be permanent. It is just to keep them outside while we clear the ditch."

They nodded and I knew that I could rely on them. We heard their horns sound and their war cries roared as they rushed the bridges. Spears and stones would be thrown but they would be an irritation only for they came with shields held aloft. We took away some of the large beams which had been placed against the gate and cleared a path for us to run at it. We heard the axes as they hammered on the gate. We held our spears at head height. I did not have my seax in my left hand, instead I held the spear with two hands.

As I had expected the Danes quickly broke down the gate. They stood for a moment in surprise and exultation. It was a fatal pause. "Charge!"

We hurtled at them. They had been working individually; we were a warband fighting together. We were able to run on the hard parade ground of the old fort. Our spears struck them and swept them away. I heard their screams as the spears tore into faces and necks. Inevitably one or two spears broke. We kept running. The land dipped a little to the ditch and we struck the armoured Danes who were rushing to gain access to the fort. We were a solid mass of armoured warriors and we were moving quicker than they were. The ones who were not impaled on the last of the spears were knocked into the stinking wet ditch. There were still weapons and branches below and they pierced skin and armour. Men who fell in there would not rise.

We kept running on the other side of the ditch. Our wild charge had demoralised the attack but now Magnus Skull Splitter ran at me, swinging his war axe and surrounded by his oathsworn. We were no longer a wedge. We were a two deep arrow. My men had spread out as we had crossed the bridge. The remaining spears were passed back and I drew Ragnar's Spirit and held it aloft. It drew them all to me. The Weird Sisters are devious. As the Danes came towards me, in the centre of the line, they converged and banged into each other; more importantly they stopped the axe men from getting a good swing. You need space to swing an axe.

A young, keen warrior out ran Magnus and he triumphantly swung his sword over his head to strike a blow which would split my head in two. I deflected the sword with my shield and stabbed him in the middle of his body. I pulled the sword sideways so that his body fell to my right and tripped the second warrior up. Cnut's sword ripped through his body.

The huge Dane stood before me. "Now I shall take your sword, your helmet and your armour. Then the world will know that Magnus Skull Splitter is the invincible warrior who wields the sword that was touched by the gods."

I stepped forward as he swung. Einar jabbed the spear from behind me and the movement distracted Magnus. I pushed up with my shield and struck his left hand. At the same time I stabbed forward and Ragnar's Spirit tore through his mail links and into his side. It came away red. I saw his face before me and I head butted him as I took another step and pushed with my shield. He was a big man but I knew my business and I heard his nose break. His eyes began to stream as his nose spurted blood. I was too close to use my sword effectively and so I punched the hilt into the wound on his side. He winced. I knew I had to end this quickly. Behind him I could see King Coenwulf's men as they raced towards us. When arrows flew from behind I knew that Arturus was protecting me. I punched again with my shield and, as he stepped back, lunged at him with my sword. His streaming eyes and blurred vision meant he did not see it coming and it plunged into his throat. He fell backwards dead. I knelt down and picked up his axe.

"Back. When I am across pull back the bridge."

I sheathed my sword and slung my shield across my back. I would use the axe to keep them at bay. I swung it before me, two handed, as Saxons tried to rush me. Two died bravely before they realised they would need spears or arrows to hurt me.

"Now jarl!"

I turned and ran. I felt a thump in my back which almost knocked me to the ground and then I was across the bridge. Half of my men formed a shield wall while the other half pulled back the bridge. I heard Arturus' voice from the ramparts. "Father! Ware left!"

I turned. I did so quickly and the movement made the spear which was stuck in my shield fall to the ground. I picked up the fallen spear and saw some of the warriors from the next bridge racing towards me. Two were struck by arrows as I threw my spear at them. I hit one and then ran towards them. I swung the axe and knocked one into the ditch. A second hacked at my side. I felt a rib crack and I grabbed his belt and threw him into the ditch. He screamed as he fell on the spear which had jammed into the bottom of the grey filmed, water filled ditch.

There were no more warriors before me but I could see the Saxons and Danes up ahead, crossing a bridge. I saw that my men had manhandled the bridge to the open gate. "Ulfheonar on me!"

They ran to join me. I saw that two wolf cloaked bodies remained close to the ditch. We had not had it all our own way. I handed the axe to Erik Dog Bite. "Take some men and destroy that bridge. The rest follow me." I drew my sword and we ran to the wall. The attackers had a couple of crudely made ladders and were trying to drive the men of Wessex from the walls. I raised my sword high. "Ragnar's Spirit!"

The men took up the cry and the man at the bottom of the ladder turned in fear. With shields held tightly we ran along the wall. The two ladders were destroyed and the warriors atop fell to their deaths as we crashed into them with our shields and our bodies. It was crude but effective. I swung my sword sideways at a warrior who lunged at me with a spear. I shattered the spear and I brought the blade back to disembowel him. I waved to Erik Dog Bite, "Take the last bridge!" There was one bridge remaining at this western side of the fort. This time it was

Guthrum's men who were assaulting the walls. They were using shields held by their fellows to help them climb up.

"Wedge!"

It was only six paces between the ditch and the wall. We filled it with our small wedge and ran, like a human battering ram, at the warriors. We careered into them, knocking warriors to the ground and landing in an untidy heap ourselves. I was on my feet and swinging even before I knew what I was swinging at. My sword hacked into the side of one warrior. At my feet I saw a Dane struggling to rise. I rammed the edge of my shield across his throat. I stood to get my breath as my men despatched the last of the ones who had survived. Erik and his men joined us. We manhandled the bridge sideways into the ditch.

"Do we go to the other bridges?"

I shook my head. I could see that they were reinforcing their last foothold on the fort side of the watery ditch. "We have tempted the Norns too much already. We will go around to the south gate. We can use fire to destroy the remainder of their bridges and hope that we have bought another day."

We trudged around the walls. We held our shields in our right arms for protection although the arrows which were sent after us were hunting arrows. They would not penetrate our armour at the range they were using them. As we reached the river I felt my heart sink. Our drekar had gone!

I had no time to speculate. We ran around to the gate which was opened by some of Arturus' men. I said nothing but ran up the stairs to the tower of the south gate. I looked at the river and then I saw them. They were heading towards Grenewic. "Do you know why my ships have left?"

The young warrior had a grin on his face. He pointed to Grenewic and my ships, "It is the rest of the army. Can you not see their banners?"

I shaded my eyes and saw, indeed, the banners of Wessex. Erik Short Toe had used his initiative and he was ferrying them across. We needed to hold just a short while and we might be saved. Even though I was exhausted I ran to the north east corner of Lundenburgh. The enemy still had bridges standing. I needed to give hope. I saw men at the top of the wall. I drew my sword and I hoped that my Ulfheonar were with me yet. I saw a Mercian plunge his sword into the chest of a young Wessex warrior. I ran and swung my sword as the Mercian stood on the stone ramparts. My sword sliced through both legs and his maimed body crashed on to three warriors at the foot of the wall. "Hope is here! King Egbert's army comes! Hold on for just a little while!"

I saw Eorl Edward and King Egbert turn. "Is it true?"

"My ships have gone to Grenewic to pick them up. These are the only three bridges left."

"Then we will hurl them back from whence they came. Men of Wessex show these dogs how we fight for what is ours!"

I saw that Bjorn the Scout was wounded, "Bjorn the Scout go to the south east corner and tell Erik to land the army to the east of the fort. We can trap these warriors and then get to Aiden."

"It is but a scratch."

I shook my head as he headed off. I had seen the blood and knew that it was far more than a scratch. "Arturus, fire arrows." I turned to Eorl Edward. "Is there any fat or oil left?"

"A little."

"Then bring it to the bridge at the west. We can trap the Mercians between the walls and your father's army."

There was just one amphora of heated pig fat and the bridge was thirty paces away. We could now use it. Suddenly Arturus said, "Put it down on the floor." It was so hot we could see it smoking. It would not take much to ignite it. He took a length of cord from his waist and tied it around the neck of the jar. "Snorri, have the arrow ready." He carefully lifted the jar to see if it would hold the weight and it did. He whirled it around his head a couple of times to gain speed and then released it. It looked as though it would miss but it smashed against the side of the head of a Dane standing on the bridge and shattered. The flaming arrow flew straight and true and ignited the pig fat. The writhing Dane spread both the fat and the flames. Soon the bridge was an inferno as warriors fled away from the danger.

"Use every arrow we have left on the last two bridges! Clear them. Arturus, let us take our men and sortie from the eastern gate."

We ran down the stairs and flung open the gate. We had no order and there were Danes outside but we had victory in our sights. I punched the first warrior with my shield as Haaken took the head from a second. The warrior I had hit fell to the floor and Arturus plunged his sword into his chest. The arrows from above were clearing the bridge and our sudden assault made them flee. We were exhausted beyond words and our arms ached but with victory so tantalisingly close we could not stop; we dared not stop. We marched forward slaying all who stood in our way. The men we faced were not Vikings they were Mercians and they had no stomach for such fighting. We were relentless. Our shields and armour made us hard to hit. Even when their swords managed to hit our mail they were rarely good enough to penetrate Bjorn's armour.

I glanced up and saw that the first warriors had disembarked from our two drekar and they were beginning to finish off the survivors who had fled our ferocious charge. We had won. The day was ours and the Weird Sisters had spun their webs.

Wyrd.

Chapter 10

We searched the field for our own dead and took them to the river to send them to the Other World. Four Ulfheonar and two of Arturus' men had died although many of our men had wounds. When I removed my armour, I discovered a broken rib as well as a couple of slight wounds where blades had penetrated the armour. We had been lucky. We laid out the dead and then returned to the field to despatch any of the Danish dying. Most of the Mercians were Christian. King Egbert could deal with those. Those of our men who were unwounded collected the treasures from the dead. The Danes of Guthrum were the richest and my men all did well from it.

We used some of the gold we had collected to buy a small boat from one of those who had hidden in Lundenburgh. We paid a fair price but the man was keen to win our favour. We laid our dead within it on top of kindling and some of the better weapons we had collected. I placed the axe of Magnus Skull Splitter on the top. Finally we hoisted the sail and loosed fire arrows into it. It sailed downstream back to the sea. Ran must have looked kindly on them for it did not sink immediately. We saw the smoke still when it was well beyond the bend at Grenewic.

I had decided we would clean ourselves up and sail home but a messenger came from King Egbert asking me to attend a celebratory feast. Arturus was to come too. Aiden, who had just returned from his healing, saw the look of doubt upon my face.

"You should attend, my lord. We can leave in the morning. They will all want to see you. Everyone said that it was you and our warriors who won the battle for the king. They want to show you their appreciation."

"I do not want to but you may be right. Erik, prepare the drekar to sail. We sail on the next high tide! Haaken and Cnut take the treasure and the weapons to the drekar. We are going home!"

They all gave a cheer as they marched from the fort to the two drekar. I saw that Tostig had a barrel of beer held on his shoulder. They had used some of the coins already.

We washed and put on the fine clothes we had brought back from Byzantium. They were beautiful silken tunics. We rarely wore them for they were too good to damage but all of our other clothes were bloody. We washed and oiled our hair and we trimmed our beards. There would be ladies present and we all knew how terrifying an unkempt Viking could appear. I strapped on Ragnar's Spirit only because I knew it would be expected of me. Arturus put his new sword into his old scabbard. I was proud of my son. He was a handsome young man. He would soon find himself a wife.

We had buried our friends and taken some time to prepare ourselves. We were the last to arrive in the hall for the feast. Embarrassingly we were greeted with tumultuous applause and the banging of beakers on the table. I had thought it would be just the king and his family but there were fifteen eorls present too. Some of them had women with them. There were two places for us next to a girl who looked to be a little younger than Arturus. I wondered if it was Egbert's daughter. I could not see his wife and I assumed that the journey had been too much for her. I allowed Arturus to sit next to the young girl while I took the chair next to Eorl Edward. He looked to be the only one who was still reasonably sober.

Before I could sit, King Egbert raised his beaker and said, "Long life to Jarl Dragon Heart and his Vikings. They are our allies and they did us a service today."

Everyone toasted us and cheered. I was glad when I could sit down. I swallowed half of the beaker of ale without even tasting it. The slaves brought in the food. I said quietly, "Edward, where is the king's wife? Was the journey too much for her?"

He lowered his voice, "She is the one seated next to Arturus, Elfrida. They married six months ago." My mouth must have dropped open. He smiled, "His other wife, Ælfthryth, decided to enter a convent and serve God."

"Truly?"

He shrugged, "It is the story we were told and who would argue with the king?"

"But she is so young."

"That is the way he likes them. My mother was but thirteen summers when he bedded her."

"Where is she now?"

"She died in a Viking raid."

"Sorry."

"It was not you and I have come to learn that not all Vikings are the same." He ate some of the food. "You were right, Jarl, we should have heeded your words more. We wasted too many arrows. It nearly cost us dear. If we had had more arrows then they might not have been able to cross those bridges they made."

"You learned and I believe that Coenwulf and the Danes will leave now."

"And you?"

"I would be gone already if it were not for this feast." I ate some of the venison placed before me. It was old and it was tasteless. I suspect it had been salted and then washed clear of salt. I was suddenly not hungry. I drank some more of the ale. As I did so I glanced at the girl. She looked happier now that she was talking to Arturus and the two of them were becoming quite animated. Egbert asked her something and she looked suddenly sullen. "She looks unhappy about something."

Edward's voice became almost a whisper, "I do not think she is happy with a marriage to a man three times her age." He looked worried, "You would not say anything would you?"

"Eorl Edward, you are the one friend I now have in Wessex. Your words are safe with me."

We were interrupted when the king stood. He was drunk. Some men can be funny when they are drunk, Haaken was one. Others can be nasty and mean. King Egbert was both of those and loud too.

"My warriors and Eorls, today I have won a great victory over not only my enemy Coenwulf of Mercia but also the Vikings who sought to attack us. The men of Wessex have shown all that they are the greatest warriors in the world!" He glanced down at Elfrida but she was talking quietly with Arturus. Egbert scowled. "We can now conquer the whole of this land. With warriors such as you behind me then there is nothing to stop us!"

While his eorls began to chant and shout their agreement Egbert leaned down and said something to Elfrida. She shook her head and he slapped her. She ran from the room weeping. My hand was across Arturus before he could move. I knew my son and I knew his temper. "No, Arturus."

"I want to kill him!"

"There are many men that we can kill and probably will. He just isn't one of them. When the moment is right and he sits down we shall leave. I, too, have had enough of this."

The room had quietened and Egbert stared at the two of us. He put on a false smile. "Jarl Dragon Heart. You may think I disparaged your men by not mentioning them. I did not mean to do so but we both know that they fight the way that they do because of the magic sword. You use it well but imagine what I could achieve, a king, if I owned it. Why I could challenge the Holy Roman Emperor himself! I will buy the sword from you. I will give you another chest of gold. What say you?"

His sycophantic eorls began to bang the table and chant even louder. The king looked at me expectantly. I stood and shook my head. "You cannot expect me to give up the sword which was touched by the gods. I was meant to have it."

"And you have done all with it that you can. I have said that I will buy it from you. Name your price! If a chest of gold is not enough then what is?"

"It was touched by the gods. It is beyond price!"

His face darkened, "You are a pagan! There is but one God. I could have you burned for blasphemy!"

He was beyond reasoning and I could see that this would get worse rather than better. I turned to Eorl Edward, "You will always be my friend but we leave now before I shed blood." He nodded. "Arturus, we are leaving!"

It took a moment or two for the king to realise what was happening. He became enraged, "Stop them! Bind them!"

Edward stood and held his arms out. "Go quickly, jarl; I will try to reason with them."

We had our swords out as we ran to the doors. Two warriors had heard the commotion and the king's raised voice and were standing there as we opened the doors.

"Kill them!"

The two warriors were not to blame and I could not draw blood. I drew my hand back and punched one with the pommel of my sword. He went down like a stunned animal. Arturus was more angry and he stabbed the other in the leg. We ran. Once we were through the next doors we turned to race across the parade ground to the river gate and the safety of our drekar.

Suddenly I heard a voice, "Arturus, wait for me!" There was Elfrida and a woman a little older than she was. They had emerged from the hall and were running towards us.

"I will not leave her to him father. He is an animal." I nodded, "Run Elfrida!" The two ran towards us.

Four of the eorls had grabbed their weapons and were racing towards us. They were drunk and they were overweight. We stood to wait for the two women. I parried the first blade and ducked under the second. I brought my sword around and it tore into the upper arm of one of the eorls. The second tried to stab me but it was a clumsy mistimed blow and he paid for it with his life as I ran him through. Arturus had killed his two although he had a cut to his arm. The two girls were at the gate already. We joined them there and then lifted the beam holding it secure. As we opened it I yelled, "Ulfheonar!"

Behind me the hall had emptied and King Egbert was leading his eorls towards us. They were drunk and they were getting in each other's way. We pushed the huge pair of gates open. Arturus shepherded the two women towards the waiting drekar. I swung my sword in a wide arc to keep the eorls at bay and then I turned and ran. My heart soared when I saw the Ulfheonar with shields and swords forming a protective shield by the side of my drekar.

"Erik, get us to sea!"

The men of Wessex were drunk but not drunk enough to risk the wrath of Vikings. The wall of shields bristled with swords and spears. They halted. As soon as I leapt aboard we cast off and the tide took us towards the sea. I glanced astern and saw Arturus with his arm around Elfrida, the Queen of Wessex, aboard the '*Josephus*'. The Norns were weaving once more.

Wyrd.

There was no pursuit and so we did need not row. The river was taking us to safety. The king had no ships with which to pursue us. The rivers and the seas were always our allies. Haaken and Cnut came aft to join me and Aiden when the danger of attack abated. "What happened then? How did you upset the King?"

"It was he who upset me. He wanted the sword. He was drunk and I would have ignored it but he threatened to have me burned as a pagan."

"He seemed happy enough to have his pagans fighting and dying for him."

"That is not how he tells it. The victory was down to the men of Wessex. It was the sword which helped him. In his mind he thinks he deserves the sword for the victory."

"The man is insane. We are well rid of him. And where now? Raiding?"

That, of course had been my original plan but it seemed that the Weird Sisters did not wish me to do so. I did not answer them. Aiden said, quietly, "And who is the girl whom Arturus took on board his drekar?"

Haaken said, suddenly intrigued, "A girl?"

"Elfrida, the Queen of Wessex."

Haaken laughed so loudly that it must have carried all the way back to Lundenburgh. "He is your son, Dragon Heart. We all knew he would take a wife soon but to take the wife of a king! That is worthy of a mighty song! You must tell us all."

He was correct. I owed it to my oathsworn. I knew not what effect this stone thrown in the pond would have. They were part of it and they deserved to understand how this thing had come about. Even as I was speaking to them and telling them of what I had learned I was already deciding that we would return home and forget the raids. Kara would need to speak with the spirits and I would need to warn our knarr captains that Lundenwic might not welcome us again.

When I had finished the tale Cnut nodded, "Arturus did right. A man may hit his wife but not before others. That is a private matter."

"And if she is young enough to be his granddaughter," Haaken shuddered, "there is something not quite right about that."

Aiden had said nothing. The river and the tide had taken us into the estuary of the river and soon we would need to row and for me to decide our direction. "This was *wyrd*, Jarl Dragon Heart. I could not foresee this but it feels right. You have decided to return and seek the advice of Kara and the spirits?"

"I have."

Behind me I heard Erik Short Toe's voice, "Then we will be heading south soon and I will need the mighty Haaken to row while he composes his verses! The wind will not be in our favour."

Soon the Ulfheonar were rowing. I heard them talking as they rowed. There were no secrets on the **'Heart of the Dragon'**. I looked astern and saw the **'Josephus'** following behind. Aiden looked astern with me.

"Tell me Aiden, you know him better than I do. You were inseparable when you were young. How can you explain what he did; what just happened? It was so sudden. I do not understand it."

"I am a stranger to women, Jarl but from what I have heard you were meant to be with the Lady Erika were you not? From what Haaken told me the whole settlement of Hrams-a knew that you were born to be together and so it turned out." I nodded remembering that midsummer when we had sat and talked on the beach for hours. "The Norns make plans for us and we do not know of those plans. If Jarl Erik and his family had not come to Mann then you might never have met her. The Norns made them land there so that you would meet her, marry her and sire Kara and Arturus. When that was done they took your wife from you to be a spirit to guide you."

"But this is different. Arturus took her."

Aiden shook his head, "From what you told me she fled with you. He did not take her, she came to you. That alone tells me that the Norns wish these two to be together."

"I am not so certain."

His voice became lower so that I had to lean in to hear him against the sound of the sea and the oars. "You have dreamed of your son taking a wife and giving you a grandchild." I looked up. He had been in my mind again. "I have heard your dreams. The spirits know your dreams and they have made this happen. This is naught to worry about. This is a cause for celebration. The spirits listen to you and they grant you your wishes. You do as they command and they reward you. This is *wyrd*!"

I looked astern. Arturus' ship was rising and falling in the waves behind us. Perhaps Aiden was right. Erik's voice sounded, "We are going to turn west. Ran is being kind this night. The wind is rising and is now coming from Norway. He is speeding us on our way. Rowers, take in the oars but prepare for a bumpy ride. We will ride a wild stallion until after dawn." He laughed. He loved the sea and its wild side. It was a challenge to him and he would meet it. I hoped that Arturus and his new bride would be as safe. It would be just like the Norns to grant us both joy and then snatch it from me. They could be cruel.

I sat down between the chests at the stern, Aiden joined me. He spread a cloak above us to give us some shelter from the spray and the wind. My Ulfheonar were doing the same between the benches. Haaken and Cnut joined us. No one said a word.

Eventually I broke the silence. "It seems that in taking the sword from Cyninges-tūn to protect my people I have now drawn more enemies upon us."

Haaken laughed again, "You, least of all, should be surprised at the Norns. They have little else to do to amuse themselves. Blame your mother and your ancestors. They were talking under Wyddfa's snowy top long before you were even a thought."

"Are the Ulfheonar behind Arturus' actions?"

Cnut shook his head and snorted, "You need to ask that? We have just seen this King Egbert; the man would be High King, hiding behind your wolf cloak and quaking when his enemies came. Had we not been there then there would be no King Egbert and King Coenwulf and his Danes would be High King! Of course they are behind you. We have emerged from this richer. We have made more on this one voyage than in the last five years. We are all rich beyond our wildest dreams. The men are eager to spend their treasure on armour and weapons. Bjorn will do well from this and we have time enough to return. It is not yet midsummer. This is a cause for celebration, Jarl."

I looked at Aiden who smiled and nodded, "Aye Jarl, Midsummer, when you married Arturus' mother. *Wyrd*!"

With that thought we curled into our cloaks and slept while Erik wrestled the ship and the sea.

I had been dreaming and it was a turbulent dream. I was being hunted by men on horses and they had long boar spears. I ran into the high places around my home but still they came after me and when I ran to the waters of Cyninges-tūn and stared at my reflection, I was a wolf.

"Jarl you must wake!" Aiden's urgent hand brought me back to the deck of the *'Heart of the Dragon'*. The drekar was pitching violently. He pointed to the steering board where Erik and two of his boys were hanging on to it as they struggled in the maelstrom of water. The Ulfheonar were at their oars. Waves were breaking over the sides.

As I stood Erik shouted, "This came from nowhere. We must find shelter." He and Aiden stared at me and I knew where Ran was sending us, Syllingar. I nodded. I was a warrior and I was a tool to be used by the gods, the Norns and the spirits. We would visit with the witch and discover what she had to tell us.

As we sailed into the labyrinth of islands, shoals and rocks the winds suddenly abated and the motion of our ship became easier. The first time this had happened we were surprised; now we expected it. We frequently sailed through these waters and we always stared at the island where the witch had her cave. We never saw either smoke or signs of habitation. This time we saw the tendril of smoke spiralling in the wind eddies rising from her island. It seemed to be a signal.

Erik pointed to the ropes. "I will have to replace some stays and shrouds. That was a fierce storm. It was fortunate that I bought new rope when we were in Lundenwic."

Arturus tied up astern of us. I waded ashore with my Ulfheonar. The storm seemed to be elsewhere as though these islands were protected from nature itself. They knew, without my words, that we might be here for some time and they lit a fire with dry kindling from the boat and began to search the rocks for shellfish. We had done this before. For the crew of the *'Josephus'* this was a new experience. Haaken and Cnut would tell them what to do.

Arturus carried the young Elfrida ashore followed by a fearful looking servant. When they were on the beach I approached them. Behind me I knew that Haaken and Cnut were grinning. They had known my son since he had been a baby and were as close as uncles to him. I said nothing. I could tell that Arturus was struggling to find the words and to explain his action. He was now a man and responsible for what he had done. I would wait.

"I could not leave Elfrida with that man! It was not right."

"So shall we return her to her family?"

The two of them looked at each other. I knew that they had not considered that nor would they. "No, father, for they agreed to the marriage." He paused as I waited for his words, "We would be wed."

I looked at Elfrida. "And you would agree to this even though you have been wed already? Are you a Christian?"

She looked at the ground, "My parents told me to say that I was Christian so that King Egbert would marry me but I follow the old ways." She took out a token from around her neck and showed it to me. It had a bronze hart with a blue stone for its eye. *Wyrd.*

"And would you marry my son?"

Her face lit up. "I would! The moment we spoke I knew that I was meant to be with him. The voices in my head told me so."

I shivered and it was not the cold. "How old are you child?"

"I have seen fourteen summers."

There were just three years between them. I saw that the servant was still shivering. "And who is your servant?"

"She is a slave from Flanders, her name is Judith."

"She looks terrified."

"Her village was raided by Danes and she was the only survivor. She hid in the woods. Other slavers from Frisia captured her and sold her to King Egbert."

"Perhaps we should free her and release her from this torment. If you come with us then she will see Vikings every day. It is not fair that she pays the price for your happiness."

Aiden said, "Let me speak with her."

My Galdramenn led her away and spoke quietly to her. He had a way with people the way some have with horses. They talk to them in a unique language and speak to their hearts. I held the hands of Arturus and Elfrida. "Then when we return you shall be married. There will be weddings on Midsummer's Day and if the winds are with us we can return in time."

They hugged each other.

"Thank you, Jarl Dragon Heart. I had heard that you were a fair man and a just ruler. They were right."

"Perhaps but, Arturus, you have sown the breeze, let us hope you do not reap the whirlwind."

"Why?" He looked puzzled. His heart had blinded his head.

"King Egbert will not take kindly to having his bride taken from him. There will be retribution."

I could see he had not thought of that. "I am sorry father I did not think."

Haaken burst out laughing. "When did a warrior in love ever think? They are contradictory. Do not worry, Arturus. If Egbert comes with that rag tag army of his then we shall send him packing."

My son looked relieved, "We are here to see the witch?"

Elfrida clutched Arturus' arm, "Witch?"

"Fear not. You need not come. My men will watch over you. Come son, Aiden."

Aiden brought back a now smiling Judith. "She is resolved and she is happier. I explained that I too was once a slave and that the Danes and the Norse are as different as foxes and wolves."

"Good let us enter the cave then. Haaken and Cnut watch over the women. Perhaps teach them more of our words." We had spoken only Saxon until then but once we were in Cyninges-tūn the two of them would need our words or they would be isolated. It would be like being in a cell if they did not.

We made our way up the path towards the entrance of the cave. We had been there before and knew its path. The glow from within told us that the cave was occupied. We heard singing as we descended into the bowls of the earth. Each time we visited I wondered why the cave did not flood in high seas. The floor was always dry as were the walls. The cave itself was around a bend and, as usual, I hesitated before turning to enter. I could face any number of warriors in combat but this was the spirit world. One day I would come and be devoured by a dragon.

"Come Jarl Dragon Heart, surely you who have defeated Magnus Skull Splitter does not fear an old woman who sings alone."

I entered and saw the same woman we had seen before. She looked to be the same age as the last time I had seen her but how could that be?

"Come, sit. Drink some of this broth. You must be cold."

We sat down and took the handmade pots with the oyster shell spoons. We ate the soup which was delicious. While we ate she spoke. "You are here because you need the advice of the spirits. They will come in the fullness of time." She smiled at us and took Arturus' hand in her own bony one. "Elfrida was meant for you, Arturus but there will be danger."

He nodded, unable to speak.

She began to sing. I did not understand the words but it was a pleasant sound. The exertions of the past days began to take their toll and I felt my eyelids drooping.

I was on the top of Mann. I stood on the high place I had used when I first became a jarl. I could see all the way to my new home across the sea. I saw a fleet of ships and they were heading towards Úlfarrston. I tried to run but I could not move and then the fog swirled in. It was a sea fret and it stopped me from seeing anything. I dared not move for fear of falling down the mountainside. I could not even see my feet. Then I felt a hand take my right hand. I looked up and saw my mother. Before I could speak a hand took my left hand and it was Erika. They said nothing but I felt myself lifted from the ground and I was flying between them.

We landed on the mountain which looks over Ulla's Mere. Here there was no fog, neither were there any ships. It was a land at peace.

"My son you have made a perfect land for our people here. Those who went before you are resting easy. So long as you hold this land then you need fear no enemies. What is was meant to be."

And then she was gone.

Erika took my hand in hers and kissed it, "Elfrida is right for our son. She is fey and has the blood of your mother's people coursing through her veins. She knows not yet what powers she has but Kara will teach her. In the darkest night, my husband, trust to your men, trust to our son but, most important of all, trust the sword. When the storm comes stand firm. You and the sword will have to go through fire and blood before our land and people will be safe. Your mother's spirit waits for you and watches over you. Remember that."

She lifted me up and we soared into the sky like an eagle and then, just as quickly as she had appeared, she was gone and I was spinning down to the earth. It grew closer and closer until I was sure that I would crash and die.

I opened my eyes. The fire was cold and the cave was empty. Arturus and Aiden slept still. I heard Arturus speaking, "Mother, come back to me, do not leave me, mother!"

I waited until he opened his eyes. Strangely, Aiden did so at the same time. They both looked around and took in the empty cave. I said nothing. Arturus' eyes were wide. "I saw mother and another woman I did not know. Aiden, you were with me and you saw."

Aiden nodded. "The spirits asked me to be your guide for they thought you might be afraid."

He nodded, "Who was the other woman who spoke with me? She was the one who said I would rule after you had joined her."

"That was your grandmother."

"It is good that you are to marry Elfrida. I am happy now." I hesitated. I did not wish to put a burden on Elfrida. I chose not to reveal all to Arturus. "Your mother wishes Kara and Elfrida to be close."

He looked up, startled, "She told me that too. Were you there, father?"

"No, but she spoke to me." I saw Aiden give the slightest of nods. He understood. "Now come, I fear your Elfrida will be worried or possibly bored with Haaken's stories."

When we emerged it was broad daylight. Elfrida threw herself at Arturus. "I thought you had been swallowed by the earth. I did not believe Haaken when he said you would be safe."

Arturus looked gratefully at Haaken. "You can trust any of our men with your lives. They are oathsworn and would give all to protect us."

"How long were we in there?"

"Half a day."

"You saw no-one leave?"

"No but when the smoke stopped rising then we knew you would not be long."

"We can sail home now."

Cnut pointed to the clear skies. "It seems the Norns say that we can go too."

Chapter 11

I was relieved to reach Úlfarrston without further incident. It was Midsummer's Eve when we saw the walls of the town. We had made good time. I was also pleased to see the knarr in port. I wanted to warn them about Lundenwic. We halted, briefly, at the wharf. I had to speak with both Pasgen and my captains. We would then sail a couple of miles up the river to shorten the journey we would need to make.

"So you are saying that Lundenwic may be closed to us?"

"No Pasgen. It will be closed to me and anyone who says that they serve me may well be treated badly." I looked at Siggi and Trygg. "It might be that all Vikings are so viewed from now on. I wish you two to trade with the Cymri for a while until we see how the land lies. As for your captains, Pasgen, so long as they do not speak well of me they may be safe. It is your decision."

They all nodded. Siggi said, "The new ploughs and wares produced by Bjorn fetch a high price."

"And you can ask for more. The merchant you sold them to doubled the price." I smiled. "And now on to more pleasant matters. Tomorrow is Midsummer Day and my son will be married. I shall hold a feast. I hope you will come."

Their faces gave me their answer.

The walk to Cyninges-tūn was not a long one but I was not certain how Judith and Elfrida would cope. I had no need to worry. They seemed excited. When Elfrida saw the Water she stopped. "This is beautiful." She looked at Olaf and his mountain. "I dreamed of this place. Before the beast took me I dreamed of such a place and an old man who looked down upon it." She frowned. "How can that be? I have never been here."

I looked at Aiden who smiled, "It means that you were meant to come here, Elfrida. This is a good sign."

Unsurprisingly Kara met us to the south of the western Cyninges-tūn. I knew now that she would have dreamed. Elfrida saw her approach and she shivered. "Who is that lady? She is beautiful and I can feel her," she tapped her chest, "in here."

Arturus looked delighted. "She is my sister and she is a volva. You two will be friends."

Kara hugged her brother first. "This is good, my little brother. This is *wyrd*!" She turned to Elfrida, "And you shall be my little sister." She put her arm through mine and said, "Come, I have made the preparations for the marriage."

Elfrida stopped, "How?"

Arturus laughed, "I told you, she is a volva and she is fey. You will get used to her reading your mind."

While Arturus showed Elfrida and Judith the settlement I took Kara into the hall and told her of our journey and trials. None of it surprised her. Then I gave her the golden torc with the blue jewels I had taken from the dead Danish warrior, Guthrum's son, Cnut. Her eyes lit up as she touched it. She squeezed my hand. "This belonged to an ancestor. I can feel its power. It speaks to me. This is a good sign. It has come home."

I wondered how she knew and then I remembered; she was a volva and her mother's daughter. It was good to be home. My dream suddenly all made sense. I needed to stay closer to home. I knew I would raid again but I had to protect the land of Cyninges-tūn.

That midsummer festival was one of the best that anyone could remember. Perhaps because we had lost six warriors and all of us had come close to death we celebrated the marriages and the hope that they brought with exuberance and joy. We celebrated long into that shortest of nights.

I left with Aiden on the day after the weddings to visit our new mines. I wanted to walk my land. The Ulfheonar and Arturus' men would be building a hall for Arturus. I knew that it would be finished by the end of the day and they would not need me. Kara spent the day with Elfrida and Judith and her world of women; the cheese and ale makers, the clothes makers and the weavers. I led the warriors and Kara led the women much as her mother had.

I was just grateful to be back in my own land and not to have to be beholden to any man. It was just a couple of hours march to reach the mines. I saw that Scanlan had had huts built for the slaves and the three overseers who ensured that they did not run whilst feeding and caring for their needs. It was a poor master who neglected his slaves. They were like horses and ponies. They were an investment.

It was quite a pleasant spot in which they lived but the mine was not. Although it had barely delved far into the earth the cramped and dirty conditions would not have pleased me. I felt the walls closing in upon me. I made a point of speaking to them all. Perhaps because we had had such a celebration I had brought a haunch of venison which I gave them for their meal and a firkin of ale we had left over. The smiles on their faces pleased me. I had been a slave. I had always tried to be a happy yet diligent one. If these slaves worked hard then I would grant them their freedom. We could always get more slaves.

I was almost reluctant to return to my hall but I knew I must. Aiden spoke to me, on the way back, about how we might use the iron. He had taken a great deal of interest in both metal working and in mining. "We can use far more of the stones and metals we have. Perhaps we could find more slaves and look for other stones we might use. The roof stones from Olaf's mountain are much longer lasting than turf. They will save work. Then there is copper. That is to be found on Olaf's mountain. We can mix that with iron and make bowls which will last longer than the pot ones. It will also mean we have to trade less for them."

We halted to look on the water at Rye Dale. "You are thinking of our dream."

"Aye Jarl. We can become reliant just upon ourselves. We have salt and fish from the sea. We have abundant timber. We have stone and metals. The less we need to find from outside the better."

We walked on and I remembered Erika and her love of lace. "There are things that the womenfolk might like which we cannot make ourselves."

He looked at me, "We have forgotten Byzantium. They have finer cloths and clothes than anywhere in Britannia or Frankia. If we send our ships further afield they will be away longer but they will return with greater riches. Each time we sail we have the problems of Mann and the stormy coasts. One voyage a year will minimise that. We could even afford to send a drekar to escort the knarr. Remember how they prized objects we took as ordinary. We can forget Britannia and Frankia. It is Byzantium where we shall make our profit." He was right. His mind had been planning since our visit to the witch. Perhaps my days of fighting were gone.

We headed back to Cyninges-tūn in high spirits. We had extracted ourselves from a difficult situation in Wessex. My son was wed and the spirits approved. We had a strategy to trade more successfully and we were home. The world was in balance once more.

Our world was shattered when we returned to Cyninges-tūn. Thorkell sent an urgent message. The men of Strathclyde had a new king and he had invaded our lands. Thorkell was besieged within his walls and war had come to our home once more. The Norns had held out a hope of peace and then snatched it away just as quickly.

I sent for Windar and gathered Scanlan, Kara, Rolf, Arturus, Haaken and Cnut for a counsel of war. Unlike that held by King Egbert mine would, at least, allow everyone to have an opinion. We would begin to plan and then allow Windar to give his views. Most Vikings would not have included a woman but a volva was special. It gave us an insight into the spirit world. None would gainsay Kara.

It was Einar Boar Slayer, one of Thorkell's oathsworn, who came to speak with us. "They came, four days ago across the river. They learned from us and built rafts. They captured our fort and slew all the warriors who guarded the eastern end of the river. Jarl Thorkell managed to bring all those who lived nearby into the stad but I saw many marauding bands heading south. Some are close to Butar's Mere. They are slaughtering our people and stealing the animals."

"You are an experienced warrior, how long before they reach us here?"

"Two days at the most."

I nodded. We would need to get to the col north of the Grassy Mere. There we could hold them and then drive them back. "Any thoughts?"

"Unless we strike quickly then we will lose all that we have built up."

"You are right Rolf." I drummed my fingers on the table. "I will take the Ulfheonar and we will stop them at the col. Arturus you will need to gather every warrior who can be spared and march them in the morning to the col. If we are not there then carry on cautiously north until you find us."

"What of Windar?"

"I want a warband from Windar's Mere and Ulla's Water to head north and meet me on the old Roman Road."

They all nodded.

"Kara, what of the spirits?"

"They warned of the danger which was coming." I gritted my teeth at the mischievous spirits. The warning had been vague at best. "We will prevail."

"Is that a wish or do you know?"

"I believe."

"Then we must trust to the iron of Bjorn Bagsecgson and the arms of my warriors." I stood, "Kara and Rolf watch over my people." I hesitated, "Watch Elfrida. This will make her feel afraid. Her new husband will be away and I know that she will find it hard."

I saw the look of gratitude on my son's face and I was pleased that I had said what I had said.

I gathered my armour and my weapons. Bjorn Bagsecgson had put the sharpest of edges upon Ragnar's Spirit. We took a pony each and left my fort and my refuge. The days were as long as they ever would be. Night would be but a few hours long. My twenty-eight warriors had had some rest and we would teach these raiders that the punishment for invasion was death. I would slaughter all; even those who surrendered. I would make them fear to cross the river again. I wanted their wives and children to be terrified of the wolves who came from the south and tore the hearts from their warriors.

As soon as we passed the Rye Dale I waved Bjorn the Scout and Snorri forward. "Find them!"

Animals skittered from our path as we rode relentlessly north. I had no doubt that they would have to stop at night but I wanted to be at the col before them. We would have the advantage of height and the land. The pass leading to it was narrow and lined with trees. It was perfect for a small band such as ours to ambush an army; no matter how large. It was not arrogance which gave me such confidence; the men of Strathclyde had come from Hibernia. They shunned armour and fought with their hearts, recklessly. They were also incredibly superstitious. The wolf warriors would increase and aggravate that fear. The spirits had been right. We had to defend this land by all means possible.

We reached the col shortly after dusk had fallen. Neither of my scouts were there but I did not worry. We tied the ponies to some scrubby trees which the lined stream meandering along the scree covered valley. "Spread out on either side. String your bows and wait for my command."

Snorri and Bjorn the Scout returned, leading their ponies. "They have camped by Leathes Water."

"Have they sentries?"

"A few." Snorri grinned. They are, like the others, drunk. They must have brought some of their fiery spirit with them."

"How many are there?"

"It is a warband of fifty. They have two warriors with mail."

Bjorn the Scout nodded his agreement. "To be truthful jarl the two of us could have disposed of them but we thought Haaken might be unhappy if he missed the chance to compose a song about it!"

When my warriors all laughed I knew that all was well. Leathes Water was less than two miles up the Roman Road. It was a narrow valley and they would have had to camp by the Water. We knew exactly where they would be. "Bjorn the Scout and Snorri, take your bows and take care of the drunken guards. The rest, we use blades and we strike silently. Let them think we are ghosts or wolves."

We trotted along the road. I had my wolf cloak over my helmet so that I looked, especially in the dark, like a wolf. Bjorn the Scout and Snorri had long disappeared into the darkening dusk. I was confident in their ability and they would stop us from blundering into their camp. If we could destroy this warband then we might surprise the rest. My two scouts appeared from the dark like wraiths. Had I not been expecting them then I might have been afeard. They signalled to the left and right. I waved off Cnut and Haaken. Snorri and Bjorn the Scout came with me.

I heard the men of Strathclyde and I smelled their fires before I saw them. They were celebrating. The screams of the young women told me that they had captives. I drew my sword. They would pay. As we descended towards the water and the trees thinned I saw the warriors. There was a huddle of them despoiling a girl. Another group were having a drinking contest. The three of us did not pause. We ran into the camp. The four men raping the girl were dispatched in four blows. I swung my sword and took the head of one then backhanded a second across the throat. They died silently. I could see, from the firelight, the rest of my warriors as they fell upon the men of Strathclyde.

We did not stop; delay was unthinkable. We raced to the next three men who were raping a girl. This time they stood as they saw us. I ripped Ragnar's Spirit into the naked groin of the rapist. The other two fell to Bjorn the Scout and Snorri. The warband was now terrified. We had sprung from nowhere. While one or two warriors tried to grab weapons and fight us, most fled. They were half drunk and they were panicked. We began to overhaul them. There is little satisfaction in killing a man who had his back to you but we needed to teach a lesson. I slashed Ragnar's Spirit across the back of one warrior. Bjorn had put such an edge on the fine weapon that it sliced through the back bone and almost cut the warrior in two. It was all over in a very short time.

"Haaken I want every head taking from the corpses and bring them with us."

He knew me too well to question me. Then I found the girls. Sigtrygg was comforting them. "Tostig Wolf hand, escort them back to my home and then rejoin us. Take the two horses the men of Strathclyde brought with them."

"Aye Jarl." Tostig might have wanted to continue on the journey with us but my tone told him to obey and he did.

After they had departed and the heads were collected I said, "We get a little sleep and then push on. We did well."

Unprompted the men began to howl and even I got shivers down my spine as the call of the wolf echoed through the narrow valley. The Ulfheonar were coming.

We reached the northern edge of the hills by dawn. The last barrier before the river lay before us. We waited there in the woods which lined the road. There was a stream which bubbled towards the water we had left earlier and we drank from that. We chewed on dried venison as we waited for Arturus.

He must have left our home before dawn for he reached us when the sun had still to give any warmth.

"My men saw the bodies of the dead raiders." He nodded towards the grisly heads strung over the ponies' saddles. "You do not usually take trophies."

"These are not trophies. I shall use them as weapons. Come we head north." I did not elaborate. There was no need he would know the reason soon enough.

We made our way in single file through the hills. I saw that the one or two farms we passed were burned out and the animals were gone from the hills. The raiders had been here. What had been bothering me, since we had heard the news, was that two years earlier we had raided and destroyed the forces north of the river. Were these the same people or had another invader come to take the land and to push south? The men we had killed the previous night had been the men of Strathclyde. They had the same clan markings and the same weapons. I knew that, in the old days of Rheged, the Kingdom of Strathclyde had been a large and powerful one stretching all the way north to the land of the Picts. Perhaps it was rising again.

We reached the Roman Road which ran east and west from coast to coast. We watched from the hills for any warriors passing along it. None passed in the time we watched.

"Harald. Wait here for Windar and bring him to Thorkell's Stad." He nodded and we led our ponies down the road. We had two of Arturus' men as well as Snorri and Bjorn the Scout well ahead of us as scouts. I did not want to be surprised.

"Why do you think the raiders are laying siege to the fort? If they were raiders then they would just sweep south and take cattle, sheep and slaves."

Arturus was correct. It made no sense. This was one of the times I wished I had brought Aiden with us. He had a sharp mind and could untangle puzzles. I said nothing but tried to work it out for myself. It took me two Roman miles to do so. The markers they placed along the road were useful in many ways.

"I think there are two reasons." I shrugged, "There may be more but there are two obvious ones which spring to mind. Either they need the fort to use as a base for they want to invade and conquer our land."

Arturus nodded, "As King Egbert did with Lundenburgh. The fort here controls the river and the northern entrance to our land."

"The second reason is more devious. It would be to draw us on and ambush us."

"Then why risk the warband you slew last night?"

"Perhaps they were part of the bait to make us over confident."

Arturus shook his head, "That is a large number of men to sacrifice."

"They were not well armed. They could have been mercenaries. Halt." I was curious now about the men we had slain.

I turned to the pony and lifted one of the heads it carried. The blood had matted the hair. I lifted it at the back and saw a tattoo on the back of the neck. Haaken saw it and spat. "Hibernians!"

He was right and Aiden would have spotted it when we had attacked them. He knew his own people. "These are hired mercenaries. It seems the Saxons are not the only ones who like to hire others to do their dying."

Three of our scouts ran towards us. I saw that Snorri was missing. "Jarl there is an ambush some two miles up the road. There are many warriors and they are lining the hills and the trees on either side. It is the last climb before the fort."

I nodded. That made sense. It was a good place to attack for if we had not known we would have trudged up the hill and been attacked when we were weary. "And Snorri?"

"He went around them to spy out Thorkell's Stad."

"Then we will wait. Were there any young trees close by the ambush site?"

Bjorn the Scout's eyes narrowed as he tried to work out the reason for my question. "There are some in the bottom of the small valley some hundred paces or so from the ambush. But they cannot be seen from the hill."

"Perfect. Then when Windar's men arrive we shall head there."

Enigmatically I left it at that. Harald brought Windar's warriors to us in the middle of the afternoon. They looked hot and tired for they had marched almost twenty miles. Windar was not with them. He was now old and corpulent but they were well led by his son, Karl.

"My father sent fifty of us, Jarl. It would take longer to summon the others."

"Do not apologise Karl Windarsson. This number of warriors will suffice for we fight tonight."

We left the road and moved through the hills and fields which were adjacent to the road. Bjorn the Scout told us when we were less than two miles from the ambush and we rested there. Our delay in arriving at the ambush would worry and unnerve those waiting. The last time they had done this my action and revenge had been swift and terrible. They would be expecting the same swift reaction. I wanted them looking over their shoulders and wondering if we had managed to ghost around them. Our scouts had not managed to get close enough to ascertain numbers accurately but they estimated more than two hundred warriors were waiting for us. There would also be a force ringing Thorkell. It was an army the size of Coenwulf's. We could never hope to match such numbers. We would always be outnumbered and we had to make up for paucity of numbers with better weapons and skill.

As we waited I walked around the resting warriors. Karl Windarrson's men had good swords and shields but only two had mail byrnies. Some had a metal helmet but many only had a leather one reinforced with leather strips. The men from Windar's Mere did not have the experience in war that even Arturus' young warriors had. They were however keen to impress and would swell our numbers. I had to make the enemy believe that they were more Ulfheonar.

Nights were short and we reached the bottom of the valley with the young saplings just after dark. We chose the stand to the north of the road. That would be our diversion. I gathered the Ulfheonar, Arturus and Karl around me and explained my plan. Their smiles and approving nods told me that they thought it might succeed. Suddenly one of Arturus' sentries hissed a warning and our hands went to our weapons.

"It is me Snorri! I though you heard me when I was a mile away!"

"What news of Thorkell?"

"His drekar is destroyed and he is surrounded. The men of Strathclyde have some Hibernians with them." He reached into his pouch and pulled out a copper torc. It was crudely made but it bore the designs of the Ui Néil clan. "I questioned the warrior who owned this before I sent him to the Other World. Silkbeard and the other Norse are making life difficult for the clan in Hibernia and they are hiring themselves out as warriors. There are a hundred and fifty warriors surrounding the Stad but they are trying to starve out Thorkell. The warriors besieging them are eating well on the lambs and sheep they captured. They are in no hurry to move in and attack."

"No, they are waiting until they kill or capture me and then they will hope to induce surrender."

Haaken laughed, "Then they do not know Thorkell."

"They do not know us at all. They think that because we do not make war on them constantly that we are weak. They will learn that we are not."

While Snorri ate my warriors moved forward and prepared the trees. Young saplings were silently bent back and pegged to the ground. Three of the heads were attached to each of the ten trees. The rest of the heads were given to the warriors who would launch the attack. Karl knew what he had to do and we left him at the saplings. I led the Ulfheonar and Arturus' men and we headed around the side of the hill. Snorri had discovered that the ambush was on both sides of the road. They had assumed that we would come down the fastest route and the trees on either side would make an ambush simple. The road also helped them for there was a slight slope to the road and warriors who had travelled far would be weary. Whoever led them had split his force. It meant that by attacking the southern band we would outnumber them. Karl and his men would keep the northern half occupied by a fake attack.

Our scouts killed the sentries silently. They crawled in beneath their wolf cloaks, rose as silently as wraiths and slit the throats of the hapless Hibernians. We spread out in a half circle and waited. Karl and his men were counting. They would then release the trees and the decapitated heads would land in the northern camp. I tried to imagine the effect of their own warriors' heads landing amongst them would have. When we heard the confusion then we would attack and Karl would bring his men to support us.

The shouts to the north shattered the silence of the camp. The men before us woke and looked to the north. As they did so I led my Ulfheonar into the camp. Arturus' men lobbed the remaining heads high into the night sky and they began to rain down on the startled warriors. I saw a chief who had wisely slept in his armour pick a head up and examine it. The distraction had worked for my wolf clad warriors were amongst them before they realised.

I yelled, "Ulfheonar!" which was the signal to attack and my warriors howled their war cry; it was the howl of the wolf! I saw the terror in their eyes as I leapt forward and slashed my sword across the throat of the chief who still studied the head. We were swift and we were terrible. Few warriors even tried to fight us for they were terrified. They fled towards the road where they met those coming from the northern camp. The men of Strathclyde tripped and fell over each other and we slew them where they lay. When Karl's men, unencumbered by armour overtook us then the flight became a rout and the enemy ran as fast as they could towards their main camp at Thorkell's stad.

They left leaving behind their belongings. They carried their weapons only. We swept through both camps and collected all the helmets and weapons we could. Haaken shook his head, "I prefer fighting Danes. There is better treasure to be had." There were very slim pickings to be had. It confirmed my view that whoever led them had kept the bulk of his better warriors close by Thorkell's stad.

Cnut snorted, "And they fight better too. We lost no Ulfheonar today my friend."

Arturus asked, "What do we do now? Attack the main camp?"

My warriors looked at me expectantly. "No, we rest here and tomorrow we march towards them and set up our own camp."

Arturus frowned, "We camp?"

"Tonight's attack served two purposes. First we cleared the road but secondly, and most importantly, we spread terror. Those warriors who survived and fled will talk of heads falling from the sky and wolves appearing in the night, seemingly rising from amongst them. Tonight, after we camp, we take it in turns to be wolves close to their camp. We keep them frightened and awake. We kill their sentries and they will wait, armed, all night for an attack which will not come. Weary, worried warriors do not fight well."

"But we normally attack at night for it disguises our small numbers."

"And they will expect that. We will attack in the morning after they have been awake all night and we are rested. Besides, Snorri will need that time to get inside Thorkell's fort. When we attack it will be from two directions. I intend to wipe out this band of raiders. None shall return home save one. That one will tell a terrible tale of wolves in the night and fierce warriors who take no prisoners. The men of Strathclyde will never dare to venture south again."

We marched the next day and camped in the hills to the east of the enemy camp which ringed Thorkell's fort. We were a mile or so away. The Roman Road cut through the heart of their camp to head towards their old fort. Snorri had left before dawn to make his way around the fort and seek entrance. He knew it well and I did not fear for him. He and Bjorn the Scout were the best at concealing themselves. He would slip past the sentries ringing the fort and be inside before they knew.

I ordered the men to build one fire for every two warriors and to move around as much as possible. I wanted our numbers disguising until the following day. They had to believe we had greater numbers than we actually had. Once the fires were lit I told the men to put damp material on the fires to make smoke. That way it would be even harder for them to see us and count our numbers. In addition, the wind was coming from the east and would blow towards their camp. It would not be pleasant for them. I had Arturus' and Karl's warriors move around the camp while my Ulfheonar slept. It would be their task to carry on the campaign of terror at night.

I lay down but I did not sleep. My mind was too filled with the events of the next day and night. If we succeeded then the rest of the summer might be enjoyable. If not then we would be waging war with the men of Strathclyde.

I must have dozed off for I was woken by Arturus. "There is food, father."

I rose although I wished for a drink rather than food. I knew, however that my body would need both. My men were also up and about. Sigtrygg came over. He still limped a little but he insisted that he should be a part of my plans for the Ulfheonar. I knew that we all carried injuries. My ribs still sent spasms of pain through my body. If we could rest for a month or so then we would all heal. "If you give me your sword, Jarl, I will put an edge on it. These men of Strathclyde have thick necks!"

While he did that I organised the weapons we had captured. I had plans for the many spears we had taken and they were stacked in neat piles to one side. They might make the difference the next day. When darkness fell we built up the fires with dry material. It would look as though we had a vast army come to fight them. I wondered why they had not come to attack us. We discovered the reason for that later that night. I sent Arturus and one of his men on a simple but silent task which would aid us in the morning.

While the rest slept half of my men stood guard and I led the other half to the camp of the men of Strathclyde. We moved stealthily and cautiously. It was as well that we did for, fifty paces from their first sentry we found a concealed ditch. They had wanted us to attack them and had prepared defences. It was why they had not attacked us. They were tempting us. We also found stakes embedded in the ground. They were well hidden in the bushes which they had also used for defence. They would break up any attack by a body of men. Our enemies were learning from us. It was the same trick we had used against Guthrum. They would not, however, protect them from individual warriors. Bjorn the Scout led ten warriors to slit the throats of the guards. They negotiated the traps which they quickly identified. It was easy enough to do; their defences made them complacent. The guards would have felt themselves protected by their defences. After a silent death my warriors brought back the heads of the sentries. I had brought some of the damaged spears and we placed them in a half circle and jammed the heads upon them. We placed them just inside the bushes as macabre sentries. Until one came close it looked like their sentries were still watching.

Then we divided into pairs. I went with Bjorn the Scout. Haaken and Einar began to howl off to the northern end of our line. Even as those in the camp heard the howl Cnut and Erik were doing the same at the southern end of the line. Bjorn the Scout and I joined in from the centre. I heard a horn from inside the camp as they prepared to be attacked. We crouched in a tiny ball beneath our cloaks as the warriors raced out to find the grisly trophies staring at them from the dark. They were less than ten paces from us but the darkness and our cloaks hid us. I understood enough of their language to hear a leader mutter something about a Viking trick, he used the word Lochlannach. Then they moved further away from the edge of the bushes. To our right Einar and Sven began to howl. And so it went as pairs of warriors howled. Once we had all done so twice then we moved back to our own camp.

We lay down to rest and to catch what little sleep we could. Sigtrygg woke me when he and the other half of the Ulfheonar went to torment the enemy. We now stood guard. It was eerie to hear such good mimics as my men emulate the wolf. It sounded realistic and yet the men of Strathclyde knew that it was we who were doing it. Suddenly I heard screams and then silence. Had something gone wrong? There was a commotion in the enemy camp and I saw flaming brands moving through towards the bushes where Sigtrygg and my warriors waited. I was about to order the rest of my men to get their bows when Sigtrygg and the others materialised before our very eyes.

He smiled as he rubbed his aching leg. "They sent some of their own warriors to try to trap us. When we rose before them and they saw our reddened and blackened faces they panicked and we slew them. I brought the men back for I saw the hint of dawn yonder." He pointed behind me and I saw the thin pale line which hinted at dawn.

"You have done well, Sigtrygg. Get a little rest. Today will be a long day."

I saw that the whole of the enemy camp was up and agitated. They had had little sleep and, as yet, they had failed to remove the heads of their dead men. That was a mistake for it would be a reminder to warriors who were already demoralised and afraid. As the sun rose and our men woke I saw the size of this warband. There were over three hundred of them. That was an estimate only but our position on the hill afforded us a good view. They would, I had no doubt, wait for us to attack them even though they outnumbered us. Their leader hoped that the traps he had laid would catch us unawares. It was not hard to understand his confidence. How else could we attack him if not through the very place where he had placed his defences?

I gathered my men around me. The Ulfheonar already knew what was expected of them. I had told them as we waited for dawn. Now I took the rest into my confidence. When I had told them of my intentions they laughed and began to bang their shields. It was a good sign.

"When we strike them keep a tight formation. Thorkell the Tall will be surprising them with an attack to the rear." I paused, "We take no prisoners. I need no slaves! All that will remain of them are the pathetic weapons they own and whatever treasures they have. When they are dead we shall sacrifice their bodies to the god Icaunis! Their bodies will be taken to Ran and they can both feast upon the dead!"

That brought an even greater cheer. All the time the exhausted warriors of Strathclyde were waiting and wondering what was coming next. We formed up and each of the Ulfheonar and Arturus' men took two of the spears. The rest were given to Karl's men. We were a mile from their camp and I had my men spread out in two long lines. The first was made up of the Ulfheonar and was flanked by Arturus' men. There were eight paces between each warrior. Ten paces behind us were Karl's men. They too were spread out. I knew that the enemy would see our formation and think we had a death wish. Their traps and tricks would hurt us and they would overwhelm us with their numbers. Their confidence grew as they formed up in tight lines five deep beyond where their traps were. Their line was almost as long as ours. They had superior numbers and they knew that all that we could do was to attack them. Each of my warriors would be outnumbered by three or four to one.

We began to move down the road towards them. At first we walked. I saw ahead the white stones which Arturus had placed along the road. They marked distances. I reached the first marker and I levelled my spear and began to trot. What I hoped the men of Strathclyde would fail to see was that, as we moved closer to each other, our frontage shrank. At each marker the men closed up a little more towards the road. It would appear imperceptible. By the time it was obvious I hoped that it would be too late for them to do anything about it. It was hard to move a large body of men quickly from the flanks when they were in line. By the time we were half a mile from the enemy we had shrunk to half of our original width and I saw the three leaders, sitting on their ponies pointing at us and waving. They started to shout instructions. It was too late.

At the marker which was four hundred paces from the enemy I began to run a little faster and Haaken and Cnut formed up behind me. It would now be clear what we were doing. We were forming a giant wedge which would punch a hole through the middle of their line. We had avoided their traps by running along the road where they could not lay traps. The ditch alongside the road afforded some protection too.

By the time we were one hundred paces from them they were trying to reorganise their lines. The few arrows they sent our way bounced off armour or struck shields. At thirty paces the Ulfheonar began to hurl our first spear. It did not matter that some would miss. The warriors of Strathclyde and Hibernia had to hold up their shields and were temporarily blinded. Just before we struck I pulled back my arm and punched forward with my second spear. It slid along a shield and the pressure of the men behind and our speed took it into the stomach of a warrior in the second rank. All of the Ulfheonar spears found a home and a hole was punched through the middle of the line. They were three deep. They were hit by a body of men which was almost a hundred strong. We were so swift that the three riders on their ponies did not have time to react and move out of the way. I drew Ragnar's Spirit and hacked at the first rider. He turned to flee to safety but my blade hacked though his leg and into the pony. The pony reared in pain, throwing the rider and clattering into the next rider. Cnut despatched him.

The third leader shouted an order and the men from the flanks came around the rear to try to form a new line which would encircle us. Suddenly a horn was heard as Thorkell led his garrison from the Roman fort less than a quarter of a mile away. I saw the face of the last leader of the men of Strathclyde. It was a mask of fury. I had outwitted him. His army was now split in two. I yelled, "Two lines! Back to back!"

We were on the road and we halted to stand back to back. We had a ditch in front of us and my men locked shields with their neighbour. Haaken was in the most precarious position for there was no one to his right. I had my shield on that exposed side. Cnut and I stepped forward to the edge of the road. We had broken through the men with armour and now faced the ones who had a shield, a spear and, if they were lucky, a helmet. The first Hibernian jabbed his spear at me and, as I deflected it harmlessly to my left, I lunged forward and skewered his half naked body on my sword. I stepped forward and twisted my sword from his writhing body which dropped into the ditch. I was ahead of Cnut and I sliced sideways to slice into the back of the warrior he was fighting. We were now forcing the two halves apart and, behind us, Thorkell's men were attacking the rear of the southern end of their line.

A rash and courageous warrior hurled himself at me with his sword held in two hands before him. Although I held up my shield the sword struck my helmet. Had it not been a full face one then I would be dead. As it was my head was forced to the side. The young warrior impaled himself upon my sword. His act of bravery seemed to encourage others and they threw themselves at our line. Had we not been mailed warriors then it might have gone badly. The blades struck metal and shields and their unprotected bodies were ripped and torn by our swords. Their attack petered out. They ran towards the north and we began to drive them, inexorably towards their home and the river which protected our northern borders. The river was less than sixty paces from them and we were like beaters driving game into a net. The most resistance was in the middle where Arturus and his men were fighting the last of the mailed warriors. There were not many but they were like a dam holding back the water. At the sides Karl and I were pushing towards each other. The men of Strathclyde found themselves attacked from all sides and, inevitably some of them broke and, joining the ones we had broken already ran to the river.

Ignoring the ones who were doomed to drown we pushed towards the warriors fighting Arturus. I need not have worried. I saw my son take a blow from a long sword on his shield and swing backhand into the mailed side of the warrior. He pulled back and struck again. I knew what had happened without seeing. The first blow had severed the mail links and the second tore into the warrior's side. He was a dead man walking. He struck at my son's shield but I saw that his blows were weakening. Arturus struck at the same spot again and the warrior crumpled and died. We kept pushing the ever-decreasing circle of warriors further and further back.

Three warriors decided to make a heroic end and they charged at me and my Ulfheonar. My wolf shield drew them on. We were tired but they were exhausted. Their final effort to charge us sapped the last of their energy. The sword which struck my shield was a weak one and I contemptuously knocked the sword aside with my shield. I feinted with my sword and the warrior parried fresh air. I swung my sword it his neck and his head joined his dead companions on the bloodied grass. That was the last resistance from our band we went to the river and I saw three men of Strathclyde clambering up the other bank. The others who had survived were being swept to the sea and their death. We needed no prisoners now. There were three who would tell the terrible tale of the slaughter of the men of Strathclyde by the wolves from the south.

Chapter 12

Although the battle was won we still had to clear the field of those who fought on beyond all hope. We turned our attention to the southern band. Even when they surrendered they were slain. They had not learned their lesson the last time. This time we would make no mistake. Finally, we met Thorkell's men. Of my former Ulfheonar, Thorkell the Tall, there was no sign. Harald Green Eye with bloodied blade approached me. "Thorkell has gone to Valhalla, Jarl Dragon Heart. He was stabbed in the back by the leader on the pony." I looked and saw the body of my captain next to the butchered leader and his pony. Yet another of the original Ulfheonar had gone to the Other World. My world was emptier for the loss.

"Did you lose many others?"

He shook his head, "Not Ulfheonar but they killed many of the people and had you not come then it would have gone ill. Thorkell had become complacent and we did not have enough supplies within the fort. We would have starved to death in a matter of days had you not come." He shrugged, "I know he believed that he had let you down. Perhaps he had a death wish."

My decisions had been the correct ones but that did not help me for I had lost another old friend. There were just two left from the original Ulfheonar, Haaken and Cnut.

We stripped the bodies and then took them to the river. As I hurled the first one in I intoned, "Great Icaunis, take these unworthy offerings in thanks for our victory today!" It was a sacrifice of sorts.

It took some time to rid the field of their bodies. Then we dug a grave for our own dead. These were not stripped but dressed and arrayed in their armour with helmets and shields. We laid Thorkell in the middle and the others around him. We put his sword and that of the chief who had slain him across his body. The shield covered his head. We placed stones on top of the bodies and when that was completed we piled earth until it was a mound and then turf on the top. It would be visible from the fort and a reminder of the sacrifices others had made to keep their freedom.

The fort was too small to accommodate us all and so the men camped outside. Arturus and I stayed in the hall for we would need to speak with the Ulfheonar who remained in Thorkell's Stad. I would need to appoint a new commander. There had to be someone to command my northern marches. However before that I needed to be clean. I had been fighting for almost three days and I reeked of blood and sweat. There were still baths at the fort. They did not work as they had in the days of the Romans but they would clean the blood away. I donned a simple kyrtle when I was clean. I felt better.

There were just seven of us seated around the table; the five remaining oathsworn, me and my son. After we had eaten we told tales of Thorkell. We told of his time in Cymru and his escape. We remembered his fierce style of fighting. A blow to the back was the only way he could have been slain. There were a few moments of silence as we each said goodbye in our own way. Then I raised my horn of ale, "Thorkell the Tall; may the ceilings be high in Valhalla!"

"Thorkell the Tall!"

Arturus and I told them about Wessex and Lundenburgh. They were both impressed that Arturus had managed to steal a queen.

"I did not steal her! She chose to come with me!"

"You stole her heart then. That is even more impressive."

I could see that he was embarrassed and I quickly changed the subject. "We will not be either raiding or trading as often as we did. Aiden has come up with a plan to trade with Byzantium once a year. Now that we have our own iron we need less from Frankia and Wessex than we did."

Harald nodded, "That is good. The land is safer when you are here."

I shook my head, "This year we have had many warriors coming to take my sword from me. It has invited death into my home."

Sven White Hair swallowed his beer, "We heard that from some traders who passed through heading north. They said that in Jorvik the tales of the sword which was touched by the gods was a constant source of conversation."

"I know and that is why I will silence that snake Wiglaf."

Einar held up a finger, "I would advise caution, Jarl. The same traders told us that Jorvik now has a Danish master. Wiglaf runs the city but it is ruled by Magnus Klak. He has powerful connections. His brother, it is said, has aspirations to be King of Denmark. They rule Jorvik with a rod of iron. Many traders, like the ones we met, have fled to find easier places in which to trade."

"Thank you for the information." I had put off making the announcement as long as I could. It had to be said. "Now I need to have one of you as a Jarl. I have my own thoughts but you know me well enough to know that I like your opinions too."

They all looked at Harald Green Eye. Sven White Hair said, "There is an obvious choice. When Thorkell sailed on the drekar, Harald ruled. We are all comfortable with that."

"And you Harald, are you comfortable too?"

"I am no Thorkell but I will do my best. Aye, I will be your jarl." We gave him the chain which Thorkell had worn. It had a golden wolf with jet eyes. The ones I gave my Ulfheonar had blue eyes.

That night I slept like a baby. It was a luxury to have a bed. We spent some hours repairing the damage to the fort and dividing the treasure up and then we left. All shared in the victory as we had all shared in the deaths. Karl took his warriors back to Windar's Mere. The battle had made them all better warriors and I was more confident about our eastern approaches. Windar had never been a warrior but his son was and that made me feel safer. We spent the day heading south. There was no hurry and more of my warriors now sported both injuries and wounds.

As we entered, at dusk, the gates of our stronghold, Elfrida ran to greet her husband. The men he led merely smiled but the Ulfheonar took great pleasure in whooping and cheering as she hugged and kissed my embarrassed son. Poor Arturus did not know which way to look. Kara glared balefully at them and they subsided. Kara was very protective of her brother. She took me by the arm and led me into my hall. "The men of Strathclyde are defeated?"

"Aye, daughter but we lost Thorkell the Tall."

"He will join the spirits for he had a strong heart. Do not mourn him for he died doing what he enjoyed."

"I also heard that there is a new Dane who rules with Wiglaf. There may be danger coming from the east."

"I will speak with the spirits. I have not felt any danger." She stroked my hair. "You are tired. I will get Scanlan to light the fire in the sweat hut. It will do you good and then a swim in the Waters will refresh you." She stood, kissed me on the cheek and added, "Aiden is keen to speak with you."

She knew me so well. I had not used the sweat hut for some time. It would be good to do so again. Aiden joined me and brought in jug of ale. "It is freshly brewed. We used some of the hops we traded the merchants of Kent. It has a good flavour."

He was right. "There are still some things we need from the land of Wessex then?"

"There may be other places we can get them. Perhaps I will sail with Siggi on his next voyage." He had grown in the years he had served me; both physically and mentally. His mind was an asset as much as my sword. "I hear from Haaken that Wiglaf now has a master."

"He was never cut out to be a leader. Perhaps he was just preparing the way for this Magnus Klak. It would not surprise me. The man is a snake."

"You still plan the winter raid?"

"I do but we will make it by sea and not by land."

"Why?"

"We cannot predict the weather. If we have storms at sea we can shelter in estuaries and bays but the high, empty land between here and Jorvik is dangerous."

"It is a shorter journey. We can be there in three days by pony. The sea voyage would take many days."

"I know. We will see what the spirits say when Kara speaks with them."

"You would not go sooner?"

"No, Aiden, I need time here with my people. I have been gone more than I have been present lately and besides, Arturus will want to come with me and he has a new bride."

"All the more reason for going by land."

Just then Scanlan entered, "The sweat hut is ready Jarl. I should hurry. Haaken and Cnut smelled the smoke!"

I laughed, "I shall use my power to evict them. Would you join me, Aiden, and we can continue our talk? The sweat and the conversation help me to see things clearly."

"I will, jarl."

Of course, the hut was big enough for six warriors and Cnut and Haaken joined us. As the sweat cleaned our skin and hair we began to relax and I talked through my plans for Wiglaf. As the day drew to a close a slave came to tell us that the evening meal was ready.

We stepped out and saw the sun setting over the Water and Old Olaf was framed in a golden light. The world was good.

"Well Jarl Dragon Heart, have you finalised your plans yet? Did our talk help?"

"Let us just say, Cnut, that I am clearer but I will wait to speak with Kara when she has sought the advice of the spirits."

I had a fitful sleep. My dreams were filled with faces from the past. Warriors who had died alongside me and for me drifted in and out of my mind in no particular order. Everywhere I turned was another face and I had no place to go to be alone. I wondered if this was the spirit world trying to tell me something but I could not piece together the threads. All that I could see were the bloodied hands of my comrades and there was fire. Perhaps Aiden or Kara could unpick the answers.

I dressed and went down to the Water. I loved it in the morning with the sun behind me picking out Olaf's features and the Water so still it looked as though you could walk upon it. Two ducks quacked their way south; the only noise on that still morning. I stayed there until I heard the noises from the people who lived on the other side of the wall. As work began I headed back to my hall. We had too many people living on this side of the Water. I had chosen this for my home because I liked the view and it was easy to defend but it was steep and rocky. The houses were small for it was difficult to make deep foundations. The land to the west was better. I decided to talk with Scanlan and Aiden about it.

The slaves brought my food and I ate alone and in silence. My thoughts and plans filled the quiet. Aiden slipped in and joined me. He and I shared the hall with my slaves. Erika and I had built it with the children in mind but the Norns had had other plans.

"I have been thinking about the western stad."

Aiden nodded as though he knew. "I think we should visit with Scanlan. There are too many crowded into this small hillside."

He nodded, "Bjorn has been thinking of moving but he did not wish to offend you."

"Offend me? He can go where he chooses but I thought he was happy here."

"He was but now that we have our own iron he needs to be on the other side of the Water. Lang's Dale is to the north and west. It would be easier to take the raw ore there. The animals struggle up our hill with the load. And he needs to have more room for his forges."

"Are there others too who wish to move?"

"I think so. When you were in the north I spent much time here and spoke to many. I think that Arturus and Elfrida should have a large hall on the other side of the Water. The dwelling the men threw up is too small for a family."

"Family!" My face must have had a startled expression for Aiden laughed.

"You are not to be a grandfather yet but that will come. Arturus' warriors could have a warrior hall built there too."

"Then that would just leave my Ulfheonar and Kara's house of women here."

"Isn't that what you wish, really, Jarl? And some of the Ulfheonar have families now and they might prefer to have a larger home on the flatter land to the west of the Water. The warrior hall should be for the single Ulfheonar."

I would need time to think but I could give Bjorn the blacksmith his answer. "I will be by the Water. I need to talk with Bjorn and then think." I descended to the fires of Bjorn and his sons.

He came out to greet me. He held a dagger in his hand. It was unpolished but ready to be sharpened. "The first weapon with our new iron. It is good metal. I shall finish this one for you, Jarl."

I held it in my hand and it was well balanced. Although a little shorter than the seax I used it had a point and two edges; it would be a handy weapon for close in fighting. "Thank you Bjorn. I think that it is a good thing if you move your forges to the western side."

"You are not unhappy?"

"I shall miss my talks with you but I can visit each day. I do not spend enough time in the western stad anyway. Go with my blessing, Bjorn."

"It will mean we can work quicker. It takes a longer time for the iron to reach us and the jetty on the other side is better for the boats. This is *wyrd*."

I smiled when I saw him hurry to tell his sons that they were moving. I did not know that my old friends were afraid to upset me. I had thought they could all be honest and open with me. Perhaps I was wrong. Kara waited in the hall for me. Aiden was with her.

"Did you tell him?"

"Aye Kara and he seemed happy." I looked at her. "You knew?"

"The spirits said nothing about Wiglaf or your quest but the dreams you had were sent by them. They sent them to me." She put her hand on Aiden's. "I think that this should be like the home you shared with Ragnar when you were a boy."

"But there were just two of us!"

"And you were happy." She pointed through the open door to the west. "That is Cyninges-tūn. This is the Wolf's Lair. It should be you, Aiden and the single Ulfheonar who live here. Rolf can guard it when you are gone. This is your home; it is not ours."

"You would go too?"

"You are away for long periods and do not see my people struggling with the goods they make. It is steep and the road in winter is impassable. There is more than enough room on the western side for all and Arturus and Elfrida can rule there. He needs responsibility."

My shoulders slumped, "Then I am no longer needed."

She laughed and it was as though Erika was in the room with us. "We need you more than ever but when you and your Ulfheonar go this winter then it is hard to protect both Cyninges-tūn and this place." She looked into my eyes and said, "It is right that we move and now is the time to build so that the halls are built before the winter comes."

There was something in her words, "It will be a bad winter?"

"It will be another Wolf Winter."

That decided me. We had lost too many of our people in the last wolf winter. "Then it is good. I will tell my Ulfheonar!"

I think I was disappointed with the enthusiasm with which the news was received. Even Cnut and Haaken seemed happy to move. Haaken confided in me, "It is our wives. They wish to be closer to other families." He shrugged, "Thanks to our raids we are rich warriors and they wish to show off our wealth to other families."

I finally understood. I was no longer a married man with a family and I liked the remote world of my Wolf Lair. I remembered how Ragnar and I had enjoyed visiting the village at the floor of the mountains but we had preferred the isolation, especially in the winter, of our mountain hut. I think that was why I had chosen this site for my home when we had first arrived.

Arturus took the news well. I think he liked the idea of being the new Jarl of Cyninges-tūn. Elfrida was delighted to be able to have a new hall built. She hugged me. "Thank you, Jarl Dragon Heart! You have made all of my dreams come true." She was a lovely girl and I knew that she and Arturus would be happy but I felt an ache inside of me knowing that I would not speak with them every day. When they visited they would be coming to a home which was no longer theirs. I would be losing the rest of my family. I had lost Erika and now I would lose Kara, Arturus and Elfrida. *Wyrd.*

Over the next few days people left. The men went first to build the new homes. The forests were filled with the sound of axes and falling trees. Each day Wolf's Lair became a little emptier. Bjorn and his smiths ferried their anvils across the Water and left the empty wooden shells where they had worked. Soon the wind and the weather would eradicate all traces of them. When the married Ulfheonar left I just had eight single warriors remaining. The last to leave were Kara and her women. It felt like inhabiting a ghost town.

It took almost a month to build the hall for the women for Kara supervised it with a tongue as sharp as ice. She wanted her brewery and her place to make cheese to be better placed than they had been on the hill. Her hall was taken down for many of the parts, such as the roof beams could be reused. My men learned not to upset the formidable Kara.

There were new tenants, however. With the warriors of Arturus gone to the new hall Rolf had a small hall he could have for his own. There were old warriors without families and old men who lived alone. They came from Cyninges-tūn where they had lived alone in empty huts. They would be Rolf's guards for Wolf's Lair. All of them liked the name and felt they had a new purpose in life. The priests of the White Christ have places they call monasteries where men work, pray and study in isolation. We did not pray but it was a similar existence. They even took to brewing their own ale. As the summer drew towards the falling of the leaves my world had changed beyond all recognition. And still Kara had not dreamed.

The sword had been forged in a storm when we had been on Mann. Cnut and I had been in the tower when the lightning had struck. The leaves had yet to fall but a storm had been brewing all day. I wondered if it would be a repeat of the one on Mann. The heat became unbearable and the air felt so heavy that people's shoulders sagged as they dripped with sweat. Night fell early for the clouds were so black it felt like night. I sat by the Water with Aiden to get some relief from the tiniest of breezes across the water.

Suddenly, in the distance, I heard the rumble of thunder and felt the first spots of rain. I stood for they were not small spots. Aiden and I turned to run for the shelter and protection of the hall for the heavens opened and a deluge dropped from the skies. We had a stone roof on my hall and I was grateful for it that night as the rain pounded so hard that, had it been turf, then we would have been soaked. Just when I thought it could not get any worse I heard more rumbles of thunder. Aiden and I went to the door to watch. I saw lightning in the distance grow closer to us. The rain continued to fall unabated and the crack of thunder and the lightning grew closer together. I saw a huge lightning bolt and it seemed to strike Old Olaf's head. I recoiled with the force for it lit up the whole valley. Were the gods punishing us? I turned to speak with Aiden but he had gone and I was alone. The storm seemed to have some mesmeric attraction for me.

Osbert, one of my slaves, hurried over to me. There was terror in his eyes, "Jarl is this the end of the world?"

"I think not, Osbert, but the gods are unhappy with something." I smiled at him. "Get to bed. I will watch and if the world is about to end then I will wake you."

He managed a smile back, "If the world is about to end then bed will be the best place for me. Goodnight, master."

I watched the storm ebb and flow across the valley. The rain and the thunder abated and then rushed back again. The wind howled and rain swirled horizontally with its force. When it did abate I heard the torrent of water that was the beck thundering down from the hillsides. I looked anxiously at Cyninges-tūn. I hoped that it would not be flooded. If it were then that would be a sign that the move had been a bad one. And then just as quickly as it had started it stopped and, as the clouds scudded away I saw that it was a new day. The storm had raged all night. I saw the timbers from one of the boats we used on the Water floating by. I could still hear the raging torrent of Bjorn's Gill behind me. I stepped out of the hall and my feet sank to my ankles in mud which had been washed down from the hills. I climbed the stairs to the gate tower and, looking outside, saw that the ditches had been filled with water. They had saved us from worse damage and I hoped that the ones at Cyninges-tūn had done the same.

I woke Osbert. "Is it the end of the world, master?"

"No the storm has passed and it is a new day. Saddle my horse for me."

Rolf was up too. "That was a storm and no mistake."

"Aye and I fear for Cyninges-tūn. Check for damage while I cross the valley."

"Where is Aiden?"

"He sleeps. Let him rest. He can do naught."

I mounted my horse and headed down the trail. It was covered in the branches and leaves smashed from the trees by wind. The gods had sent us a message. I hoped that one of my dreamers knew the answer. When I reached the northern end of the Water I saw that the deluge had flooded the trail. The water came up to my horse's haunches. Had I been riding a pony I would have struggled. In all the years we had lived here I had never experienced such a storm. Was this the beginning of a bad winter? Would we have another Wolf Winter?

There were farms and houses outside of Cyninges-tūn. Two had been destroyed by the storm. I could find no trace of the people and I hoped that they had taken shelter in my daughter's hall. One family whose home had survived were already clearing up. I saw that they had a stone roof and their stone home was built into the hillside.

"Are your family safe, Sven?"

"Aye Jarl Dragon Heart but it was only the stones from Old Olaf that kept us safe." He patted the grey stone walls."

"If you need any help then send to Cyninges-tūn."

He nodded, "How did they fare?"

"I will soon discover."

There had been damage. As I rode to the wooden walls I saw that the jetty had been torn apart and there were no ships to be seen. Bolli would have much work to make good the damage. I wondered how our drekar had suffered in the estuary. That would have to wait. The gates of Cyninges-tūn had been torn asunder by the force of the storm and I feared the worst. Surprisingly all of the new buildings, Kara's hall, Arturus' new home, all still stood. Scanlan was already organising the clear up of the fallen trees. The ditches looked to have stopped most of the flooding but there were still parts which were under water.

I tied my horse to a post and headed for Kara's hall. She was not within but her women sent me to Arturus' hall. "The Lady Elfrida had a bad night, Jarl Dragon Heart."

It must have been terrible for her. She was in a strange place and the storm would have frightened strong warriors. It was the gods unleashing their power. When I entered Elfrida was crying and she was being comforted by both Arturus and Kara.

Kara rose to greet me. "She dreamed and it frightened her."

I saw that Kara too was hollow eyed, "And you dreamed too."

She nodded, "I will speak with you later. Elfrida's dream was more urgent." She lifted her chin, "Elfrida you must recount your dream again for the jarl. It is important."

She shook her head, "If I tell you then it will come true and he will come to get me."

Arturus kissed the top of her head, "Fear not Elfrida. Jarl Dragon Heart is here and he will protect us all. He has the sword touched by the gods."

She looked up at me and nodded, "I dreamed that I was on the top of Old Olaf. The storm came and I sheltered in a cave. I was not alone. I thought it was a wolf but it was not it was a bear and it came to get me. I ran but I could not escape. It grabbed me and I saw its teeth were stained with blood. I closed my eyes and prepared to die. When I opened them the bear had changed into Egbert.

I thought I was going to die and then a wolf leapt from the dark and I remember no more." She grabbed my hand, "Jarl, father, do not let the bear get me! Do not let Egbert take me back. I would rather die than submit to him!"

"Fear not, Elfrida, for I am the wolf of your dream and we will stop Egbert. You are safe here. Arturus and his men are a wall around you while you are here and he is going nowhere." Elfrida smiled and buried herself in Arturus' arms. He looked at me quizzically. "We will talk later Arturus."Come daughter let us leave them."

Once outside she asked, "Did you not dream last night? The gods were as close as they will ever be and the night was filled with the spirits."

"I watched the storm all night. I could not sleep."

She nodded, "But you know what Elfrida's dream means."

"Aye, Egbert is coming for her. I had thought we were too far from his grasp."

"He may not come himself but he can hire warriors. You did not think that you would escape punishment from him, did you? He will send men and we need to be watchful."

"And what of Wiglaf?"

She gave a sad smile, "Last night I wrestled with many dreams. I too saw the bear but it was not Egbert, it was a Viking and it made no sense until I heard Elfrida's dream. As for Wiglaf, you cannot take Arturus away from Elfrida. My brother will need to watch her." She sighed, "I think that this will be a task for a small number and not an army."

"Then I will be crossing the land in winter."

She stared into my eyes, "Aye and remember this will be a wolf winter." She paused, "Perhaps you will be the wolf. You have much to think on, father and I wish that I could be of more help. It seems our world rests upon your back. It is not fair."

I laughed, "Do you think the Norns like a fair world? It is the world into which we are born and we have to do the best that we can. I am happy. I will be able to enter Valhalla and face Butar, Ragnar and the others with my head held high. I will look my grandsire, the Warlord, in the eye and know that I did my duty."

Unusually for Kara, she looked tearful and she threw her arms around me. "He will be proud of you as we are all proud and honoured that you are our jarl."

"I must go to Úlfarrston and see how my ships have fared."

She nodded, "What did Aiden dream?"

"I know not."

"Then see him before you travel to Úlfarrston. There may be dangers."

I had learned to heed my daughter's words. I only had my sword with me. I mounted my horse and rode back as swiftly as I could. By the time I reached Wolf's Lair my Ulfheonar were all helping Rolf to put it in some sort of order.

Aiden looked happy to see me. "We must talk Jarl." I went into my hall with him. "There is danger coming. I saw Danes climbing Úlfarrberg. It is Egbert's work."

"I know, Elfrida had the same dream. I go now to Úlfarrston. We must see how the ships have fared."

"There is more. Josephus came to me."

"And?"

"And I must travel to Miklagård. I know not why but it is important." He paused, "It concerns the sword. I saw it burning again and it was covered in blood."

"Was I holding it?"

He shook his head, "No, Jarl, and that is what worries me."

"Then this was meant to be. You shall travel by sea whilst I go to Jorvik by land. The Norns have decided this."

He nodded, "It is *wyrd*."

Chapter 13

I took some of the Ulfheonar with me when I went to the drekar. They insisted. Sigtrygg, Snorri, Bjorn the Scout and Erik Dog Bite were more than enough to protect me from any danger. Aiden came too. Instead of the longer journey around the Water we headed south along the trail which followed the ridge. We used this eastern route for it was less prone to flooding. By noon we had reached the river. Bolli was already hard at work. The *'Josephus'* had been damaged. An uprooted tree had driven into her hull. He and Erik Short Toe were hauling her on to the bank to drain her. *'The Heart'* had suffered less but she looked the worse for wear. Erik shook his head. "The gods were angry last night jarl but do not fear. We will be ready to sail in a week or so."

I nodded. "The next voyage you take will be to Miklagård with Aiden. I shall be sending the knarr there too. You need not rush the job. You have half a month to prepare."

"You will not be coming?"

"No, Erik, I have other work to do." Bolli was shaking his head at the damage. "You will have much work to do on the Water, Bolli, not a ship remains afloat."

"I should be happy for that means more gold but I hate to see any boat destroyed."

"Do your best and if you need gold before you begin then just ask."

"I know I will be paid, jarl."

"What of the knarr?"

They both shook their heads. "We know not."

I dreaded riding into the estuary and discovering that they had been destroyed too. That would be too much to bear. I was relieved to see them both bobbing up and down on the tide. Siggi and Trygg left their boats to greet me.

"I am pleased that you were spared."

"We arrived this morning and missed the worst of the storm."

"It was not out at sea then?"

"No Jarl. If it had been then we would not have survived. We hove to and watched the gods hurling their lightning at the mountains."

Something in the tone of Siggi's voice made me ask. "Where did you sail from?"

"Lundenwic."

My warriors and Aiden gathered closer in. "You were not harmed?"

"King Egbert was not there. When we were in Cymru we heard that he had taken an army into Mercia to punish King Coenwulf. We risked it."

"Were you welcomed?"

Trygg nodded, "The people of Lundenwic speak of you and our men fondly. We did good business. It is why we hove to. We did not want to risk the gold and cargo we carried."

"Eorl Edward came to see us and he gave you a message."

I already knew what it was. "He warned you that King Egbert has hired mercenaries to take back Elfrida!"

All of them clutched their hammers or their wolves. Siggi asked, "Are you fey now as well as your daughter?"

"No Elfrida and Aiden dreamed the danger. Did he say when?"

"They left Lundenwic fourteen nights since."

"Then they will be close. We will need to prepare."

"There is more Jarl. The Eorl said they needed little inducement for the warriors wanted the sword too. They are led by a Dane called Bothvar Bjarki. He came from Jorvik. He wears a wolf skin. He is Ulfheonar."

"*Wyrd*. And his men are they Ulfheonar too?"

"No, but Eorl Edward said that this Bjarki is a berserker. He has killed many men. He knows of your reputation and he told King Egbert that the world only had room for one wolf and it was him. He swore to slay you himself and bring back Elfrida." He paused, "The king wants her back or her body and that of Arturus. Your son is in danger too."

I knew that. The storm made sense now. "You have done well. Prepare your ships for I wish you to go to Miklagård with Aiden. *'The Heart'* will guard you."

Siggi and Trygg nodded. Siggi said, "These Danes are all killers. You must be careful, Jarl. There were fifty of them left Lundenwic."

"We will deal with them when they come." I clasped their arms, "You have done well but I must return to my home. Warn Pasgen of the danger."

We rode hard to reach home. I first told Arturus, privately of the dangers. It would not do to alarm Elfrida. "What will you do?" He had become far calmer since his marriage and I could see a change in my son.

"I will send word to Windar. If they left Lundenwic then they will, more than likely come through the valley of Windar. He should be warned. I will send some of my men to occupy your old fort. If they do not come past Windar's Mere then they come up along past Hawk's Stad."

"You do not want to sit behind your walls and sit out a siege?"

"No, my son. I intend to meet this Bothvar Bjarki in the open."

"He is a berserker."

"And that is why I will meet him in the open for my men have discipline and it sounds as though he has none. I do not want to risk any of my people. Berserkers and their followers never know when to stop. Do you think my warriors would slaughter women and children?"

"Of course not."

"A berserker would. They would not know how to stop themselves. We need to find these enemies and put them down as one would a mad dog."

Even Kara was taken aback when I told her the news. "The spirits did not know the severity of the threat father. I am sorry."

"Do not worry. I will deal with our enemies. I am just happy that we knew it was coming."

My Ulfheonar were summoned back to Wolf's Lair. They could return to their families when the Danes were dealt with. They all understood and came forth willingly. It was Rolf and his old men who concerned me. If I guessed wrongly

117

then they would be slaughtered. They could not stand up to a berserker warband. It made me more determined than ever to find and stop this wild Dane.

Rolf and his men were not worried about this mad Dane. If anything, they looked forward to defending their home against such a monster. Our decision to move the majority of my people to Cyninges-tūn had been a good one.

"Rolf let us prepare the ditches for defence. I know they are full of water but we need to embed stakes."

He grinned, "A little water never hurt. We will not let you down, Jarl."

"I know but I hope to stop them before they actually get here. You are my last line of defence."

He rubbed his hands. "I had thought that I had fought my last fight! I hope I am wrong!"

This was an anxious time for we had not yet fully recovered from the raids by the men of Strathclyde. I sent Sigtrygg and six Ulfheonar to Arturus' old fort to watch for danger from the south and west. I went with Aiden to tell Windar of the danger. I wore my armour all the time now and rode my horse. Until we found the would be abductors we were in a state of war.

It was late when we reached Windar's Mere. Most of the people lived beyond the walls of the old Roman fort for this was a peaceful place. Inside the halls had but six warriors, including Karl. "There is danger, Windar."

"Not the men of Strathclyde again?"

"No, old friend, your son and I disposed of them. Danes have been sent by King Egbert to take back Arturus' bride."

"Do you think they will come here?"

"They could and remember they are killers. Have you a signal to bring your people within these walls?"

"Aye but if they come from the south and they are killers they may overrun those who would warn us."

Karl nodded, "I will take some men on ponies and watch the road from the south."

"I have men at the Hawk's Stad. It may be that they head in that direction."

"Aye well I will light the beacons if they come this way."

I clasped his arm. "Do not be reckless. These are Vikings and not the men of Strathclyde. These are fierce warriors."

"I believe you Jarl but we will not let them come unannounced. You will have warning. Do you need warriors to aid you?"

"I would say yes but it is coming to harvest time and I know that every farmer will have work to do. I will rely on the Ulfheonar and Arturus' men."

We stayed the night and enjoyed the hospitality of Windar. I now knew why he was so large. There was enough food to feed a warband! We would have to name him Windar the Fat. He had a good heart but he was no warrior.

Aiden and I left early and we headed down to Hawk's Stad. Sometimes we do things and know not why. Our actions are directed by powers we do not understand. We were riding through the Dale of Grize where the biting insects swarmed like clouds of evil. When our horses neighed we knew it was something more than midges that they had sensed. We stopped and dismounted. We tied our horses to a tree and moved down towards the road. I heard voices and we stopped and watched. A file of warriors was moving through the woods towards Cyninges-tūn Water. I knew before I saw their arms that it was the Danish war band. We froze as we watched the column pass. There was little point in moving for we might alert them.

When they had passed I turned to Aiden. "Ride first to Karl and tell him where the Danes are. Then ride to Wolf's Lair. I want the Ulfheonar and Arturus' men ready to march towards Nibth's Waite."

"And what will you do, Jarl?"

I pointed to the ridge. "I will ride over the ridge and get to Sigtrygg and my men. We will fall back towards Nibth's Waite."

He nodded. I knew that I could rely on him. We mounted. He went north and I went west. It meant I had to traverse the forest which was infested with biting insects but it meant that I could avoid the Danes. They would follow the old road and that had fewer midges. It was strange that a biting insect could have such power. I rode my horse hard. I had to reach the fort. I did not want some act of reckless bravery from any of my men.

I had just crested the rise when a movement to my left caught my eye. I halted my horse and peered down the slope. There were two Danish scouts there. They both wore wolf cloaks but I could not see armour beneath. I drew my sword and galloped down the slope. They heard me but the annoying insects and the trees hid me from them until I was almost upon them. I veered my horse towards the nearer of them and swung my sword as he tried to stab me with his spear. He jabbed it at my leg, which had a metal greave. Sliding harmlessly off I was able to hack into his neck. I blocked the axe from the second scout as he tried to decapitate my horse and I yanked the reins around so that I was able to slice across his unprotected neck. His helmet had no aventail and he died swiftly. I kicked on; they were close to the fort. Scouts were normally sent half a mile in front of a war band. I had a short time only to reach the fort and extricate my men.

I was relieved to see the fort and that there were no Danes nearby. I kicked my horse's flanks as I descended the trail. The gate of the small fort was open. I did not dismount. "Quickly! The Danes are coming. Fire the fort!"

I did not want the Danes to have a place to which they could retreat. We could always rebuild if we had to. The last thing I needed was a warband of fifty warriors in my land and occupying a fort. My men threw the seal oil all over the walls and hall. Using flint and kindling they soon had a fire going and we spread burning brands around. It would attract the Danes but, by then, we would be gone.

"Quickly leave now. They will see the smoke and they will come."

My men had brought ponies and they quickly mounted and trotted towards the Water. Behind me I heard a roar as the Danes appeared along the road and spied the burning fort. I was able to trot and still keep up with the galloping ponies. I frequently glanced over my shoulder to make sure I was still safe but we were outdistancing them. We now knew where they were and I just hoped that Aiden had reach Cyninges-tūn and brought Arturus' men. My Ulfheonar alone would struggle to defeat these warriors.

We waited by Nibth's farm at the southern tip of the water. He and his family came out when they heard our mounts. "Take your family and get to Cyninges-tūn. Enemies are coming."

He picked up his sword, "I can fight!"

"I know my friend but I need you to take your family to safety. Arturus' men are coming and the rest of my Ulfheonar." He nodded. They gathered their belongings. "Take our ponies for we shall not need them and they will speed your journey." They took them and hurried north. Had the storm not destroyed it they could have used their small boat but I saw its wrecked remains lying forlornly on the sand.

There were just seven of us and it was not enough to hold back the Danes who were coming. I thought that my Ulfheonar might reach us soon but Arturus had further to come. The storm had hurt us badly. If it had not been for the storm then Arturus and his men could have sailed down the Water and be with us even now.

"Why here, Jarl?"

I pointed to the flat ground. "Here we can form a shield wall. It is the only way to break the attack of a berserker. The ground is still swampy from the rains and there are many places where an unwary warrior can sink into a muddy hole. We will wait here and, when they come we will feign flight and flee to the higher ground close to the trail to Cyninges-tūn. We know to pick our way west but they will not. When they see our few numbers they will be eager to finish us off."

Snorri nodded. "Then Bjorn the Scout and I will find the best trail to the higher ground."

"Find three. If they follow us I do not want them to see us in single file. They will know the path that way."

The two scouts were still to the west when Haaken and Cnut appeared and Ulfheonar reached us. They had their bows with them. I explained my plan. "Aiden will have sent Arturus by now. We will see him before too long."

We all peered towards the north, vainly seeking the sight of Arturus and his mailed warriors. Snorri and Bjorn the Scout reappeared. "We have found the trails. You are right Jarl. The ground sucks at your feet if you step from the path. If they come at us recklessly then they will suffer."

"Then we will make them reckless. When we run follow either Snorri or Bjorn the Scout. We form up on the road. They will have to climb that steep slope. If they drive us from the road then we fall back into the trees and work our way to Old Olaf."

Just then Erik Dog Bite shouted, "The Danes! I see them."

"Form up in two lines and string your bows." I was the only one without a bow and so I drew Ragnar's Spirit. As I had guessed they must have spent some time approaching the burning fort cautiously expecting an ambush. It would have come as a surprise to see so few of us standing before them.

Snorri pointed north. "I see Arturus. He is more than a mile up the Water."

I could not worry about that. We had to delay the Danes and then irritate them into a premature attack. Their leader formed them into a boar's snout. With two points of attack it was intended to outflank us. I took the opportunity to annoy Bothvar Bjarki.

"Bothvar Bjarki, go home! The King's wife chose to leave him. You are working for a faithless man."

I saw the huge man clad in an enormous wolf skin which covered his head. He appeared to have no armour but he carried a long sword and a large shield. He laughed, "He pays well and besides I would have done this for nothing. You and your little boys are not true Ulfheonar. We are real wolf warriors and when I have torn your heart from your body I will take your sword and then destroy your people. Who knows I may even take the pretty young queen for myself!"

"Leave now, Bothvar Bjarki, or be prepared for you and your wild men to leave your bones in my land."

His answer was instantaneous. "Charge!" They came at us at a fast walk for he was trying to keep them together.

"Release!"

In the time it took for them to cover a hundred paces and come to within fifty paces of us my men had released three flights of arrows. As far as I could see only two of the enemy had fallen but I knew we had had many hits. These were tough men. Unlike us some of them fought without armour.

"Run!"

To the Danes it must have seemed as though they had terrified us with their charge. We each followed either Snorri or Bjorn the Scout. We could see the pattern for we were amongst it but the Danes just saw the twenty warriors running away from them. I turned my head to watch as often as I could. They were trying to keep their formation but already it was breaking up as eager warriors tried to close with us. The beck which led from the Water was wide, but, at this time of year was shallow. The flood waters from the storm had made both sides the muddy quagmire. Snorri and Bjorn the Scout led us across the stones hidden beneath the waters of the beck. I paused in the middle and saw that we had increased our lead. The road was now less than five hundred paces away.

Once we crossed the river we had to negotiate the worst part of the crossing. Had it not been for Snorri and Bjorn the Scout we would never have made it. As the land began to rise it became firmer but the climb became harder. I felt the weight of my armour and the exertions of the run as I began to pant. I smiled to myself. I was truly becoming a wolf!

I was the last to reach the road and my men had formed in one long line with a space for me in the middle. Bothvar Bjarki and his Danes were now spread out. I saw that at least eight were either stuck in the mud or struggling to cross the beck. Even as we watched I saw a heavily mailed warrior pitch forward in the mud as his foot caught on something. Bothvar Bjarki was berating his men for being women. It was not the way to lead.

As soon as they were in range my men released carefully aimed arrows. They sought bare flesh and warriors whose eyes were on the treacherous ground and not on the line of warriors two hundred paces from them. Our arrows found flesh and warriors clutched at arms pierced by arrows or tore them from their legs. Two could not tear anything for they had been killed by the arrows.

When they reached the bottom of the slope Bothvar Bjarki and half of his men did something which surprised us. They halted and, while their fellows protected them they began to bite the edges of their shields. "They are preparing to go berserk. Half of you have your shields and swords ready. The rest target the berserkers."

I had seen this once before but then it had been one warrior. They were working themselves up so that they could go on a killing frenzy. Aiden had told me that he thought they had some potion smeared on the edge of their shields to make them immune to pain.

Tostig's voice came from the left of our line. "Arturus is less than four hundred paces from us."

We had hope. Suddenly the Danish line erupted as they hurled themselves at us. They might have had the desire to reach us quickly but the steep slope meant that they struggled to stay upright. Four of the berserkers were struck by arrows before they were halfway up the slope. Still they climbed to get at us their bodies oozing blood. One of the younger ones, fitter than the rest, made straight for me and, even though his arms had arrows in them he swung his war axe one handed at me. He was below me and I jumped over the axe head as he swung it. He took another step forward and I swung Ragnar's Spirit. The sharp blade, which had yet to taste blood that day, took his head off in one blow. Even a berserker cannot fight without a head. His falling body took the legs from a second berserker who tumbled down the slope.

It was too close for arrows now but my men had the advantage that the Danes were below us. I could hear them struggling for breath as they tried to clamber the last few steps to the road. I punched one warrior back down the slope with my shield as another swung his sword at my legs. If I had not been wearing the metal greaves I had been given in Miklagård then I would have lost my legs. As it was I was able to swing my sword and cleave his head in two. The pressure was mounting, however, as the Danes forced us back. And then the berserkers launched themselves at us.

The mad warriors had no regard for their own lives and I saw that one was fighting naked! We fell back in the face of the onslaught. A wound did not slow them. A lost limb did not impair them. You killed them or they would keep on fighting even though they were dying. Few warriors could stand against them. You could deal with a single berserker but here there were eight or ten of them. Most men would have fled before them but my Ulfheonar would prove who was the stronger.

I saw Einar the Swift fall to the ground as a berserker plunged his sword into his leg. Sigtrygg swung his sword and took the warrior in the neck. Even with his life blood spraying around him he tried to finish off Einar. Then I had to give all of my attention to Bothvar Bjarki for the mighty warrior barged Tostig aside with a contemptuous blow from his war axe. Tostig tumbled down the bank.

The Dane's axe came at head height for we had fallen back from the steep edge and Bothvar Bjarki was a big man. I ducked and jabbed forward with my sword. It gouged into the knee of the berserker but he did not seem to feel it. Aiden must have been right; they must have taken a potion. Perhaps the potion gave power to their arms for Bothvar Bjarki did not pause in his swing and he brought it against my shield. The force of the axe and the berserker's height meant that I was forced back. As I stumbled backwards I saw arrows beginning to rain upon the Danes. Arturus had reached us. I had not time to look for him. Bothvar Bjarki brought his axe over his head to swing it down on me. A warrior wielding a Danish war axe usually tired after a few blows but Bothvar Bjarki was getting stronger. I took the blow on my shield which gave an ominous creak. It was well made but these blows would have felled a tree and I felt my arm begin to numb.

I stabbed upwards as I reeled back and the tip of my blade caught his arm. I do not know what I managed to cut but his swing became less powerful. When he hit my shield a third time it hurt my arm but the shield remained whole. I took heart and instead of recoiling I pushed forward with my shield so that he could not swing. I wanted to get in close to him. Our faces were close together and I saw that he had filed his teeth. He roared at me. "You are the trickster they say you are! You are the spawn of Loki!"

I did not answer but pushed my sword forward. We were too close for me to be able to stab him but the edge of Ragnar's Spirit tore down his side. I felt it grate on his ribs. He roared in anger and then head butted me. I fell backwards and I was slightly stunned. As I lay prostrate on the ground I saw him raise his axe in a triumphant swing and bring it down towards me. Had he connected then I would have been gutted like a fish. I had no choice. I threw my sword like a huge dagger at him. It hit him in the chest and, as I rolled to one side, he fell to the ground. His own weight drove the sword into his chest and his heart. I jumped to my feet, took his axe and decapitated him. I threw the helmet away and held the skull by his long lank hair.

"Behold! Bothvar Bjarki the berserker is no more! Ulfheonar!"

It gave heart to my men who began to howl. I saw Arturus leading his men in a wedge to fall upon the demoralised Danes. Haaken and Cnut urged on the Ulfheonar who survived and they began to hack their way through the oathsworn Danes who all died with their chief. I rolled the body over and retrieved my sword. I was about to rejoin the fray when I saw that they were all dead. King Egbert's hunters were gone. Elfrida was safe.

The warriors all began to bang their shields and roar with the exultation of victory. I looked at the Ulfheonar who would fight no more. Karl the Bold, Sven Four Fingers, Erik Dog Bite and Einar all lay dead. Tostig Wolf Hand, Snorri, Bjorn the Scout and Sigtrygg all had wounds which would keep them from fighting for some time. But we had won and I silently gave thanks to the spirits who had protected us. We were at the very edge of Old Olaf's mountain and I knew that he had aided us. My Ulfheonar had done well but this had been our severest test. Had Arturus and his warriors not arrived things might have gone badly for us.

Arturus and Cnut helped to search the bodies. Cnut came to me with a puzzled expression upon his face. "These warriors have no treasure upon them."

Haaken laughed, "That is the problem with berserkers, they have nowhere to keep things."

"They must have been paid by King Egbert. I cannot believe they have spent it. And where are their cloaks? Arturus they must have a camp somewhere. Take your warriors and find them. I suspect they may be either at Grize's Dale or Hawk's Stad. If you hurry you may catch them."

Eager to please, Arturus led off his warriors at a steady lope. We bound the wounds of the injured. "Cnut, you appear to be unwounded. Go to Cyninges-tūn and fetch carts and Aiden. There is no rush to leave here."

After we had bound the wounds of the wounded and given them water we looked at the weapons we had captured. The axes showed that the warriors of Bothvar Bjarki had spent much gold upon them. They all had intricate carvings upon them and that of Bjarki was inlaid with gold. These were not weapons to melt down nor were they weapons which we could use. We would take them back with us and decide how best me might employ them.

It was getting towards dark when Cnut arrived back. He had brought men from the stad as well as Aiden. We laid the dead on one cart and the wounded on the other three along with the weapons.

"Where is Arturus?"

"I sent him to find the camp of these Danes. I am not worried. He will be able to handle guards. Come let us get back for we have done much work here today."

As we walked, or rather trudged, up the road to Cyninges-tūn my men chanted one of the rowing chants in honour of the dead who would never share an oar or a bench again. Ulfheonar were not easy to replace and when '*The Heart of the Dragon*' sailed again half of the crew and more would not be Ulfheonar. I knew that we could not retain all of our warriors forever. We would be reunited in Valhalla but I would miss the faces which had faced me on so many voyages. My world was changing.

Arturus and his men arrived back at Cyninges-tūn after dark. They brought with them two horses and a string of ponies. They also had the treasures the Danes had left with their guards. "They were not the best of warriors but we slew them. I did not think you would want them as slaves. They died with their swords in their hands."

The Danes had indeed been rich. It seemed they liked gold more than even we did and there were many gold bracelets and torcs. We found the gold given to them by King Egbert. His image was on each coin. One day I would take some of those coins and throw them in his face. I smiled at the thought of him waiting, over the winter, for the return of the Danes and his child bride. He would worry that they had taken her for themselves. The word of their fate would take many months to reach Lundenwic.

Kara and her healers took our wounded to their hall. Elfrida had shown some skill in that area and she helped. As Aiden and I prepared to leave for Wolf's Lair with the few Ulfheonar who lived there she came up to me and hugged me. "Thank you, jarl. I will honour the warriors who died to protect me and I will care for those who were wounded. I am happy that I chose to come here. It is *wyrd*.'

Chapter 14

I was no longer a young man and it took longer for my body to recover from the fight. The crack to my leg had done some damage as had the axe blows to my shield and arm. It would be a month or more before I was recovered enough to even consider my journey to Jorvik. My men too had suffered much. When the message came from Bolli to tell me that my drekar was ready I had already chosen the ones who would journey with Aiden. I summoned all of my warriors and Arturus to Wolf's Lair. "Some of you will be travelling with Aiden to Miklagård. I will need six warriors to go with me to Jorvik. I am leaving Arturus to protect your families when we are gone. I will take Snorri, Bjorn the Scout, Sven Sharp Blade, Arnulf Bjornson, Harald Finehair and Siggi Siggison with me to scotch the snake, Wiglaf."

The ones I had chosen looked delighted whilst the rest scowled. As I had expected many of my warriors wished to be with me.

Sigtrygg shouted the loudest, "Jarl, I have always been your first choice for such danger."

"And if you had not suffered such wounds in the last months you would be my first choice again. You need time to recover and rowing to Miklagård will help you recover." I pointed to my Galdramenn, "And you have my healer with you to watch over you as you will protect him."

Haaken looked affronted, "And what of us, Jarl Dragon Heart? We have no wounds."

"No, but you now have families and besides you are my most experienced warriors. You will have twenty warriors on the drekar who need training and guidance. That will be your task." I sighed, "This is no Tynwald. I am jarl and I have made my decision. Haaken and Cnut you need to choose the warriors who will row with you. Choose those who are single and who might make good warriors."

When they had all left me I sat with Aiden and we spoke of the voyage. "We have goods to trade with the Greeks, Aiden, but what do we seek in return?"

"We know that we can buy the spices which are so valuable elsewhere. We can sell those in the lands where we traded them last time; the ones who fight the men of Frankia. I would also trade for the garments which are finer than we can produce. They too can be sold for a profit. Then there are the wines. If we cannot trade with the Franks then we have to go there for wine. The Musselmen shun wine."

"I can see that both cargos would be light but what do we have that they want?"

"Animal skins. We have hide and fleece. Both are of high quality and we have many of them but it matters not. Thanks to the gold from King Egbert," he laughed, "and the gold which King Egbert gave to the Danes, we have more than enough gold to pay for what we want." He paused, "The real reason is to gather that which is free and even more valuable. Knowledge. The priests of the White Christ know much but even they learn from the Greeks. Our first visit merely whetted my appetite. It will take time to make all the trades we need and I can study in their libraries and their buildings." He waved his hand at my small hall. "We know that the buildings in Miklagård are many times bigger than this. How do they build them? What are the secrets of the Roman cement? How do they build so well in stone?"

I held up my hand. "Enough. Will you have enough time there to do so much?"

He laughed, "You know that I am a quick learner. There will be time enough." I nodded and peered into the fire. "And what of you Jarl Dragon Heart. Will you be able to get inside Jorvik with so few warriors?"

"I believe that the Norns sent the berserkers. They are our way in to Jorvik. We will go in disguise. We take Danish axes and helmets. We wear their rings and their scabbards. We use their cloaks. We become Danes. If Wiglaf is attracting them with the promise of my sword then we should be able to mingle easily with them. We will use their ponies too. I am certain that this berserker will have travelled up the Roman Road to Jorvik first. The animals may well have come from there. Do we still have the Danish mail? It is poorly made but it will disguise us. Is it still here in Wolf's lair?"

"I think it is. We gave it to Rolf to use for his guardians."

"And I will need a new shield which does not have a wolf upon it. Rolf can make one of those too."

"He will enjoy that, jarl. He hates being idle."

Aiden and the Ulfheonar left the next day. The hall felt lonely without him and we rattled around Wolf's Lair which was now empty save for Rolf and his guardians.

We spent the next month preparing for the journey. We chose the best of the captured mail for us. Our own was too good and was a different style. It marked us out. I found a Danish helmet which had a mask for the eyes and a nasal. Rolf made me a shield which was as strong as my old one but this had red spots painted upon a black background. I remembered the design when we had fought Guthrum's men. We took spare cloaks. The Danes had all left their cloaks at the camp they had made and Arturus had brought them. We had two each for it would be cold in the empty lands. Finally we chose the spears we would use. We did not take bows. Most of the warriors we had fought had not used them and we needed to appear Danish. I hoped that we would not need them.

The weather was against us and our departure delayed by early snow storms. Although they did not last they made the trails we would use impassable. Eventually the sun shone. The day we were to leave Kara and Arturus came to see us off. We were each riding a pony leading a spare with our armour and weapons upon it. I embraced Kara. "Have the spirits sent any warning?"

"No, father but sometimes they do not. Take care. You do not need me to tell you how dangerous this is. You are entering the lair of the bear and he is dangerous."

"But we are the wolves and this pack is the best. Arturus watch over my people and be aware that Egbert may send more warriors."

"Fear not father. I have a wife now and soon, I hope a family."

"A family?" I must have appeared a little eager.

Kara shook her head, "Perhaps, father. Do not get your hopes up. When you return then we will know more. We will both watch over our people for you."

We took the trail down the eastern side of the Water. We would follow the Roman Roads which criss crossed the land. Until we reached the high divide we would be travelling amongst people who knew me and owed me fealty. Once we crossed into the empty lands then we would be in danger and would need to be alert. We rode side by side. It was more natural that way. Although our weapons and armour were on the spare ponies we kept a watch for danger. When we passed the bodies of the Danes, Arturus had slain we took it as a reminder that we had to be constantly upon our guard.

I rode next to Snorri. I had known him since he had been the ship's boy. He had trained Erik Short Toe for me but he had proved to be so skilled as a scout and a warrior that his course was chosen for him. I knew he was eager to be off scouting. "We are playing a part, Snorri. If anyone watches then I want them to see seven Danes who wish to sell their swords to the highest bidder."

He smiled, "I know Jarl but it is hard. Bjorn the Scout and I have ranged ahead so often that it feels unnatural to be riding here next to you."

I was aware that the others were listening. "I chose all of you because you six have great skills when it comes to concealment, moving quietly but, most importantly, you can kill close in. I do not anticipate that we will have to fight in a shield wall. If we do then we will have failed. We need to get to Wiglaf when he is alone, kill him and leave. If we can do so without anyone being the wiser then so much the better. We seven are going to do something which might seem impossible to those who do not know us. I know that we will succeed."

The weather, over the last seven or eight days, had begun to deteriorate. The temperature had dropped and rain clouds constantly filled the skies. Rain showered upon us making us cold and wet. It made us huddle beneath our Danish cloaks. However it disguised us for no one could see our faces or know of our identity. We were just seven weary travellers. I hoped that if we were seen we would be taken for Bjarki's returning warriors.

It took two days to reach the eastern side of the empty lands. There the temperature plummeted even more and we were grateful for the fire we built each night. That was the first night where we kept a watch. Until then we were in empty lands or our own lands. Now we were in enemy territory. Here we had no friends. It also meant that we had someone feeding the fire all night. I insisted that each of us took it in turns to stand guard. It meant we all had a few hours sleep and it was no hardship.

When I stood my watch it happened that the clouds cleared and the stars came out. After I had put more wood and kindling on the fire I stared into the heavens. Were my mother and my wife watching me from above? I often thought, at such times, about my ancestor, the Warlord of Rheged. From what we had discovered he too would have crossed these empty lands as he fought the Saxons. Had they been empty lands then? Had he camped and watched where I watched now. I had only seen an image of him painted on a cave wall but since I had held his sword, now kept safely in Wolf's Lair, I felt an affinity with him. He too had led warriors who were a band of brothers. He had fought against great odds and he too had kept his people safe. I was continuing a proud tradition. When I fell in battle then my son would do the same. It was meant to be.

The brief interlude of a cloudless window in the sky was not repeated and dawn brought a flurry of sleet and snow which drove in savagely from the east. It made visibility difficult and it made the going harder as the sleet and snow made the cobbles on the Roman Road, slippery. We were forced to slow down. The last thing we needed, on that steep road which passed over precipitous drops, was for one of our ponies to slip. Consequently, we did not manage to travel as far as we would have liked. Fortunately, we found shelter in a cave above a twisting and roaring river. I suspect in normal times it would have been a gently bubbling stream but the recent rains and the snow had made it a torrent.

When we awoke it was to find a covering of snow on the land. That was bad news. We would be leaving clear tracks. Our progress would be clearly marked for all to see. Hitherto we had been hidden. We had passed and seen no one. It was as though we were invisible. Now, however, as we entered the land ruled by Wiglaf and Magnus Klak, we were letting our enemies know that there were strangers in their land. We would have to be even more cautious.

We saw farms and villages now dotting the vale. Many were Saxon but, from their design, we knew that some were Danish. We avoided all of them. I dare say that we were spotted but the fact that we passed through their land would reassure them of our peaceful intent. Magnus Klak might rule the town but outside the walls of the city life went on as though he had no power at all.

We reached the outskirts of Jorvik at night. There was no snow on the ground here although it was cold and miserable. It had been a year or so since we had visited and the town had sprawled even further out from the walls of the fort. That aided us for there were more places to hide. We had one major problem, where would we camp? If we were playing swords for hire then we could not be seen to be throwing coins around for beds and stables. We found some land which had once had houses upon it but the blackened ground showed that it had been burned. There were the remains of part of the roof which gave us some shelter from the drizzle and, by placing the ponies to one side we had shelter from the wind. There was some scrubby grass and weeds which had grown up and they munched happily on that. Once again we took it in turns to watch and feed the fire. We would begin our search for Wiglaf the next morning.

I was the one on duty when the three drunks staggered by. I was huddled in my cloak and they took me to be asleep. They saw the ponies and the packs. They moved towards them. I slipped my seax from my belt and, as the first one tried to untie a pony, I stood and pressed the tip into his neck before he even knew I was there. "Tell me, friend, why I should not slit your throat for the thief that you are?"

My men were awake and up in an instant and the three drunks found themselves surrounded by seven heavily armed men. The three were Norse, as we were, but their clothes were shabby and none had a sword, just a seax each. "I am sorry. We thought you were asleep. We mean no harm. We are three warriors fallen on hard times."

I nodded to my men and we sheathed our weapons. "Come and sit by the fire. Now that you have wakened us you can, at least, entertain us with your story."

They nodded gratefully and sat as close to the fire as they could get. We came here with our Jarl, Einar the Cautious. We were looking for work but our jarl fell foul of Magnus Klak who had him slain. We were the only ones of his men to escape."

Snorri frowned, "How did you three escape? Did you betray your jarl?"

"Not in the way you think. We were gambling and drinking when the jarl and the others were taken. By the time we found out what had happened their heads were on the gates of the fort."

"And why did this Magnus Klak have your jarl killed?"

"The Lord of Jorvik wanted us to go raiding Northumbria and our jarl said he wanted to go to Cyninges-tūn and find the sword which was touched by the gods." My men were learning how to deceive and not one cracked his face.

"Where is this Magnus Klak now then? Perhaps we should be worried."

"He has gone north to raid the lands north of the river. He left ten days ago. We came out of hiding when we heard he had gone."

"And why did you not leave the city?"

They all shrugged, "We have no money."

Bjorn the Scout said, "Enough money for beer."

"We were paid in beer for unloading a knarr which came from Wessex."

We had heard enough but we could not just get rid of them; they might report us to someone else. We needed them to leave of their own volition. "Is there any work then for swords and good warriors?"

The talkative one looked at us. He was the least drunk. "You are looking for work? Your clothes and weapons suggest that you are successful. Why do you come here? This is not a good place. If we had the money then we would be gone quicker than a Saxon when there is fighting to be done!"

I shrugged, "We had the promise of work from Bothvar Bjarki but we missed our meeting with him and we know not where he went."

They stood, suddenly sober, "You would fight with Bothvar Bjarki the berserker. I am sorry my friend but you are too dangerous for the likes of us. We are sorry if we offended you."

They took off like startled deer. "It seems we have arrived at the right time. Klak is not here nor is his army. This will be our best chance to get to Wiglaf."

"Aye jarl, but we need to find him yet."

There was slightly less need for vigilance if Magnus Klak's warriors were not present. I also realised the impression that Bjarki must have left. We could use that. He and his men had had a wolf token around their necks much as we had. The difference was that theirs was a crude poorly made iron one with little detail. We had worn them instead of our own to create the illusion that we were Danes. Now I had my men display them outside their mail. I wanted all to think that we were Bjarki's men. The site we had chosen the previous night was too close to the gate. We led our ponies north until we had passed the last rude hut. We found a bend in the river where there was a stand of trees. They were willows and their fronds dipped down to the river. They afforded a degree of safety.

"Jarl, we are far from the bridge here and the river is both wide and deep. How will we cross?"

"We will not. When we have done the deed, we will flee north and then head west. I hope we are not discovered but if we are then I want a trail which heads north not west. I want to protect our land as long as I can."

We left Arnulf and Harald on guard with the ponies while we went to scout out the whereabouts of Wiglaf. It did not take us long to discover that he was safely tucked up inside the old Roman fort. The last time we had come to the town the gates had been open; guarded but open. Now they were barred and guarded. We walked the length of its walls and all of the gates were closed. Towards the river and the wharf were many stalls and tables selling food and ale. The river trade was profitable. We headed there. Gossip was rife and we were good listeners.

At one stall we haggled over some pickled fish and stale bread, acting the part of impoverished warriors. We went to the next stall and bought some poor beer. The ale wife who served us was inquisitive. "What are five well armed Danes doing here when there is work to the north and the west? I would expect you to have much gold and not these copper coins."

I feigned ignorance, "North and west?"

"Aye Prince Klak has taken an army to humble the men of Northumberland in the north and Jarl Bjarki has gone to take the sword of the Dragon Heart to the west."

She knew of my sword. I was glad that I had exchanged my fine scabbard for a plainer one taken from a dead Dane. I nodded, "We were supposed to meet Jarl Bjarki here but we were delayed. He has gone?"

"Aye a month since." She laughed, "I expect him back soon with the sword in his scabbard and coins in his purse." She leaned forward and said, conspiratorially, "They say that he has gone to bring back the daughter of King Egbert of Wessex, abducted by the Dragon Heart. You are his men what do you know of that?"

I shrugged, "We were just sent word that Jarl Bjarki had need of swords and we would be well paid." I shook my head, "And now we have no gold and the jarl is gone. *Wyrd*."

She took our empty horns, "*Wyrd*. More ale?"

"Until we find work we cannot afford any. Who do we see around here for work?"

She pointed to the fort, "Wiglaf rules in Prince Klak's place. You should ask him but he is a mean spirited man. He will not pay overmuch. They say he still has the first coin he earned. He keeps the gates closed because he does not wish to pay men to work for him. Still he may want five such warriors as you. You look as though you know your business."

"Thank you for the ale and the information."

We headed down the river back towards our camp.

Snorri's sharp eyes scanned around us for any danger as we headed back to our camp. When we were out of earshot he said, "You have a plan?"

"I have a plan."

We had bought some of the pickled fish for Arnulf and Harald. "I want you two to go to the fort when you have eaten and ask the guards if you can see Wiglaf. If they ask why then say you are hired swords. Hopefully they will invite you in and you can find out where Wiglaf lives within the fort. You need to ask an exorbitant fee for your swords so that he orders you to go. Then you return here and we can plan our raid."

"Why Arnulf and Harald, jarl. No offence but Bjorn the Scout and I are the best at concealment."

"And Wiglaf knows you. He does not know Arnulf and Harald. If they find nothing then you and Bjorn the Scout may well have to get inside and find him but that way is dangerous. Let us try this first. Can you do this?"

They were both eager to prove themselves. "Aye Jarl."

"We will wait here. That ale wife has sharp eyes. Despite her disparaging comments about Wiglaf I would suspect she sells information. Her stall is perfectly placed."

The two of them left for the gate and we spent the time preparing our weapons and planning the raid. "We will climb the walls during the night. We know that during the day there are eight guards on the gate. He must have others inside but it is likely he will just have two on each gate tower at night. From what we were told he does not pay o'er much. I would be surprised if there were more than twenty guards in the whole fort."

Siggi nodded, "The guards did not look the best. They were Saxon. At least the ones at the northern gate were."

"You have good eyes Siggi. I saw that the ones at the western gate were also Saxon." Snorri smiled at me. "Perhaps we just assault the fort. If seven Ulfheonar cannot take twenty Saxons then we ought to take up farming!"

"We will wait until our scouts return, Snorri, before we take on the world."

They returned at noon. Both looked very pleased with themselves. "Did he see you?"

Harald smiled, "No but we saw the leader of his guards, Osbert of Bebbanburgh. He told us that he hires the men for Wiglaf. Wiglaf, it appears spends all his time in his quarters. He has female slaves there and he conducts his business though his steward, Aethelward. He fears for his life."

"You did not find him then?"

"We did better, jarl. Since this Magnus Klak came then all within the fort fear for their lives. He has a quick temper and the heads around the walls testify to that. Osbert fears that when he returns he might wish to be rid of Wiglaf. The two of them fear for their lives. We asked a ridiculous amount of gold and Osbert said he would pay it. Apparently the ale wife was not wrong but merely misinformed. Wiglaf wants killers around him. When I said that we had five more blades he almost bit my hand off. "

Arnulf nodded, "When Jarl Bjarki passed through Wiglaf tried to hire him and his men. He said he would return with the sword and then consider the offer. Wiglaf is building up his strength while Klak is away."

"I wonder why he does not flee Jorvik."

"Where to Bjorn the Scout? He cannot go back to Lundenwic and Rorik, his protector is dead. This makes sense. He could not be seen to be hiring swords while Klak was here and Magnus Klak has taken all of the swords which were available. This may be our chance. Perhaps this was ordained and planned by the Norns." I strapped on my sword, "Did you tell him where we camped?"

Arnulf looked shocked that I would think such a thing, "Of course not. He said we should return as soon as possible."

"Then we will head back in late afternoon. If we can gain access during the day then we can do the deed and flee under cover of darkness."

"There is still the problem of you, Jarl. He will recognise you. As soon as you are seen then the game will be up."

"Then, Bjorn the Scout, you will have to be jarl and I will suddenly feel unwell because of some bad pickled fish. Snorri will have to stay with me."

"How does this help us?"

"I am guessing that we will be taken to Wiglaf. He is the one who will recognise me. I know not this Osbert of Bebbanburgh; he is Northumbrian. When you are taken to meet with him then Snorri and I will eliminate the other guards."

"But there may be twenty or more!"

Snorri laughed, "Aye, Arnulf but we are Ulfheonar. It is a good plan and it might work. If not then what a glorious tale to be sung around the fires at night."

"If we fail, Snorri then the world will just see seven heads adorning the walls of Jorvik and no one will sing our song."

Siggi pointed to the ponies. "What of these?"

"We will need all of us for they are expecting seven of us. We leave them here. They will be here unless the Weird Sisters have something else in mind for us."

We spent the rest of the day ensuring that our mail, weapons, straps, helmets and shields were all in working order. The helmets had not been specially made for us like our own and we each had an extra padded cap to make them fit better. My shield, seax and my sword were the only items I had which were mine. I had a Danish dagger strapped to the inside of my shield. Who knew what we might encounter?

We decided that Bjorn the Scout should be the jarl for the day. He, like Snorri, was quick thinking and confident. He was also of an age with me and the few flecks of grey would add to the illusion that he was jarl. Arnulf approached the guard he had met earlier. He was stationed at the North Gate which kept us well out of sight of the ale wife who might be suspicious. "These are the men of whom I spoke. Bjorn the Scout is our leader."

The guard did not seem suspicious. "Osbert said to take you to the guard house."

He led us through the gate, which slammed ominously behind us. The guard house was, in fact, the old praetorium from the old Roman fort. We had seen them before. As we walked in I kept my head down and I saw the secret stone under which the legion had kept its treasures.

I glanced up as Osbert spoke. He was not a young man. He may have been a warrior at one time but his paunch showed that he had not fought for some years. "You did not lie, Arnulf. Your friends look like handy warriors. Well, have you agreed to my proposal?"

Bjorn the Scout spoke. "What do we need to do to earn this gold you offer?"

"If you agree then I will tell you. It is a generous offer, is it not? Now that the jarl has gone north there is little other work here."

"We could wait for Jarl Bjarki to return. We have fought alongside him before."

"It is some time since he left. Perhaps he slew Dragon Heart or was slain by him. Who knows? It may be he returned to Wessex by sea or by the west coast. You could wait here all winter and not see him. We offer gold for your purses now."

Bjorn the Scout turned to us as though consulting, "It seems like a good offer should we take it and then find out whom we have to kill?" We all nodded and grunted our approval. "We agree. Gold first and then you can tell us what we need to do."

He counted out a healthy pile of golden coins which Bjorn the Scout counted and then put in his purse. He was playing the part well. Wiglaf was extorting much money from the merchants of Jorvik. He had not changed.

"You will enjoy working for Wiglaf. We pay for nothing and anyone who argues is punished. "He grinned evilly, "And if you wish women then it can be arranged. Magnus Klak lets him run the town so long as he has enough men to fight then he is happy. He takes a tenth of all that people produce. Our master is a good tax collector." Osbert leaned forward, "My master has decided that he wishes to leave Jorvik and take his treasure with him. It needs must be before Magnus Klak returns and asks for an account of the taxes. We leave in five days. We need to secure a ship."

"Why not buy one?" Bjorn the Scout held up the heavy purse, "There appears to be gold enough."

"Let us say that my master has a need for as much gold as we can carry."

"And will we be taking all the guards in the fort? How many others are there?"

Bjorn the Scout was very clever. Osbert would not see anything amiss with such a question but we would find out how many guards we had to deal with.

"At the moment there are twenty but I shall go now and dismiss the seven worst ones. Now that we have real warriors the old can be discarded. Wait here while I see to that and set the eight sentries for the night. I will introduce you to the others and then we will go and see the master."

When he had gone none of us were foolish enough to speak of what we had heard. This could be a trick and he could be outside listening to us. Instead we chatted about what we would spend our money on. We laughed and we joked. We played the part of hired warriors eager to spend and to waste our coin. They would not know that we were Ulfheonar.

Osbert returned a while later with two other warriors. "This is Sigismund and Tadgh. They too were warriors who fought in a shield wall." We nodded to the two Saxons who looked slightly less overweight than Osbert but it had been many years since they had faced a foe in a shield wall. "The master will have finished his meal now and we will go to see him."

This would be the tricky part of the plan. As we crossed the old parade ground I doubled up. "What is the matter?"

"I had some pickled fish from the stall by the river. It did not taste right at the time."

The three of them laughed unsympathetically, "That would be Aled's stall. I would not buy from him." He waved to the far corner. "Over there is where we use. We will be in the Great Hall."

Snorri said, "I will come with you, for I, too, feel as though the world is about to descend from my arse!"

This seemed to tickle the three men even more. They were still laughing as they led my men to meet with Wiglaf. I could trust them to overpower the three guards and subdue Wiglaf. Snorri and I had the other guards to dispose of. We saw the eight men who were on guard. Pairs of them stood by each of the gates. They looked at us briefly and then went back to staring from the walls. We headed, not for the cess pit, but for the hall where the light glowed in the darkening fort. That would be the barracks the men were using. We heard them as we approached. They were playing a game of dice. As we appeared at the door they glanced over suspiciously then one said, "You must be the new Danes Osbert has hired." He spat into the fire, "Swords for hire!"

Another growled, "Leofric was my friend and he is now without work because of you."

I drew my seax, "Do you wish to make something of it Saxon? I have gutted enough of your kind before now and one more will not trouble me." He stood and I noted that Snorri had silently drawn his own seax and was standing behind one of the dice players.

"I am not afraid of a Dane even if he does have a shirt of mail."

He drew his own dagger. I smiled as I whipped my seax across the throat of the Saxon who had remained seated. "Perhaps you should have been." My hand darted across and into his throat. He did manage to try to stab me but my mail deflected the blow. Snorri's Saxon lay in a widening pool of blood.

"Do we take the sentries now, jarl?"

"No, They can see each other and we will need to take them all at once. Let us see if Bjorn the Scout has Wiglaf."

I noticed the silence as we left the barracks. The guards had been making a noise. I hoped that the sentries would not investigate the sudden silence. We could do nothing about it but at least the odds were now better for us.

As we approached the Great Hall I could hear the keening and moaning of women. Osbert had told us that Wiglaf liked young women. I hoped that they had not been hurt. When we stepped through the doors we saw the three slain Saxons and three young girls huddled in the corner sobbing. They were naked and had bruises upon their bodies. Wiglaf was cowering in his chair. I could see that one of my men had struck him.

Bjorn the Scout said, "He tried to use the girls as a shield. A real hero is our Wiglaf."

I took off my helmet and Wiglaf's eyes widened, "Dragon Heart!" He tried to sink into the wooden chair.

I ignored him, "Snorri, cover the girls and then bind and gag them. I do not want them screaming when they see what I intend. Be gentle."

Arnulf and Harald went to help him. They smiled and spoke gently to the three girls. I would release them before we left but I did not want the eight remaining guards alerting. I turned to Wiglaf, "Yes Wiglaf. It is Dragon Heart. Did you think your gold had paid for my head? The men you sent are all waiting now in the Other World but I do not think you need to fear their wrath for you will be going to Hel. You will not be given a sword to help you to Valhalla."

He took out his cross of the White Christ. "I am a Christian!"

I ripped it from his neck, "Then I hope your White Christ likes liars and those who abuse young girls."

"What will you do with me?"

"What do you think?" I drew the Danish sword I had brought. "This is not the sword you sent your warriors to fetch. But it was wielded by the warriors you despatched to kill me. It is freshly sharpened." His mouth started to open.

I saw that the girls had been gagged and I brought my blade across his neck. His head bounced from his body and rolled across the room. I felt no satisfaction in what I had done. He needed killing. If I had not then more men would have been sent to get to me and one day someone I loved would be hurt.

I went over to the wide eyed girls. "You will not be hurt but we must go and do something else. We will return and you will be freed. I give you my word. Do you understand?" They nodded. "Good." I picked up the head. They did not need to see that. I deposited the head in the praetorium. We then strolled across to the barracks. I noticed that the guards watched us, briefly and then returned to their duty.

"Harald and Arnulf go to the guards on the north gate. Tell them that Osbert asked you to relieve them. Pretend that you are unhappy about having to do a duty. When they come then Snorri and the others will deal with them. Bjorn the Scout come with me."

We headed for the praetorium. I moved the table and ran my dagger along the edge of the stone which I knew marked the hidden cellar. We lifted the heavy covering; it took both of us. Once it was up we took the candle which burned in the corner and examined the treasure room. There were four chests within it. They were not large but they were heavy. We lifted them out. Each one was filled with coins. This is what Wiglaf was going to steal. This was Magnus Klak's treasure. We replaced the stone and left the chests in the praetorium.

As we left the guards on the western gate shouted to us, "When will we be relieved?"

Bjorn the Scout waved and shouted, "When I get to the barracks. My men are still eating. Just be patient."

As we entered we saw that the two sentries had been despatched. "Sven and Siggi go to the east gate and relieve the guards there. That will just leave four and we will need to use something different for them." They left. "I will visit the stables. Those chests look heavy."

"What about the last four guards?"

"When you have disposed of these two then Snorri join me in the stables and Bjorn the Scout go to Arnulf and Harald. When you see Snorri and I mount the stairs to the south gate then you and Arnulf head for the east gate. If we strike quickly we may be able to silence them but if not then we will just run."

I left and passed the two relieved guards. One of them said, "About time someone else took a duty!"

I nodded, "Aye well you shall have a long rest now. You deserve it" As I approached the stables I heard a horse whinny. I entered and saw that there were four small packhorses. They were a little bigger than a pony but they had broad backs. They would do. I fitted their halters and was just fitting their panniers when Snorri joined me.

"What is the plan, Jarl Dragon Heart?"

"The south gate faces the river and there are people there. We must trick the men into the tower so that we can kill them out of sight of the others. Then we release the girls, pack the gold and head for our ponies."

"Gold?"

"The gold belonging to the town which Osbert planned to steal."

He shook his head. "If you steal it then Magnus Klak will know we took it and will come after us."

I shook my head. "Before we leave we will take the bodies and put them in the river. They will be taken to the sea. Klak will think that Osbert was murdered by his men and they fled with the gold."

"It is still a risk."

"A small one." We headed for the southern gate.

We climbed the stairs to the stone ramparts and approached the surly sentry. "About time."

As we neared them the two guards tried to move past us, down the stairs. I shook my head, "Not so fast, we need to know where things are. We are new after all."

"There is not much to see."

"Then it won't take long will it?"

As they led us into the tower I slipped my seax into my right hand. The first warrior turned to tell me something and I ripped my blade across his throat. Snorri did the same and we laid both men on the floor. We quickly left the tower and headed towards the last gate; the east gate. I saw Bjorn the Scout and Arnulf approaching from the other side. The two guards moved towards them and that allowed us to reach the gate unseen. We heard the suspicious guards. "What is the problem?"

"No problem, friend."

I know not what they saw but the two of them turned and ran back into the safety of the gatehouse. They ran into our blades and died at our feet. "Arnulf get back and pretend you are on guard. Bjorn the Scout and Snorri stay here. I will go to the south gate and when it quietens down we will get rid of the bodies and release the girls.

I had no idea how long we had been in the fort but it was now dark. As I reached the river gate I peered down and saw that there were still people moving around. There were not many but it would take some time for it to be quiet enough for us to open the eastern gate. I saw that there were fewer ships than the last time we had been there. Perhaps that was the time of year or, perhaps, the draconian regimes which now ruled Jorvik. Soon, however, it all became dark. There were clouds and no moon.

I gathered the others and we opened the eastern gate. There were few huts on this side of the fort and we carried the bodies from the barracks and the walls and slipped them into the river which was fast flowing because of the rains. If they were washed ashore it would be far downstream and we would be long gone. We packed the pack horses with the chests and then returned to the Great Hall. While my men disposed of the bodies I released the girls.

"Are we free to go, lord?"

The eldest had the courage to speak to me but she was terrified. I took off my helmet and smiled. "Aye you are. How did you come to be here?"

"Our fathers owed tax they did not have. Wiglaf had them executed and our mothers sold into slavery to pay the taxes. We were kept here."

"Have you homes to go to?" They shook their heads. I reached into my purse. "Here are coins for each of you. Find a boat and sail to somewhere you can start again."

They took the money. I stood to leave and they whispered amongst each other. "Lord, can we not come with you?"

I looked at them in amazement. "I am a Viking. Are you not afraid? You saw what I did to Wiglaf."

"Wiglaf was an animal and deserved to die. We have heard of you, Jarl Dragon Heart. It is only those like Wiglaf and Lord Klak who speak badly of you. Others speak of your land as a good place to live. What have we here? We have no families. Our mothers could be anywhere and in the eyes of the people we are nothing more than whores. What will our lives be like if you leave us?"

I thought of Elfrida and Kara. These girls were of an age with them. I could not leave them. "It will be a hard journey and there will be dangers. I cannot promise that any of us will survive."

They smiled, "We will take that chance."

138

"Then gather warm clothes and you will need something on your feet. There was snow in the high passes when we came east."

We hurried to the stables. My men looked at me open mouthed. I said, "It is my decision but I believe the Norns have done this. It is *wyrd*."

Snorri smiled, "I should not be surprised. Come ladies; you will be safe so long as we live. We are Ulfheonar."

I picked up Wiglaf's head. I had planned on leaving it on a spear with a gold coin in his mouth as a message. Now I had to get rid of the evidence. With the horses and the girls gone then Magnus Klak might just believe his tax collector had gone.

Chapter 15

We left by the north gate. Snorri stayed inside to bar the gate again and then he slithered down the wall. It would add to the puzzle we had made. As we passed the small river which fed the Ouse I dropped the Saxon's head into the fast-flowing waters. It would rejoin his body and those of the other dead sentries and find their way to the sea. We neither heard nor saw anyone as we headed back to our ponies. They were still there where we had left them. By rearranging some of the equipment on the pack horses we were able to give the girls a pony each. If they could not ride when they mounted then they would soon learn. I rode behind the three of them for the first few miles. I had to help them to adjust their cloaks to keep themselves warm. It was cold; not quite freezing but not by much.

I was heading for the Roman Road. I knew that there was an old fort close to it. It would provide shelter. If we could rest there for the day then we might avoid prying eyes. We had been lucky coming east; I knew that we could not count on that same luck going back. The weather turned against us. Winds drove from the east and instead of heading north west across the vale, towards the road; I led us in the lee of the hills. It was more sheltered. Had it just been the seven of us then I would have risked the wind but we had the girls. The Norns! I wondered, idly, if these three young girls were the Norns in human form. It would not surprise me. However the change in route proved propitious. We passed a small farm, which I avoided and found a sheltered dell behind a small knoll in the foothills of the eastern hills. The wind passed over and I decided to camp there. A fire was out of the question. The smoke would swirl all over the hills and, in the daylight, mark our position. Sven kept watch from the small round topped hill. We used our spare cloaks to create a shelter. It kept the rain from us and the dark colours hid us.

The rain and the wind began to abate and I contemplated leaving the shelter when Sven hurried down. "There is a warband coming from the north. I think it is Magnus Klak."

I turned to the eldest of the girls, Eanfrith. "Would you know Magnus Klak?"

She shivered and I knew it was not the cold. She nodded, "Aye, lord. I have seen him."

"Come with us then." I left my helmet and we hurried back to the round topped hill. We bellied up and Sven held up his hand to stop us going too far. The grass and plants hid us from view but allowed us to see the cavalcade coming down the road from the north. There were just three mounted warriors and the rest were all Danes. I could see, in the middle, a crowd of slaves. Mail covered warriors brought up the rear.

I whispered in Eanfrith's ear, "Which one is Magnus Klak?"

She whispered back, "The one on the black horse with the heads hanging from his saddle." She buried her head in the grass.

"He is passing us and cannot harm you. Stay here until they are gone." I hoped I was right. Had I been the Warlord I would have had scouts out. Perhaps it showed his confidence that he did not. It was a mighty warband and it took some time for it to pass us. I wondered if he was hurrying to get to Jorvik before dark. He had over twenty miles to go. I prayed that he would not stop and camp close by. That would be a disaster. I waited until they were out of sight before we moved. We slithered down the bank and rejoined the others.

"Come, we have little time to lose. They have passed us. We will head west and try to make the old hill fort in the hills. There is shelter there. I wish to try the empty lands in daylight."

Snorri and Bjorn the Scout left us to scout to our south in case Magnus Klak had any of his warriors out hunting. I slapped the rumps of the girls' ponies and we rode hard for twenty miles until we reached the foothills of the empty lands and the old abandoned hill fort. Snorri and Bjorn the Scout reached us when it first rose before us. At one time it had been used as a village. That was before the time of the Saxons. The remains of the huts were still visible but were of little use save as something to break the wind. It was a sad place for people had lived here for many hundreds of years. It had one great advantage. We could see for miles. Even though there was still an hour or two of daylight left I decided to make camp and risk a fire. The girls were blue with cold and we had gone since the previous day without hot food. A hungry warrior makes mistakes. Siggi had a fire going, using dried and dead wood. Snorri managed to bring down a couple of plump pigeons and we added those to the stew made from dried mutton, herbs and some wild brambles we found. The bubbling stream gave us water.

Once night fell I had the men put cloaks around the fire so that it could not be seen and, once again, we took turns to watch. We learned much as we spoke with the girls. One was called Freya and the youngest, who was the same age as Elfrida, was called Anya. They told us that they had been in the fort for less than half a year. They knew of Wiglaf's plan to send warriors to seek my sword but I discovered that Magnus Klak had come up with the plan. He was Rorik's cousin. I had hoped that the feud would die with Wiglaf but it seems I was wrong. I just hoped that I had muddied the waters by hiding the bodies in the river.

It also turned out that Bjarki was related to Magnus. The plot thickened. Guthrum and the Danes were fighting for Coenwulf while other Danes were helping Egbert. I could almost see their plan. They were ingratiating themselves into the two royal houses. There would come a time when they would show their true colours and fight as one against all Saxons. Although that would not bother me I now knew that they were casting glances at my land. I had thought that, with the demise of Rorik we were safe. I had thought wrong.

I must have been silent for some time. The girls were asleep, Harald was on watch and Snorri asked, "What are your thoughts, Jarl? I can see that you are troubled."

"We will have trouble from the Danes of Jorvik. I know it. And I do not have an answer."

Snorri laughed, "I do."

"Well go on then enlighten me." I was genuinely intrigued. I was used to this from Aiden but not Snorri.

"Do what we have just done. Cross the empty lands and raid the Danes. Hurt them before they hurt us." He waved his arm around the hill fort. "Our warriors can use refuges like this one. From here, using ponies we could raid as far as the coast or Jorvik. We could use our drekar as you planned to come up the Ouse and attack their shipping."

"That is a good plan but it might just provoke the Danes into a major invasion." I explained my theory to him.

He smiled, "I think you do yourself a disservice, jarl. If you were the Danes which land would you choose to attack? The south where the priests of the White Christ make all warriors women and they have riches beyond compare, or the land of the Dragon Heart where you fight fierce mailed warriors and the riches are not as great."

"You have given me much to think on."

I had the middle watch and saw nothing but, just before dawn I was awoken by Bjorn the Scout. "Jarl, men approach. I think they are Danes."

"Wake the others." I saw that Harald and Arnulf were already awake. "You two take the girls and the pack horses and head west. We will follow when we have dealt with this problem."

They said nothing but hurried away. I went to the old earth wall of the fort and joined Bjorn the Scout. I could hear the horses or ponies as they snuffled in the dark. The sky would be lightening soon and we would be able to see them whilst remaining in the dark. The others joined me. We were all armed and ready for war. Whatever came from the dark we would fight; no matter what the odds were. The Weird Sisters had ensured that we could not flee as we would have done had the girls not been with us. We would see what sort of web they had devised. Sound travels a long way at night and the Danes were some way off yet. I turned to Bjorn the Scout and said quietly, "How did you know they were Danes?"

He chuckled quietly. "You remember that stream we passed yesterday about a mile away."

"The one with the deep pools?"

"Aye, well I heard a splash and someone curse Loki. It was in Danish and it was loud."

I heard our horses as they clattered on the stones on the road which led north from the hill fort. I heard a Danish voice shout, "They are escaping! After them or Klak will have our heads!"

That confirmed who they were. The road leading north was to the south of the hill fort. It wound around the ramparts and ditches. I led my men towards the rampart which overlooked the road. We lay in wait. Bjorn the Scout and Snorri had their slingshots with them. They had not used them for some time however, in the dark, they could be an effective weapon. There was just enough light to make out the ten riders on ponies who were three hundred paces away. This needed timing well. The Danes would have assumed we had all fled north. I hoped they would not be looking to their right.

The road up which the twelve Danes travelled climbed and their ponies slowed as they struggled up the slope. They were not travelling as fast as they would have been on horses. We each had a spear. While Bjorn the Scout and Snorri slung their stones the rest of us hurled our spears. It was still dark and they were moving. One pony fell with a spear in its neck and it spilled its rider. A stone hit a second pony making it gallop off to the east. The other stone and two spears hit warriors. The rest stopped and prepared to charge up the hill towards us. Bjorn the Scout and Snorri threw another stone each and then picked up their spears.

The Danes had no mail. They had helmets and small shields. As they clambered the steep bank we waited. The two spears jabbed out and punched two warriors to slip and slide down the slope. The first rays of dawn illuminated us and the Danes stopped. They were not expecting Vikings. The delay was fatal. I took two steps down the rampart and brought Ragnar's Spirit down on the nearest warrior's head. He tried to protect himself with his small shield but it merely slowed the strike. My blade came away bloody. It was time to take the offensive. I ran down the slope. Two warriors, one wounded were trying to clamber back up. My shield stunned one while my sword stabbed the unprotected middle of a second. There had only been five of us but the Danes were no match for us.

Four remained alive although three of them would not last long. The fourth had been stunned by a stone. I put the tip of my sword to his throat. His eyes opened, groggily. "You are not Wiglaf!"

That explained everything. Klak had believed that Wiglaf had stolen his gold. He had sent warriors to find him. "No Dane, my name is not Wiglaf. I should kill you for trying to attack us when we are just out hunting." It was a lie but I intended to let this warrior go. "I will let you live but warn your jarl that not all of this land belongs to him and if he sends men to places he does not know he may well lose them."

He nodded, "What is your name? You are not Norse."

I smiled, "No, but I was brought up a Viking.

I am he who can walk through walls
I am a shape shifter
I am the witch seeker
I was born in fire and blood
I go into the bowls of the earth and speak with the dead."

All Vikings like a riddle. Mine was not a very good one but I wanted Magnus Klak to be uncertain of my identity. He might waste time trying to fathom the answer.

Snorri nodded to the warriors who were dying. "Should we give them a warrior's death?"

The Dane nodded. My men slit the throats. "We will leave you to burn or bury them and we will leave you one pony but the rest we take as were geld!"

The man was so grateful to be left alive that he simply nodded and we rode north, rather than west. I did not want an accurate report of our destination in case Klak followed us. Once we were out of sight I turned west and headed for the empty lands.

"Do you think that Klak will believe his story?"

"He has no reason to doubt it but the Norns have made this web so entangled that I know nothing any more. We will have to wait to see what the spirits say. Now, Snorri, find our companions and let us get home."

We found them three miles up the road. My warriors knew their duty and they had done exactly what I had asked. I knew their hearts and swords would want to be with us but they obeyed. I was proud of them. We told them what we had learned as we spent the day crossing the empty lands. The spare ponies meant that we travelled faster than we might have otherwise and we reached the borders of my land just before dark. We camped at the old deserted fort which overlooked the river. The burnt out timbers told us that there had been fighting here long after the Romans had left. It was deserted now but the river gave us water and the grass provided food for our animals while the walls, or what remained of the walls, gave us protection from the wind.

I was tired but I did not sleep well that night. Strange visions of high towers and knives in the night disturbed me so much that I was grateful when Sven woke me for my watch. I let Arnulf and Harald sleep I had no wish to return to the tormented tossing and turning. I lit a new fire from the burning embers and had some herb infused water ready for us to drink. My men were concerned that I had allowed them to sleep but they said nothing. However they sensed that I wished to get home and we reached Wolf's Lair just three hours after we left our camp at the Roman fort.

If Rolf was surprised at the presence of the three girls and the chests then he said nothing. We left two chests in my hall. One would be for me, one for my men but the other two I would take to Cyninges-tūn. We left eight of the ponies there too and then headed down to the other side of the Water. Our village had burgeoned beyond the original walls following the earlier move. My people shouted their greetings as we rode through their homes. The gates of the stad were open and we rode in. We dismounted, pleased to be off the backs of our mounts. Scanlan greeted me first.

"It is good to see you, Jarl. Your son took his men down to Úlfarrston this morning. He will be back tonight."

"Trouble?"

He laughed, "No, Jarl Dragon Heart but he takes his responsibilities seriously. He rode to Windar's Mere the day before yesterday."

"And my daughter?"

"Still in her hall."

I frowned, that was not like Kara. "There is a chest of gold there, Scanlan. See that all share in its bounty. I have another for my son and Kara."

I turned to the girls. "Come with me, Snorri, fetch the chest. The rest of you can return to the hall if you wish. I shall stay here a while." I smiled at them, "You have done well and I was honoured to lead you."

They unsheathed their swords, raised them and shouted, "Ulfheonar!"

The noise brought Kara and Elfrida from Kara's hall. She gave me a wan smile. She noted the girls but said nothing. She embraced me, "It is good to see you and, at least part of my dream is explained, come within and tell me all." She smiled at the girls, "Elfrida, take these girls into the hall. They must be tired, hungry and thirsty. I will see them when I have spoken with my father."

Eanfrith took my hand and kissed it, "Thank you Jarl Dragon Heart. The words they speak of you are not lies. You are a noble man. We thank you for saving our lives."

As we went inside I told her of our journey. Snorri deposited the chest and then left for he knew we needed to speak. We sat at her table and her slaves brought us beer, freshly made cheese and warm bread. I finished my tale and then began to wolf down the food.

"You did right to bring the girls here. You are a kind man."

Kara allowed me to eat. She topped up my horn whenever I drank. When I had finished I saw, for the first time, the dark shadows beneath her eyes.

"The spirits?"

She nodded and drank some beer herself. "I had a troubled night. The spirits came and told me of danger. I saw you fleeing and I saw the girls. Then you disappeared and I saw Aiden. He was drowning. Then he was being taken to the heavens and he was strapped to a cross like the White Christ. He disappeared and you and the Ulfheonar rose like wraiths from the ground. All the time our mother's voice kept speaking of danger." Her voice caught. She paused, "And I saw the sword covered in blood and fire. You were lit by fire too! And I saw our grandmother burning in our old home." She buried her face in her hands and began to sob. This was not like Kara. Then I remembered that she had been so small and had not seen my mother's death. None of us had. The stad at Hrams-a had been raided, my mother and the old blacksmith, Bjorn the Scout's father had been killed in the attack. How had she seen that?

"I am safe but I take it that Aiden is not?"

"He is not back yet. When I spoke with Arturus this morning he said that he would go to Úlfarrston and prepare the *'Josephus'* for sea."

"The ocean is a large place to search for one Galdramenn."

She smiled for the first time that morning, "He wanted to do something. He hated not being able to help. You, Aiden and the Ulfheonar were far from home in danger and he felt guilty."

"Perhaps Aiden is safe, although like you I do not understand it and the picture of my mother burning disturbs me. Has Mann and her warriors returned to haunt us again?"

"It may have." She banged the table, "We can do nothing yet so let us deal with matters we can affect. What would you have me do with the girls?"

"Heal them. They have been cruelly treated by the Norns and the world. They are alone. I could not leave them there. I could not imagine what their lives would have been like. They are good girls and they have spirit."

She smiled and put her hands on mine. "Even if you were not my father I would still say that you are a good man. I will care for them. And the chest?"

"That is for you and Arturus. I gave one to Scanlan for the people. I have one and my warriors have one. Use your share how you will."

"We have little need for gold but I am sure that we could use it." She stood. "I feel better for our talk. We will find out soon what has happened to Aiden. Of that I am certain. I have just realised that I did not see your ship or Haaken and the others in trouble and we know that your men would watch out for Aiden. Perhaps this is a dream of what is to come."

"Perhaps. I will speak with Bjorn and then return to my hall. I feel the need for the sweat hut."

The smiths were hard at work when I arrived. The huge smith came from his forge and, after dousing his head in the waters of the Water he clasped my arm. "I am pleased that you are returned safely. I did not like to think of you in danger wearing only this Danish mail!"

"We were lucky and did not need mail but you are right. This is heavy and uncomfortable." I led him towards the Water. "My daughter dreamed of Hrams-a and the raid. She saw my mother burning."

His face showed his pain at the memory. "I was the only one who witnessed that. She was not there."

"I know."

"That was the worst day of my life."

"And mine. Listen Bjorn, we need to prepare in case this is a premonition of worse to come. Have spear heads and arrows prepared." He nodded, "And, when you have a quiet time I would have six more wolves casting in gold. We took coin from the Danes and I would reward my men."

"I know about the coin. Scanlan came and gave me my share but it seems over much to me."

"Without you Bjorn we would have perished long ago. It is your weapons which help to make my warriors as strong and feared as they are."

My warriors and I basked in the heat of the sweat hut all afternoon. It cleared not only our bodies but also our minds. We spoke quietly of what had happened in Jorvik and the journey. We discussed how we might have done things differently. We spoke of the deprivations of other men. Despite what the world thought of warriors such as we my men had a code which they lived by. It made us different; it made us unique.

That evening we ate well in the warrior hall for Rolf and his men had been hunting and joined us for a feast. I even enjoyed more ale than was good for me. We sang songs of the old days and the old battles. Rolf regaled the young warriors with tales of being a hired sword in Frankia before I had made him my oathsworn. He told them of the deaths of his warrior brothers and how he had become crippled. I saw them as they looked from Rolf to me and began to understand this complicated world in which we lived.

We were about to retire when Haaken and Arturus burst in. "Jarl Dragon Heart, it is Aiden. He has been taken!"

I closed my eyes. The Norns were weaving once more.

Wyrd!

Chapter 16

I could see that they were both distraught and that would not help me to find out the facts. "Sit down and drink some ale."

"But did you not hear father? Aiden is taken!"

"And I want to find out how. That will not be helped if you two are not calm. Can we do anything about it tonight?" They looked at each other and shook their heads. "Then sit and drink." They sat and Snorri poured them some beer.

"Haaken, I assume that you told Arturus what happened." He nodded, "Then you tell me for we need to know exactly what happened."

Arturus glanced up at me. He understood the implied criticism. It was the truth. Arturus' version would have been second hand. I needed to know what had occurred from the one who had witnessed it.

Haaken spoke calmly and quietly. "We had a good voyage and the winds helped us to fly across the sea. We made Miklagård in fourteen days." He smiled, "We sailed out of sight of land and passed through the Pillars of Hercules without spying a single vessel. Aiden spent three days in the libraries and we traded well. The voyage back was going well but near the witch's cave a storm blew up and sent us out to sea towards the edge of the world. Even Erik Short Toe thought we were doomed. Aiden was the only one who said we would survive. When it abated we headed for the Sabrina and put in at Casnewydd. Other ships were there. That was when we saw the drekar."

I held my hand up. "Did you know the drekar?"

"No. The only reason it seemed unusual, to Aiden at least, was the fact that it was undamaged."

"And had you seen any other ships on your voyage; any other danger?"

He shook his head, "No, we saw but four other ships all the way back from Miklagård. It was a pleasant voyage."

I nodded and a thought came to me. "What about the voyage out?"

"We saw the usual drekar between Angle Sey and Mann but when they saw *'The Heart'* they did not close with is. They were all Threttanessa. We were much bigger than they were."

"When Aiden saw the drekar what did he do?"

"He took Ulf and Einar with him and went to see the king's man in the fort."

"Why?"

Haaken looked puzzled as though that was the first time he had thought of the question. "I know not. He just said that he wanted to ask the king's man some questions. Erik had us buy the wood and rope to repair the three ships and Erik went into the town and we never saw him more."

Arturus interrupted, "Tell him about the bodies!"

"Patience Arturus, I am beginning to get the picture already. Carry on, Haaken."

"Aiden and the others had not returned when we had finished our work and so we went into the town to find them. We thought they might have gone to buy ale or to trade."

I knew that Aiden would never have done that. Had I been there… I wasn't and there was little point in worrying about what might have been. I had to deal with the reality. "And you found their bodies."

"Aye, how did you know?"

"And you found much blood close by showing that they had fought off their attackers." I smiled at their amazement. "You said Aiden was taken. I could not see Ulf and Einar standing idly by while he was taken."

"You are right. We went up to see the king's man but he had not seen Aiden or our warriors."

"And when you returned to the ship the drekar had gone. In fact it had sailed while you were repairing the ship."

"You did not need my words, jarl, you knew what happened. I would gamble that you even know where he is now."

"Do you father?"

I nodded. "I do not have the second sight but your sister dreamed last night. I know where they have taken Aiden. It is Mann. The drekar you saw, think back, was it one which you saw close to Angel Sey."

Haaken frowned and then shook his head sadly, "It was and Aiden must have recognised it. Why did he not say something?"

"Because he wanted to make sure that the drekar was there legitimately. He could not have expected to be attacked in the town. They must have been waiting there knowing that the men of Cymru are our allies. There is little else for a drekar to do in winter. We will sail for Mann tomorrow."

I walked back to my hall. Arturus rode back to Cyninges-tūn. Haaken shouted, "I will follow." He stopped me. "I have failed you Jarl Dragon Heart. I am sorry. This was the first voyage where Cnut and I commanded and we let you down. Aiden has paid the price."

"He is alive."

"How do you know?"

"Why else risk taking him aboard their drekar? If they wanted him dead then he would be. They want him alive and that I cannot work out just yet. And you did not let me down. If I had not gone after Wiglaf then I would have been on the ship and it would have been my fault."

"No, Dragon Heart for you, like Aiden would have been suspicious. We were not. We are warriors and not thinkers."

"And I am glad for that. We will need those skills when we rescue Aiden."

I went to bed that night and slept but a little. Aiden was as dear to me as Kara or Arturus. If he had been taken then that was down to me. He had been taken because he served me. All on Mann knew that my Galdramenn was as useful to me as my sword. This was aimed at my heart and it had broken flesh.

The next morning, I summoned Rolf. "I will have to leave you again and this time I fear danger from both the east, Klak, and the south, Mann. If you hear of danger bring in those from the farm or go to Cyninges-tūn. Wolf's Lair is not worth dying for."

"Do not worry about Aiden, Jarl. He is tougher than most warriors, we both know that."

"I know Rolf but I blame myself."

"You cannot do that. This is just *wyrd*."

My men and I took all of our weapons: bows, spears, swords, daggers. We were going to war. We halted at Cyninges-tūn so that I could speak with Kara. She buried her head in my shoulder. "I should have seen this. I believe you are right, father he is on Mann."

"And we both know where too."

"Hrams-a."

"Aye. This is the work of the Norns. Watch over my people for I fear Klak may visit his vengeance upon us some time. It will not take long for him to work out who took his gold. I just hope it is after the winter."

She looked at me and said quietly, "Arturus?"

I shook my head, "I leave him here. For what we do I need one boat crew. I shall take some of his warriors with me."

"He will not be happy."

"He will obey. I will not lose two of my family."

"Aiden is not lost."

"Not yet."

I did not tell Arturus as he and his warriors rode with us to Úlfarrston. I would tell him when we reached the port.

Erik Short Toe had spent the previous afternoon and the morning finishing off the repairs to his ship. The '*Josephus*' was also ready for sea. The two knarr also bobbed up and down in the estuary. What concerned me however was the reception awaiting me. Not only were my captains there but Pasgen too and some of the fishermen from Úlfarrston. Pasgen approached me.

"Jarl Dragon Heart, one of my fishing boats was stopped in the early hours of the morning and it went to the fishing grounds. It was a drekar from Mann."

I knew what was coming but I had to ask the question. "Is this the fisherman?" The man and Pasgen nodded, "What did the Viking say?"

"He told me to tell you that he will trade your Galdramenn for the sword which was touched by the gods. He said to come to Duboglassio. You have two days to comply." The man looked fearful as though he thought I might take my anger out on him. "I am sorry, jarl."

I smiled and gave him a silver coin from my purse, "It is not your fault. Take this coin for your lost catch. Tell me did he give a name?"

"I heard one of his men call him Jarl Erik Redbeard."

I frowned, "Have any of you heard of him?"

Most shook their heads and then Siggi said, "There was an Erik Redbeard lived in Orkneyjar on one of the far islands."

Trygg said, "I think it is where the oathsworn of Sven Knife Tongue fled after they left Hrossy."

It all became clear, "Then this is a blood feud. They mean to kill me. Thank you." I turned to Arturus, "I will take your best warriors and we will double crew *'The Heart of the Dragon'*."

"No, I must come with you!"

"Erik prepare the ship for sea, Arturus come with me." I led my reluctant son out of earshot. "You have to stay here. This may be a trick to lure me away from my land."

"Then do not go. Aiden will not want you to exchange your sword for him."

"I know and I have no intention of giving into their demands. Remember Hibernia?"

He nodded. "Then you go, knowing that you will die?"

"No I go to rescue Aiden as I would rescue you." I paused, "As I did rescue you. But I will not fall into their trap."

"But Duboglassio has a good fort with clear views of the approaches and they will expect you to come at night."

"They think that I will have to travel from Cyninges-tūn. We have gained half a day because Haaken brought us the message. And I will not be going to Duboglassio. I will go to Hrams-a."

He looked confused, "Why there?"

"Because the spirits told your sister that is where they would be holding Aiden. He will be in the watch tower on the hill and there will be a cross already there."

"A cross? Why?"

"For they mean to crucify him. At least that is what the spirits told Kara."

"And if you are wrong and they lie?"

"Then Aiden will die and I will have lost someone as dear to me as you are. But I think this is the work of the Norns. The sword was forged in that tower and we return to its place of birth. It is *wyrd*." He nodded. "Now pick your best warriors and watch over our people while I am away."

Once the crews were aboard I went to Siggi and Trygg. "I want the two of you to sail one of your knarr with your best warriors and follow us. When we go ashore I want your men to guard the drekar. If there is trouble then take her away from the shore."

"You fear a trap?"

"Oh there will be a trap which is why I am not going to Duboglassio. We are going to sail to the northern shore and land out of sight of those who live there. There is nowhere to moor my ship. Tomorrow morning, take the two vessels to Hrams-a. I will be there."

They rushed to sort out their ship. I boarded mine. The drekar was fully laden and every oar had twice the number of rowers as they normally had. Every warrior had mail of some description. We would likely be outnumbered on Mann but I knew the island and I had the best warriors with me.

"Erik, cast off and set sail for Mann."

We headed due west, towards Hibernia. Erik knew the island as well as I did and he brought us towards it from the north west. It was the only course which we could take and remain unseen by the two settlements. I knew that there might be isolated waites and other farms but they would just take us for another sailing to the west of Mann. It was a popular route. Even if they carried a message to Erik Redbeard we would be ashore and at Hrams-a by the time they could reach us. I was aware that, this time, I was gambling with someone else's life and not just my own.

We reached the island in the early afternoon. I saw smoke from a turf covered house. There were Norse people on the isle. We headed in for the beach which lay on the other side of the headland. It was well hidden from the settlement. It was a small beach and we disembarked where the water was chest height. "Erik I am taking all of the warriors with me. Siggi and Trygg have crew and they will come aboard. Stand off shore and out of sight to their forts. Come for us tomorrow when the tides and weather are right. By then we should have accomplished what we came for. If not then you can pick us up and we shall sail for Duboglassio."

"We will manage, jarl." His face wrinkled up, "Save Aiden, Jarl, he is a good man and a friend. I would not lose him."

"Nor will we."

Fifty warriors stepped ashore. The moment we landed Snorri and Bjorn the Scout leapt off like greyhounds. I turned to Sven Gold Beard, the leader of Arturus' warriors. "Your warriors will form the second line behind us. I fear that when the alarm is given there will be warriors coming from all over the island. You will have to protect our backs."

He smiled, "It will be an honour, Jarl Dragon Heart."

As we climbed I saw the old wooden tower rising in the distance. Although below the top of the mountain it was a good vantage point. We had had a fort there when Prince Butar had ruled but it had since fallen into disrepair. The only part which remained was the tower. We moved in the lee of the slope so that we were shielded from view by the trees and shrubs which dotted the hillside. We each wore our wolf cloaks which made us harder to see. Sunlight does not reflect from an animal skin.

We were less than three miles from Hrams-a when Snorri and Bjorn the Scout materialised from the ferns. "It is as you feared Jarl. They have a cross built close to the tower. I did not see Aiden but there is a drekar close by the beach and its crew are waiting."

"They must be guarding Aiden well away from Duboglassio."

Haaken was not so certain. "The cross may be there to execute him if we do not come."

"Then why erect it here? And besides there is Kara's vision. When have you ever known her to be wrong?"

"Never!"

"Tell me Bjorn the Scout, was there still a patch of dead ground where the hall stood?"

"Yes, how did you know?"

"In the dream Kara saw my mother dying. She was not here then. It was the spirit of my mother which summoned us." I took out my sword. "Now we become Ulfheonar. Arturus' men will guard our backs. We find Aiden, kill these warriors and sail home."

"You will not punish this Erik Redbeard?"

"There will be a time for this but not yet. We do not have enough warriors yet. Snorri and Bjorn the Scout, take scouts and eliminate any sentries. We will follow." As they trotted off I said, "Sigtrygg, take five warriors and occupy the tower. You can keep watch there for any other warriors."

I led the rest of my Ulfheonar; there were not many of us, and we trotted through the ferns towards the old stad of Hrams-a. The ridge hid it from our view. Had these warriors had any sense then they would have had sentries there. When we neared the top of the ridge we flattened ourselves and peered through the ferns. I could not see my men but I knew that they would already have disposed of the sentries above the beach. I saw the huddle of warriors and spied the smoke from their fire. The port still had its jetty and they were on the beach to one side. Their backs were to us.

I waved my men forward and we slithered and crept towards the shore. We came upon Snorri and the others just at the edge of the ferns and the bushes. "Have you seen Aiden yet?"

Grim faced he said, "Aye Jarl Dragon Heart. If you look at the fire. They are roasting his feet."

Snorri had sharp eyes and he was right. I could see my Galdramenn being poked by the warriors. They were laughing and jeering at his pain. We could wait no longer. I jabbed my spear into the ground raised my sword and then ran towards the drekar and the fire. Bjorn the Scout and Snorri did not run. They strung their bows.

As the warriors realised they were being attacked they grabbed their weapons and turned to face us. One of the men closest to the fire raised his sword to end Aiden's life. An arrow took him in the chest. I ran as though I had wings on my feet. I was the first to reach the flimsy shield wall. My shield bowled over two of them as my sword ripped into the side of another. One of Bjorn the Scout's arrows hit the second warrior who attempted to kill Aiden. My Ulfheonar were showing no mercy to the men of Mann and when Arturus' men flooded over the ridge all fight went from the enemy and they fled to the drekar which had its sail lowered and was already beginning to move away from the jetty.

I left my men to finish off the warriors who were attempting to flee and I pulled Aiden away from the fire. The bottoms of his feet were scorched from the flames. I wondered if he would ever walk again. "It hurts, jarl but they will heal. Just do not expect me to walk too far this night." Even though he must have been in excruciating pain he was still my Galdramenn.

I cut the bonds which bound his hands and handed him a skin of water. "I will return in a moment," I ran to the jetty. Only a handful of warriors had made the safety of the ship and even as they sailed towards Duboglassio arrows were still pitching men from the ship. It mattered not. Erik Redbeard would know that his plan had failed. He would be upon us in a matter of hours and our ships would not be here until the next day.

We would worry about that later. We had time now to see to Aiden and then to plan. "Sven Gold Beard, strip the bodies of any weapons, armour and treasure then give their bodies to the sea. Tostig. Take the Ulfheonar and join Sigtrygg. Build a beacon fire. When Redbeard attacks then we will light it and try to attract the attention of Erik Short Toe. You should find some old timbers from the fort. They should burn."

Haaken and Cnut joined me with Aiden. Haaken said, "I am sorry you were captured, Aiden. It was our fault."

"No Haaken, it was *wyrd*. The Norns planned this." He looked at me. "These warriors are from Orkneyjar."

"I know."

"They have as Redbeard's right hand men, the oathsworn of Sven Knife Tongue."

"You are certain?"

He gave a grim laugh and pulled open his tunic to show where they had carved a crude dragon on his chest using a knife. "Oh yes and they took great pleasure in reminding me that I was at their mercy. This whole plan is their idea. Their leader is Torgil the Cunning. Redbeard is just a brute of a warrior who rules with an iron fist. He does not know it but they are using him."

"Then this was a trap?"

"Aye. I have tried to communicate with the spirits but I did not know if it worked."

"It did, Kara saw this and that is why we did not go to Duboglassio. How would the plan have worked? "

"You would have seen one small drekar in the harbour. The other three were on the other side of the headland to the south west of Duboglassio; close to where Olaf and Rolf ruled. They have watchers on the two headlands and they would have lit fires to summon the drekar. These warriors would have taken me to the hillside and nailed me to the cross. Redbeard seemed amused by the thought of killing a Hibernian that way. For some reason he thinks that all Hibernians are Christians. I think Torgil planted that idea. Torgil certainly chose this site. He said it was fitting that the place where you lived and your mother burned to death should be the place their whelp, as he called me, should perish. He also liked the idea that it was the closest place to Cyninges-tūn. It would be the last place I saw before I died and he hoped it would be seen from our land as a reminder of his cunning. If I were Redbeard I would fear Torgil more than us. Torgil is using him."

"And how many men does Erik Redbeard have?"

"He had a hundred and thirty but you have killed many here. He has perhaps a hundred left but there are more spread around the island."

"Do not worry Aiden, Erik Short Toe brings our ship back tomorrow."

"Then we need to survive the night."

"And something tells me that we were meant to be there, at the tower."

All three of them nodded and murmured, "*Wyrd*!"

Chapter 17

Haaken and Cnut carried Aiden up the hill. I collected our spears and joined them. My warriors were tough men but they all felt the pain Aiden was enduring. He was as much a warrior as they were. Tostig had just finished building the fire. It was quite high as there had been some large timbers for him to use. I pointed to the cross, "Tear that down and throw that on the fire too."

I gathered them around me. "Erik Redbeard will be coming here soon with his warriors. They will come to finish us off. We will be outnumbered by two to one and we have no means of escape until tomorrow." I pointed to the tower, which now looked a little unstable. Cnut and I once stood sentry here on top of this tower and then Odin sent his lightning bolt to make my sword the most powerful weapon in the world." Even the Ulfheonar could not resist looking up at the tower, now framed by thickening clouds and a darkening sky. "We were meant to come here. The Norns sent us to face Bjarki and his wolf warriors and now they send us back here to see how we fare against the men of Orkneyjar. They are testing to see if we are worthy warriors. Many of you have fought on this isle and on this mountain before." I pointed to the Garlic River. "Bjorn the Scout earned the right to be Ulfheonar there in that very valley when even the great Sweyn could not find him. Redbeard has made a mistake if he thinks he can best us here. This was our land and we can show the men of Orkneyjar that when it comes to fighting, they are children and we are the warriors!"

They all gave a cheer and began banging their shields. It told the island that the Ulfheonar had returned.

"Rest now. They cannot be here in less than two hours. Have food and try to sleep. We form a circle at the top of this hill. Arturus' warriors and Ulfheonar standing side by side. We let them come to us. Use the hill, your bows, your spears and finally your swords to drive them hence."

As the men heeded my words we made Aiden as comfortable as we could. He was in pain but he told us that the healing would begin when he returned to Kara's house of women. "Cnut, come with me."

Tostig pointed up at the skies. "It will rain tonight, Jarl. We will never light the wood if it is wet. I saw some oil in the old settlement. I will pour that on top and then cover it with the cloaks of the dead warriors."

"Good thinking Tostig."

He shrugged, "I have no desire to be on this island any longer than I need to be. I wish to be back in Wolf's Lair with a fine fire burning!"

I led Cnut to the tower and we climbed. Even though it was now old and rickety I knew that we would not fall. I still had Ragnar's Spirit strapped to my side. By the time we reached the top darkness had fallen but I could see, a way off in the distance, lights as the men of Orkneyjar trekked from Duboglassio. They were many miles away yet. They would have to ascend the mountain and then drop down before climbing again. It would sap energy from legs and make their arms weary from carrying weapons.

"We will not be able to see them approach."

"The lights they carry, Jarl, will help us."

"Then if Redbeard is a fool for we will know where he is but if, as Aiden says, Torgil the Cunning does the planning then when they reach the mountain they will douse their lights. I will send Bjorn the Scout and Snorri up here with fire arrows and flints. When the lights are doused they can watch and loose fire arrows to light the night."

Cnut pointed to the skies. "I fear, Jarl, that tonight it will rain and there will be a storm."

I laughed and patted him around the shoulders, "Then that is perfect. Remember the last storm here?"

We descended both laughing at the circle we had just made. It had started here and it would end here. I sat next to Aiden and pulled my other cloak around my shoulder. My wolf cloak was warm but the drizzle had begun and I knew that soon I would be soaked to the skin. I smiled, "Something amuses you Jarl?"

"Aye Aiden, the thought of those warriors trekking through this. It will become harder. Do you remember when we lived here?"

"I do. If there were clouds on the horizon then it would soon rain and if there were none then it had just been raining!"

"How are the feet?"

"They will recover."

"And did you discover anything new in the libraries of Miklagård?"

"I did and they should be in my chest on the drekar."

"It was taken to Wolf's Lair."

"My trials had driven it from my mind but I now know the secret of the Roman Cement. I know how the Romans were able to build such high buildings. In short I can make our lives and our world much better."

"Good."

"And your mission?"

"Wiglaf is dead!" I told him of our adventures concluding with the hill fort and returning with the three girls.

"I think you are right Jarl. The Norns did send them." He pulled the cloak I had given him tighter around his shoulders for the rain was now drumming down upon us. "Why do you think that the Weird Sisters take such an interest in us or, more specifically, you, Jarl?"

"I know not but the caves beneath Wyddfa showed me a thread which travels back through time. Perhaps the sisters weave that web to make the future stronger. I think they just use me to their own ends. We are mortals and we have to live this life we are given. It may be we find all when we die and that is why the sprits are there." I pointed to the tower. "When the fighting begins then you take shelter there."

He nodded, "I will take a weapon. I cannot move but they shall not take me without a fight."

The intensity of the rain was increasing and the wind began to swirl. The tower began to creak alarmingly. "Come, we will build a shelter there now. Haaken, Cnut."

155

We helped Aiden to the shelter of the old tower and used some of the timbers Tostig had not needed to prop up a cloak. It made a drier sheltered place for Aiden. The tower protected us from the worst of the wind.

Sigtrygg descended from the tower. "The lights went out Jarl. It may have been the rain." He chuckled, "I do not envy Snorri and Bjorn the Scout their eyrie tonight." He huddled closer to the old wooden walls of the tower. "It moves at the top! I confess I was hanging on."

I nodded, "It always did so, even when new. It will stand a little longer." I cupped my hand. It was hard to make myself heard above the wind and the torrential rain which was lashing down relentlessly. "Snorri, Bjorn the Scout, up into the tower." As they went I shouted, "Stand to! They are closing."

I went to the southern side of the hill. It was the direction many of them would use. If they had any sense then they would send some men along the Garlic Valley and others around our western flank. I had many of Arturus' men and some Ulfheonar there. However neither route was easy. The Garlic Valley was steep and slippery whilst the western approach was over a rock filled scree. In this rain their footing would be uncertain.

We stood quite close to the tower. The ground fell away before us. When they reached us they would be tired from their march and I hoped that the last few steps would afford us an advantage. The spears we brought would reach over the shields and a falling man was like a tumbling rock. He would begin an avalanche of bodies.

Bjorn the Scout came slithering down the rickety ladder from the wooden tower. "We cannot light arrows, jarl. They are close. We caught sight of them less than five hundred paces away."

"Use your arrows anyway and then get down here."

As he scurried back up there was a distant rumble of thunder out to the west and then a short while later a flash in the western sky. It was a momentary flash but Haaken shouted, "I see them."

Our archers prepared their bows. I dropped my cloak and pulled the wolf's head over my helmet. They would see Dragon Heart and his wolf warriors when they ascended and they would feel the fury of my sword. There was another rumble. I counted in my head and when I reached fifteen there was another flash and I saw the men from the north less than a hundred paces away coming up the slope.

"Release!"

The archers loosed their arrows. I heard shouts but we could see nothing. We would have to wait either for another flash or to spy them when they closed. Snorri and Bjorn the Scout joined me. "We can do little up there. Besides I am not certain that Odin would touch my sword. He is more likely to rid the world of me!"

"Take your places then."

"There is one thing though, Jarl. There are only seventy or eighty of them. We were able to get a rough estimate from the flashes."

I frowned. Had the rest fallen by the wayside? "Tell the men to the north to keep watch. Aiden maybe right and this Torgil may be a more cunning opponent than we have met before."

We saw them before the next rumble. I pulled my shield tight to my body and held my spear with its head pointed down. Even in the dark and with the rain falling I could see them as the rain glinted off the metal of their helmets. They were less than ten paces away and I could see them struggling for their footing. Inevitably it was the young ones who wore no or little armour who were the first to reach us. One giant, with a helmet, a shield and a spear pointed his weapon at me as he launched himself the last few paces towards me. He lunged with his spear. It slid off the slick surface of the shield and I stabbed down over the rim of his shield. The blade went through his eye which was staring at me. As it struck bone I twisted and pulled. His body tumbled backwards and rolled down the hill scything down others who were struggling to climb.

It gave me a respite. There was another rumble and, again I counted to fifteen. In the flash I saw Redbeard. He had his mail adorned oathsworn in a wedge and they were thirty paces from me. Unlike the young giant I had just slain these were coming more slowly and cautiously. Around me some of the warriors on the flanks were pressing my warriors and they were being forced back.

I looked around me. Sigtrygg, Haaken and Cnut were there along with some of Arturus' men. "Form a shield wall around me! Redbeard is coming for me. If we can defeat him and his oathsworn the rest will fall."

Haaken and Cnut flanked me and Sigtrygg stood next to Cnut on my right. The other three were Arturus' men. Proud, no doubt, to be making this stand with the vaunted Ulfheonar. There was another rumble and this time I only counted to ten before the flash lit up the hillside as though it was daylight. I thought I heard Aiden shouting something but the wind and the rain took it away. Of more importance was the proximity of Redbeard. He and his fifteen oathsworn were less than five paces away.

He had done this before for he stopped to allow his men to get their breath for the final push. "You have no honour, Jarl Dragon Heart. You sneak from the hills and murder my men! You are a Nithing! I will tear the sword touched by the gods from your dead hands and then be the most powerful warrior in the Western Seas."

A spear was hurled and an arrow was loosed from behind me and two of the warriors at the rear of the wedge tumbled down the slope to the valley below.

"If Torgil the Cunning has finished with you." I saw the frown pass over his face. Aiden was right. "He is not with you is he? He lets you sacrifice yourselves on my blade and he hopes to finish me off then. You are being used, Redbeard! It is Torgil who leads and not you! You have been duped. This is all working to the advantage of Torgil."

I almost laughed as I saw him working it out. Just then there was a crack of thunder and five beats later a flash of lightning. His face contorted with rage, Redbeard yelled, "Charge!"

It is hard to get up to speed quickly in mail on a slippery slope. I knew the men with me and I shouted, "Strike!"

We stepped forward and all stabbed down with our spears. Redbeard was an old and wily fighter. He punched aside the head of my spear; which went, instead, into the neck of the warrior behind. The warrior's dying hands clutched at the haft and he tore it from my hand as he rolled down the hill. The wedge was broken. I was drawing my sword as Redbeard stabbed up under my shield. He used the hill to his advantage. Although I managed to bring my shield down he still scored a hit on my left knee and I felt the warm blood as it dripped down my leg.

He roared in triumph as he saw the blood on his blade. I heard Aiden's voice wailing behind me on the other side of the tower but I could do nothing about it. I had my sword in my hand as the lightning lit up my sword and there was another crack of thunder, closer this time. Redbeard seemed mesmerised by it. I brought it down and he just managed to get his shield above him. He was a powerful warrior and his next blow smashed into my shield and forced me back a few paces. He was able to step up and face me on the same level. He now had the advantage for I had a wounded leg. I could feel the blood sloshing around inside my boot.

He grinned. "Now you see, Dragon Heart, you are outnumbered and the gods have forsaken you. Here you will die!"

Predictably he swung on his last word and I was expecting such a move. I was already turning. I planted my left leg which was injured and spun around so that his momentum took him and his sword into my shield and then fresh air. I brought Ragnar's Spirit round to hit him in the middle of the back. I penetrated only links and his padding but the blow hurt him. He was an experienced warrior. He tried to sweep his shield at me. I stepped back on my right leg and planted that behind me. Once again, the speed of my move had taken me away from the force of the blow. More importantly it had opened him up.

There was another flash of lightning and then but a few heartbeats later a crack of thunder. The centre of the storm was almost upon us. He glanced up when the sky lit and I lunged forward. The tip entered his side and I twisted as it sank through the mail, and the padding finally tearing into his side. He brought his own sword down on my blade but all that did was to drive my sword down and open his wound even more.

"Tricky little bastard aren't you! Torgil said to watch out for your tricks."

I heard Aiden shout, again, "Jarl!"

It was more than my life was worth to turn. I had to end this and end it swiftly. Aiden was in trouble. I had to use my injured left leg. I had no choice. I stepped forward and punched with my shield. The boss hit his wrist and he had to step back. The ground was slippery with mud, blood and rain. He began to overbalance and I took my chance. I brought Ragnar's Spirit over from behind me. I put all my weight into the blow. The tip struck his nose and carried on to slice open his face. I found myself falling forward and the sword continued to slice down into his throat. As all my weight landed on my sword it drove the point through his neck and pinned his wriggling body to the ground.

I had to push myself up with my shield. I sensed a weapon coming from my left and I rolled to my right, leaving my sword impaling Redbeard. The axe cracked into my shield and forced me to the ground. I took the dagger from the back of the shield and slashed wildly. It struck a bare leg and the man shouted. I flipped the dagger so that I held its tip and threw it. Ragnar must have guided my throw for it struck his neck. I struggled to me feet and pulled my sword from the body of Redbeard. I glanced around as I gathered myself. The skirmish had become a series of fights to the death between two bands of oathsworn. I knew that I should help my men but Aiden needed me.

I moved around the tower and was just in time to see Sven Gold Beard decapitated by a warrior I recognised. It had to be Torgil the Cunning. He had four oathsworn with him and was moving towards Aiden. There were two bodies lying close to Aiden. Aiden had managed to get to his feet and his back was to the tower. He had used his dagger well but now he had no weapon in his hand and the five warriors were moving towards him. I saw a spear lying on the ground and I threw it at the nearest warrior who was racing towards me. It hit him in the chest with such force that it threw him back into the second warrior. I ignored my injured leg. Aiden was in mortal danger. I fended off the blow from the first of Torgil's oathsworn while I sliced sideways at the other. It was a lucky blow and it hacked through his upper arm, cutting through to the bone. The warrior I had knocked over was below me and I dropped to my knee and brought the metal edge of my shield across his throat. The pain in my left leg almost made me pass out and I could hardly move. My weight almost severed his neck.

The last of the oathsworn had regained his feet and ran towards me with his sword held high. There was no way that I could avoid the blow. Suddenly two arrows flew from behind me and both struck him, one in each eye. As I ran to reach Aiden I saw that Torgil had grabbed him and was using him as a human shield. There was an enormous flash of lightning which lit the whole hillside and a crack of thunder almost at the same time.

Torgil laughed, "It seems you are lucky, Dragon Heart, but your archers will not strike me." He held his sword at Aiden's throat. My Galdramenn looked calm. I advanced toward them. "Do not come too close, Dragon Heart. Your Irish friend has a short time to live. Do not take away his last few moments of life." He laughed, "You avoided my first trap but I have you now and when Redbeard and his oathsworn reach you…"

It was my turn to laugh as I took a step closer. He backed away closer to our signal fire. "Redbeard and his oathsworn lie dead. You have lost, Torgil the Cunning. Release my Galdramenn. He can do you no good."

He took another step back and found his progress impeded by the wood of the fire. "It will give me pleasure to end his life and you will not leave me alive. I know that. This will not bring Sven Knife Tongue back but you will mourn his loss for the rest of your life."

I raised my sword as he moved his hand away from Aiden's throat to allow him to give more power to the cut which would end the life of my dear friend. A number of events all happened at once. It seemed that they happened in slow motion. Aiden flung his head back and butted Torgil in the face. Torgil's hand dropped and Aiden rolled away. I threw Ragnar's Spirit at Torgil. There was a crack overhead and I hurled myself at Aiden to knock him away from Torgil. There was an enormous flash as the lightning hit the tower and lit the whole hillside as though it was daylight. The man from Orkneyjar looked at the blade sticking from his chest and grabbed the hilt to pull it from his body. I rolled Aiden away and saw the tower burst into flames and begin to fall towards us. Aiden's burned feet and my injured leg meant we had to roll. As my head came up I saw the burning tower strike Torgil, the sword and the oil-soaked wood. It went up in a huge conflagration. Torgil had been leaning against the wood and his body was covered in oil. He began to burn. His hands were stuck around the blade of the sword and I realised that it had pinned him to the fire. I watched as his face began to melt and his mouth opened in a scream which never came. It took him but a few moments to expire and we lay there watching the burning body of Torgil The Cunning.

My men ran over to lift us up. Miraculously the rain had ceased and the storm had gone. Odin was finished with us. I hoped that the Norns had too.

"That was either extremely brave Aiden or incredibly foolish."

He shrugged, "I was a dead man either way but I knew that Odin would not let you suffer here of all places. The spirit of your mother watched over us all."

I turned to Haaken, "Is it over?"

"It is over. Redbeard's oathsworn fell with him and you despatched the last of Torgil's. The others had no loyalty and they are gone. We did not pursue them."

I shook my head, "No, we will quit this place and return home."

Aiden shook his head, "Not yet jarl, we must wait for the fire to die. It seems that Odin wanted the blade tempered a second time, this time in blood and fire. You now have an even stronger sword."

We spent the rest of the night healing the wounded; they were brought to Aiden. The warriors who were untouched collected the treasures and weapons after they had taken the bodies of our dead to the beach to await our ships. We would bury them with honour in our home, in the valley of Cyninges-tūn. I had lost Ulfheonar. Tostig Wolf Hand, Bjorn Carved Teeth, Karl Bollison, Sven Sharp Blade, Einar Siggison and Leif Knutson. Many others, like me had serious wounds but we would heal over the winter and we would return stronger.

It was just before dawn when our ships appeared below us. I went to the fire which still glowed and burned at the bottom. The blackened, charred body of Torgil the Cunning lay grotesquely over it. I went to see if the sword could be removed; the wood and the leather from the hilt had been burned away. It was now a single piece of metal. I touched the tang and it was merely warm.

160

I turned to Aiden and my oathsworn who were there, "It is just warm."

"Then pull the sword from the fire, jarl and let us go home."

I grabbed the tang and slid the blade from the fire. The marks left by the burning, bleeding hands of Torgil had left an imprint on the sword it looked as though there was a dragon writhing on the blade. Ragnar's Spirit now had its own heart of the dragon forged in blood and fire. Redbeard and Torgil had tried to take it from me and come closer than any and yet they had only succeeded in making it stronger.

Wyrd!

Epilogue

Our homecoming was a mixture of joy and pain. The pain was in the bodies of the dead who were reverently carried from the two ships and the eyes of their families. The joy was in our return and in the news that Elfrida was with child and I would be a grandfather. As we silently trudged back to Cyninges-tūn I realised that we had experienced all of life in one day. Death was ever present and sometimes we were the width of blade away from oblivion. We could be in the depths of despair and yet, if we hung on, then great joy could take us unawares. The storm had cleared the skies and we saw, reflected in the Water, the face of Old Olaf the Toothless and he seemed to be smiling. I had no doubt that Ragnar had told him that his Spirit now inhabited a dragon's body.

Aiden and I had insisted upon walking; the constant pain was a reminder that we lived still and yet should have died. Haaken, who was ahead, turned to wait for us. He stared beyond us to the south and Mann, "Do you think we shall ever go back?"

"There is no need. The tower is gone and Odin has finished his sword making. We were meant to go there. It was not just the sword which went through fire and blood. We all did and, like the sword, we are stronger still. I have finished with Mann. We may have fewer warriors but there are new ones yet to be trained." I smiled, "Perhaps my grandson will become a great warrior like his father."

Aiden said quietly, "I think he will aim higher, Jarl Dragon Heart. He will become as great a warrior as the greatest Viking of all, Jarl Dragon Heart who wields the sword touched by the gods, twice. Whoever risks combat with you faces certain death."

It was unprompted but every warrior took out his sword and yelled, "Ulfheonar!" and howled like wolves. We told our land that we were back!

The End

Glossary

Áed Oirdnide –King of Tara 797

Afon Hafron- River Severn in Welsh

Bardanes Tourkos- Rebel Byzantine General

Bebbanburgh- Bamburgh Castle, Northumbria

Beck- a stream

Blót – a blood sacrifice made by a jarl

Byrnie- a mail shirt reaching down to the knees

Caerlleon- Welsh for Chester

Casnewydd –Newport, Wales

Cephas- Greek for Simon Peter (St. Peter)

Chape- the tip of a scabbard

Charlemagne- Holy Roman Emperor at the end of the 8th and beginning of the 9th centuries

Celchyth- Chelsea

Cherestanc- Garstang (Lancashire)

Corn Walum- Cornwall

Cymri- Welsh

Cymru- Wales

Cyninges-tūn – Coniston. It means the estate of the king (Cumbria)

Drekar- a Dragon ship (a Viking warship)

Duboglassio –Douglas, Isle of Man

Dyflin- Old Norse for Dublin

Ein-mánuðr- middle of March to the middle of April

Fey- having second sight

Firkin- a barrel containing eight gallons (usually beer)

Fret-a sea mist

Frankia- France and part of Germany

Garth- Dragon Heart

Gaill- Irish for foreigners

Galdramenn- wizard

Glaesum –amber

Gói- the end of February to the middle of March

Grenewic- Greenwich

Haughs- small hills in Norse (As in Tarn Hows)

Heels- when a ship leans to one side under the pressure of the wind

Hel - Queen of Niflheim, the Norse underworld.

Here Wic- Harwich

Hetaereiarch – Byzantine general

Hoggs or Hogging- when the pressure of the wind causes the stern or the bow to droop

Hrams-a – Ramsey, Isle of Man

Icaunis- British river god

Itouna- River Eden Cumbria

Jarl- Norse earl or lord

Joro-goddess of the earth

Knarr- a merchant ship or a coastal vessel

Kyrtle-woven top

Leathes Water- Thirlmere

Legacaestir- Anglo Saxon for Chester

Lochlannach – Irish for Northerners (Vikings)

Lothuwistoft- Lowestoft

Lundenwic - London

Mammceaster- Manchester

Manau – The Isle of Mann (Saxon)

Marcia Hispanic- Spanish Marches (the land around Barcelona)

Mast fish- two large racks on a ship for the mast

Melita- Malta

Midden- a place where they dumped human waste

Miklagård - Constantinople

Nikephoros- Emperor of Byzantium 802-811

Njoror- God of the sea

Nithing- A man without honour (Saxon)

Odin - The "All Father" God of war, also associated with wisdom, poetry, and magic (The Ruler of the gods).

On Corn Walum –Cornwall

Olissipo- Lisbon

Orkneyjar-Orkney

Pillars of Hercules- Straits of Gibraltar

Ran- Goddess of the sea

Roof rock- slate

Rinaz –The Rhine

Sabrina- Latin and Celtic for the River Severn. Also, the name of a female Celtic deity

St. Cybi- Holyhead

Scillonia Insula- Scilly Isles

Scree- loose rocks in a glacial valley

Seax – short sword

Sheerstrake- the uppermost strake in the hull

Sheet- a rope fastened to the lower corner of a sail

Shroud- a rope from the masthead to the hull amidships

Skeggox – an axe with a shorter beard on one side of the blade

South Folk- Suffolk

Stad- Norse settlement

Stays- ropes running from the mast-head to the bow

Strake- the wood on the side of a drekar

Suthriganaworc - Southwark (London)

Syllingar- Scilly Isles

Tarn- small lake (Norse)

Temese- River Thames (also called the Tamese)

The Norns- The three sisters who weave webs of intrigue for men
Thing-Norse for a parliament or a debate (Tynwald)
Thor's day- Thursday
Threttanessa- a drekar with 13 oars on each side.
Thrall- slave
Trenail- a round wooden peg used to secure strakes
Tynwald- the Parliament on the Isle of Man
Úlfarrberg- Helvellyn
Úlfarrland- Cumbria
Úlfarr- Wolf Warrior
Úlfarrston- Ulverston
Ullr-Norse God of Hunting
Ulfheonar-an elite Norse warrior who wore a wolf skin over his armour
Volva- a witch or healing woman in Norse culture
Waeclinga Straet- Watling Street (A5) Windlesore-Windsor
Waite- a Viking word for farm
Woden's day- Wednesday
Wulfhere-Old English for Wolf Army
Wyddfa-Snowdon
Wyrd- Fate
Yard- a timber from which the sail is suspended

Historical note

The Viking raids began, according to records left by the monks, in the 790s when Lindisfarne was pillaged. However, there were many small settlements along the east coast and most were undefended. I have chosen a fictitious village on the Tees as the home of Garth who is enslaved and then, when he gains his freedom, becomes Dragon Heart. As buildings were all made of wood then any evidence of their existence would have rotted long ago, save for a few post holes. The Norse began to raid well before 790. There was a rise in the populations of Norway and Denmark and Britain was not well prepared for defence against such random attacks.

My raiders represent the Norse warriors who wanted the plunder of the soft Saxon kingdom. There is a myth that the Vikings raided in large numbers but this is not so. It was only in the tenth and eleventh centuries that the numbers grew. They also did not have allegiances to kings. The Norse settlements were often isolated family groups. The term Viking was not used in what we now term the Viking Age beyond the lands of Norway and Denmark. Warriors went a-Viking which meant that they sailed for adventure or pirating. Their lives were hard. Slavery was commonplace. The Norse for slave is thrall and I have used both terms.

The ship, '*Dragon Heart*' is based on the Gokstad ship which was found in 1880 in Norway. It is 23.24 metres long and 5.25 metres wide at its widest point. It was made entirely of oak except for the pine decking. There are 16 strakes on each side and from the base to the gunwale is 2.02 metres giving it a high freeboard. The keel is cut from a piece of oak 17.6 metres long. There are 19 ribs. The pine mast was 13 metres high. The ship could carry 70 men although there were just sixteen oars on each side. This meant that half the crew could rest while the other half rowed. Sea battles could be brutal.

The Vikings raided far and wide. They raided and subsequently conquered much of Western France and made serious inroads into Spain. They even travelled up the Rhone River as well as raiding North Africa. The sailors and warriors we call Vikings were very adaptable and could, indeed, carry their long ships over hills to travel from one river to the next. The Viking ships are quite remarkable. Replicas of the smaller ones have managed speeds of 8-10 knots. The sea going ferries, which ply the Bay of Biscay, travel at 14-16 knots. The journey the *'Heart of the Dragon'* makes from Santander to the Isles of Scilly in a day and a half would have been possible with the oars and a favourable wind and, of course, the cooperation of the Goddess of the sea, Ran! The journey from the Rhine to Istanbul is 1188 nautical miles. If the *'Heart of the Dragon'* had had favourable winds and travelled nonstop she might have made the journey in 6 days! Sailing during the day only and with some adverse winds means that 18 or 20 days would be more realistic.

Nikephoros was Emperor from 802-811. Bardanes Tourkos did revolt although he did not attempt a coup in the palace as I used in my book. He was later defeated, blinded and sent to a monastery. Nikephoros did well until he went to war with Krum, the Khan of Bulgaria. He died in battle and Krum made a drinking vessel from his skull!

I have recently used the British Museum book and research about the Vikings. Apparently, rather like punks and Goths, the men did wear eye makeup. It would make them appear more frightening. There is also evidence that they filed their teeth. The leaders of warriors built up a large retinue by paying them and giving them gifts such as the wolf arm ring. This was seen as a sort of bond between leader and warrior. There was no national identity. They operated in small bands of free booters loyal to their leader. The idea of sword killing was to render a weapon unusable by anyone else. On a simplistic level this could just be a bend but I have seen examples which are tightly curled like a spring.

The length of the swords in this period was not the same as in the later medieval period. By the year 850 they were only 76 cm long and in the eighth century they were shorter still. The first sword Dragon Heart used, Ragnar's, was a new design and was 75 cm long. This would only have been slightly longer than a Roman gladius. At this time the sword, not the axe was the main weapon. The best swords came from Frankia and were probably German in origin. A sword was considered a special weapon and a good one would be handed from father to son. A warrior with a famous blade would be sought out on the battlefield. There was little mail around at the time and warriors learned to be agile to avoid being struck. A skeggox was an axe with a shorter edge on one side. The use of an aventail (a chain mail extension of a helmet) began at about this time. The highly decorated scabbard also began at this time.

The blood eagle was performed by cutting the skin of the victim by the spine, breaking the ribs so they resembled blood-stained wings, and pulling the lungs out through the wounds in the victim's back.

I have used the word saga, even though it is generally only used for Icelandic stories. It is just to make it easier for my readers. If you are an Icelandic expert then I apologise. I have plenty of foreign words which, I know, taxes some of my readers. As I keep saying it is about the characters and the stories.

It was more dangerous to drink the water in those times and so most people, including children drank beer or ale. The process killed the bacteria which could hurt them. It might sound as though they were on a permanent pub crawl but in reality they were drinking the healthiest drink that was available to them. Honey was used as an antiseptic in both ancient and modern times. Yarrow was a widely used herb. It had a variety of uses in ancient times. It was frequently mixed with other herbs as well as being used with honey to treat wounds. Its Latin name is *Achillea millefolium*. Achilles was reported to have carried the herb with him in battle to treat wounds. Its traditional names include arrowroot, bad man's plaything, bloodwort, carpenter's weed, death flower, devil's nettle, eerie, field hops, gearwe, hundred leaved grass, knight's milefoil, knyghten, milefolium, milfoil, millefoil, noble yarrow, nosebleed, old man's mustard, old man's pepper, sanguinary, seven year's love, snake's grass, soldier, soldier's woundwort, stanchweed, thousand seal, woundwort, yarroway, yerw. I suspect Tolkien used it in the Lord of the Rings books as Kingsfoil, another ubiquitous and often overlooked herb in Middle Earth.

The Vikings were not sentimental about their children. A son would expect nothing from his father once he became a man. He had more chance of reward from his jarl than his father. Leaders gave gifts to their followers. It was expected. Therefore, the more successful you were as a leader the more loyal followers you might have.

There was a warrior called Ragnar Hairy-Breeches. Although he lived a little later than my book is set I could not resist using the name of such an interesting sounding character. Most of the names such as Silkbeard, Hairy-Breeches etc are genuine Viking names. I have merely transported them all into one book. I also amended some of my names- I used Eric in the earlier books and it should have been Erik. I have now changed the later editions of the first two books in the series.

Eardwulf was king of Northumbria twice: first from 796-806 and from 808-810. The king who deposed him was Elfwald II. This period was a turbulent one for the kings of Northumbria and marked a decline in their fortunes until it was taken over by the Danes in 867. This was the time of power for Mercia and East Anglia. Coenwulf ruled East Anglia and his son Cynhelm, Mercia. Wessex had yet to rise.

Bothvar Bjarki was a famous berserker and the Klak brothers did exist. I did not make either name up! Guthrum was also a Dane who lived in East Anglia.

Slavery was far more common in the ancient world. When the Normans finally made England their own they showed that they understood the power of words and propaganda by making the slaves into serfs. This was a brilliant strategy as it forced their former slaves to provide their own food whilst still working for their lords and masters for nothing. Manumission was possible as Garth showed in the first book in this series. Scanlan's training is also a sign that not all of the slaves suffered. It was a hard and cruel time- it was ruled by the strong.

The Vikings did use trickery when besieging their enemies and would use any means possible. They did not have siege weapons and had to rely on guile and courage to prevail. The siege of Paris in 845 A.D. was one such example. The Isle of Mann is reputed to have the earliest surviving Parliament, the Tynwald although there is evidence that there were others amongst the Viking colonies on Orkney and in Iceland. I have used this idea for Prince Butar's meetings of Jarls. The blue stone they treasure is Aquamarine or beryl. It is found in granite. The rocks around the Mawddach are largely granite and although I have no evidence of beryl being found there, I have used the idea of a small deposit being found to tie the story together. There was a famous witch who lived on one of the islands of Scilly. According to Norse legend Olaf Tryggvasson, who became King Olaf 1 of Norway, visited her. She told him that if he converted to Christianity then he would become king of Norway.

I use Roman forts in all of my books. Although we now see ruins when they were abandoned the only things which would have been damaged would have been the gates. Anything of value would have been buried in case they wished to return. By 'of value' I do not mean coins but things such as nails and weapons. Such objects have been discovered. Many of the forts were abandoned in a hurry. Hardknott fort, for example, was built in the 120s but abandoned twenty or so years later. When the Antonine Wall was abandoned in the 180s Hardknott was reoccupied until Roman soldiers finally withdrew from northern Britain. I think that, until the late Saxon period and early Norman period, there would have been many forts which would have looked habitable. The Vikings and the Saxons did not build in stone. It was only when the castle builders, the Normans, arrived that stone would be robbed from Roman forts and those defences destroyed by an invader who was in the minority. The Vikings also liked to move their homes every few years; this was, perhaps, only a few miles, but it explains how difficult it is to find the remains of early Viking settlements.

The place names are accurate and the mountain above Coniston is called the Old Man. The river is not navigable up to Windermere but I have allowed my warriors to carry their drekar as the Vikings did in the land of the Rus when travelling to Miklagård. The ninth century saw the beginning of the reign of the Viking. They raided Spain, the Rhone, Africa and even Constantinople. They believed they could beat anyone!

There was a King Egbert who did indeed triumph over King Coenwulf. He founded the power base upon which Alfred the Great built. It was also at this time that the Danes came to take over East Anglia and Yorkshire. The land became, over the next 50 years, Danelaw. I have made up Elfrida and his marriage to her but the kings of that time had many liaisons with many women. Some kings sired up to twenty illegitimate children and many legitimate ones. The practice continued into the late middle ages. Wives were frequently taken for political reasons. The inspiration for the abduction comes from the story of the Welsh Princess Nest (Nesta) who, in the 12th century had two children by King Henry 1st and was then married to one of his friends. She was abducted by a Welsh knight who lived with her until her husband recaptured her and killed her abductor.

Harald Klak became King of Denmark in 826 but I made up his brother.
I used the following books for research

- British Museum - 'Vikings- Life and Legends'
- 'Saxon, Norman and Viking' by Terence Wise (Osprey)
- Ian Heath - 'The Vikings'. (Osprey)
- Ian Heath- 'Byzantine Armies 668-1118 (Osprey)
- David Nicholle- 'Romano-Byzantine Armies 4th-9th Century (Osprey)
- Stephen Turnbull- 'The Walls of Constantinople AD 324-1453' (Osprey)
- Keith Durham- 'Viking Longship' (Osprey)

Griff Hosker **March 2015**

Other books
by
Griff Hosker

If you enjoyed reading this book, then why not read another one by the author?

Ancient History

The Sword of Cartimandua Series (Germania and Britannia 50A.D. – 128 A.D.)
Ulpius Felix- Roman Warrior (prequel)
Book 1 The Sword of Cartimandua
Book 2 The Horse Warriors
Book 3 Invasion Caledonia
Book 4 Roman Retreat
Book 5 Revolt of the Red Witch
Book 6 Druid's Gold
Book 7 Trajan's Hunters
Book 8 The Last Frontier
Book 9 Hero of Rome
Book 10 Roman Hawk
Book 11 Roman Treachery
Book 12 Roman Wall
Book 13 Roman Courage

The Aelfraed Series (Britain and Byzantium 1050 A.D. - 1085 A.D.)
Book 1 Housecarl
Book 2 Outlaw
Book 3 Varangian

The Wolf Warrior series (Britain in the late 6th Century)
Book 1 Saxon Dawn
Book 2 Saxon Revenge
Book 3 Saxon England
Book 4 Saxon Blood
Book 5 Saxon Slayer
Book 6 Saxon Slaughter
Book 7 Saxon Bane
Book 8 Saxon Fall: Rise of the Warlord
Book 9 Saxon Throne
Book 10 Saxon Sword

The Dragon Heart Series
Book 1 Viking Slave
Book 2 Viking Warrior
Book 3 Viking Jarl
Book 4 Viking Kingdom
Book 5 Viking Wolf
Book 6 Viking War
Book 7 Viking Sword

Book 8 Viking Wrath
Book 9 Viking Raid
Book 10 Viking Legend
Book 11 Viking Vengeance
Book 12 Viking Dragon
Book 13 Viking Treasure
Book 14 Viking Enemy
Book 15 Viking Witch
Book 16 Viking Blood
Book 17 Viking Weregeld
Book 18 Viking Storm
Book 19 Viking Warband
Book 20 Viking Shadow

The Norman Genesis Series
Hrolf the Horseman
Horseman
The Battle for a Home
Revenge of the Franks
The Land of the Northmen
Ragnvald Hrolfsson
Brothers in Blood
Lord of Rouen
Drekar in the Seine

The Anarchy Series England 1120-1180
English Knight
Knight of the Empress
Northern Knight
Baron of the North
Earl
King Henry's Champion
The King is Dead
Warlord of the North
Enemy at the Gate
Warlord's War
Kingmaker
Henry II
Crusader
The Welsh Marches
Irish War
Poisonous Plots
The Princes' Revolt

Border Knight 1182-1300
Sword for Hire
Return of the Knight
Baron's War
Magna Carta

Modern History
The Napoleonic Horseman Series
Book 1 Chasseur a Cheval
Book 2 Napoleon's Guard
Book 3 British Light Dragoon
Book 4 Soldier Spy
Book 5 1808: The Road to Corunna
Waterloo

The Lucky Jack American Civil War series
Rebel Raiders
Confederate Rangers
The Road to Gettysburg

The British Ace Series
1914
1915 Fokker Scourge
1916 Angels over the Somme
1917 Eagles Fall
1918 We will remember them
From Arctic Snow to Desert Sand
Wings over Persia

Combined Operations series 1940-1945
Commando
Raider
Behind Enemy Lines
Dieppe
Toehold in Europe
Sword Beach
Breakout
The Battle for Antwerp
King Tiger
Beyond the Rhine

Other Books
Carnage at Cannes (a thriller)
Great Granny's Ghost (Aimed at 9-14-year-old young people)
Adventure at 63-Backpacking to Istanbul

For more information on all of the books then please visit the author's web site at http://www.griffhosker.com where there is a link to contact him or you can Tweet him @HoskerGriff

Made in the USA
Columbia, SC
31 October 2020

23777728R00096